MIGNON G. EBERHART
CASA MADRONE

WARNER BOOKS

A Warner Communications Company

The author wishes to acknowledge her indebtedness to many newspapers, magazines and books, too numerous to list here, but especially to Gertrude Atherton's *Golden Gate Country*, to Herb Caen's *San Francisco*, and to the *San Francisco Earthquake*, written by Gordon Thomas and Max Morgan Witts; any errors of fact in this novel are due solely to the author, as well as the entirely fictional characters, some streets and two houses.

One

"It's in his letter," Scott Suydam said. He turned to the window that looked over Fifth Avenue; his shoulders made a solid block against the light from the window. "About the accident, I mean." Surely there was no sense of evasion; certainly his voice was perfectly steady. "He thought it would be simpler for me to bring the letters rather than send them by mail. A telegram is too abrupt and impersonal. I had some business in New York, so he asked me to see you and give you his message."

Aunt Flo Bel rustled her letter, rereading it. It had been properly addressed to her although it concerned Mallory. Mallory's own letter lay on the table beside her. It, too, was proper. It was not, she thought vaguely, really a love letter; however, it had been written by the man soon to be her husband.

"He regretted being unable to come," Scott Suydam said flatly.

Aunt Flo Bel eyed him. "What *was* the accident?"

"Just an accident. He told you about it, I suppose. In the letters. He has sent his private railway car. He told you that, too, I'm sure."

Was it there again? Mallory asked herself: a kind of too well-controlled steadiness as if to conceal some remote uneasiness. Oh, no; she was letting her imagination, nerves, whatever, suggest things. The fact was simple. Richard Welbeck, whom she was so soon to marry, had had an accident which prevented his crossing the continent for their wedding; consequently, he had asked her to come to San Francisco, where the marriage ceremony would be suitably performed.

Aunt Flo Bel's still-lovely face was perfectly calm; her once bright red hair was barely touched with silver, like an added sheen; it was neatly arranged—a high pompadour and a charming knot of very abundant hair above her straight shoulders and slim neck. She still wore widow's black; her dress accommodated itself to her small waist and swept downward in graceful folds; there was a touch of white around her neck. Just now, watching her, Mallory felt that there was the barest flicker of relief in Flo Bel's brilliant blue 'eyes between their sweeping dark eyelashes. She might be thinking of the enormous expenses the wedding—as planned, here in New York—would have entailed. Already the trousseau had been an extravagance; probably there were debts galore for that. Flo Bel was still trying to pay for the truly shocking cost of Mallory's debut.

Actually, Mallory had met Richard Welbeck, the fabulously rich Richard Welbeck, at a small dinner party preceding that event, but the expense for the debut had not really been wasted, Flo Bel had assured her.

Now Flo Bel was tapping her small hand, ringless at present except for the broad wedding ring, upon the arm of her chair. Perhaps she, too, sensed something not quite candid, something withheld. Oh, nonsense, Mallory told herself.

Scott Suydam stood perfectly still at the window, not turning to look at either of the two women, yet she knew that he was keenly aware of them and the room.

It had been a lovely room. Now only its shape was lovely; it was octagonal and beautifully proportioned. Once it had been almost as famous as the Bookever fortune; it was called the Fragonard room for the panels around the walls. Now the panels were gone. Gone were the graceful French tables and fauteuils and the Aubusson rug, made to fit the room. Gone were the delicate silk curtains, woven for the room by order of Uncle Peter Bookever.

Yes, Mallory had been very lucky to meet Richard Welbeck, and lucky indeed, Flo Bel said firmly, to engage his interest, and then, before he went home to San Francisco, to receive a formal proposal of marriage after he had first, properly, spoken to Flo Bel. The wedding had been planned for April the eighteenth, three days after Easter. Mallory wondered sharply if it was too late to cancel the elaborate plans that had been made.

8

Flo Bel's lips had tightened a little; she looked down again at Richard's letter. Scott Suydam did not move. At last Flo Bel said, "This accident. He doesn't say how it happened."

Scott Suydam spoke now, precisely yet still over his shoulder. "In his own home. Fell down the stairs. Broken leg. Must be in a cast for some time." He paused, took a long breath and turned around to face Flo Bel. "He regrets it very much. He hopes that you will permit the marriage to take place in San Francisco. His cousin Dolores will be happy to act as your niece's chaperon and hostess."

Flo Bel's long eyelashes drooped a little but her eyes gleamed through them. Flo Bel was still a beauty, even though she was touching fifty, a rather fragile beauty but a beauty. She sat upright, her figure distinguished and firm in the ugly straight chair which had replaced the former cushioned fauteuil. The Fragonard room had been only a setting for her elegance; it had not reflected her true personality. She was in fact steel. She said now, icily, "I myself will chaperon my niece."

Scott Suydam sent one glance at Mallory. It was rather a shock in a strange way; it was as though he were looking at her, seeing her, for the first time. His eyes were sharp and probably saw a greal deal—perhaps too much, Mallory thought suddenly and rather uneasily. "No matter," he said. "Richard said only—that is, he requested me to escort Miss Bookever."

Flo Bel's fine eyebrows lifted. "Without a chaperon! Dear me, Mr. Suydam, he could not have meant that. No, no, if Mallory decides to accept this changed plan for her marriage, then naturally I shall accompany her. Dear Richard must have so intended."

Mallory glanced down at her own letter from Richard, a rather formal letter, regretting the accident, entreating her to forgive his inability to return to New York, asking her to come to San Francisco, where his cousin would arrange their wedding. His friend Scott Suydam had volunteered to act as her escort, his private car would bring them west—and he was her most loving Richard Welbeck.

Scott Suydam seemed to make up his mind, and unexpectedly looked rather relieved in turn. "I think it an excellent idea, Mrs. Bookever. I'm sure Richard would have suggested it if he"—he did falter a little here, but went on quickly—"if he had not been in such pain. It was a very bad fracture, you know. Oh, he has good care but— It is unfortunate, of course. I do regret—"

"Naturally," Flo Bel said crisply. "Now then, Mallory, this is entirely your decision."

There was no decision to make; it had been decided long ago. Perhaps, indeed, years ago. She replied, "Yes, certainly, Aunt Flo Bel. After all, it is Richard's wish."

Surely Flo Bel's lovely forehead cleared a little, that or the steely look in her blue eyes softened. Scott Suydam accepted Mallory's agreement with a slight bow in her direction but did not look into her face. "Then I'm afraid you may be rather hurried—your preparations, I mean. Richard had planned for the car to leave two days from now, but if that is too soon..."

"Not at all." Flo Bel was firm. "We shall be ready. Anything which cannot be packed, indeed much of my niece's trousseau, can be sent on separately."

"Yes, certainly." Scott Suydam bowed again. He hesitated, came with one stride to Mallory, took her hand briefly, still without looking at her, and allowed Flo Bel to walk with him out into the great hall with its bare and echoing parquet floors.

Without really intending to, Mallory rose and went to the window overlooking Fifth Avenue. Her long, full skirt, soft green cashmere, for Flo Bel had never permitted her to wear black, rustled softly as she moved, and the glass of the window was cool on her face; if she pressed against it a certain way she could see anyone emerging from the huge and impressive front portico. She did: Scott Suydam, complete with gray topper, pale-yellow kid gloves, black coat, striped trousers, the very picture of a fashionable young man—or even, she thought irreverently, an ambassador. Well, in fact that was what he had been, an ambassador from Richard. At the corner he paused, removed his gray topper and touched his forehead with a white handkerchief, drawn swiftly from some recess of his gray waistcoat. He had clearly not enjoyed the errand he had undertaken, and probably had felt the unexpected strength that lay below to Flo Bel's elegantly feminine and charming grace.

Flo Bel came back into the room, sank down into her chair, permitted her backbone to relax and said thoughtfully, "I can't help wondering how such a very crippling accident could happen."

Mallory had jerked swiftly away from the window, conquering a foolishly guilty qualm for what was, really, merely natural curiosity. She said, tritely, "Accidents will happen," and got down to the important immediate subject. "Flo Bel, can we cancel Delmonico's? And the church and the awning and the bridesmaids— Oh, for heaven's sake, the bridesmaids!"

"I'll see to all that."

"Especially Delmonico's. They charge so much. And the orchestra and florist for the reception and—"

"I'll see to all that."

A wave of compunction struck Mallory. It was by no means the first since Flo Bel had undertaken all her expenses during these last few desperately difficult years.

"You've spent far too much money on me."

"What else could I do?" Flo Bel was a typical Victorian in her realistic assessment of facts. "There we were. Nothing left after your uncle's collapse and death. One of us had to marry money. There was only old Frank Graham for me. I couldn't really take advantage of his age. And in fact, his children would certainly have opposed my marriage to him."

"You could have managed them." Mallory spoke with certainty.

"I expect I could have. But then, you, Mallory, made things come out all right. I wanted a good marriage for you, of course. It had to be. You couldn't have gone to governessing or—or—well, I can't think of anything else you are qualified to do, and you aren't really qualified to do that." Mallory started to speak. Flo Bel knew what she was going to say. "Yes, you can speak reasonably good French, but only reasonably good. You can dance. You know how to enter a room, how to behave at dinner parties or balls, what to do—more important, what not to do. But no, I can't say you are fully qualified to undertake a governess's work. Besides, I don't know who would employ you unless it was some newcomer who was willing to pay—a pittance, at best—for a step up socially. No, that was not for you. Nor," she said frankly, "for me."

"You've done far too much for me," Mallory said again.

"Certainly not. After all, we did adopt you legally. I admit I did have other plans for you." It was not in Flo Bel's nature to feel sorry for herself or to shrink from facing anything she had to face, but just now she sighed. "A finishing school in Paris, the school I was sent to. Presentation later in London, the Court of St. James's. Perhaps even an English title, though that has been overdone, really. Too much good American money flowing into too many bad castles. Well, that's all over now. Get to your packing, Mallory, dear. Have Gorham bring down two trunks from the trunk room. And those two big grips your uncle used. I'll write the notes, all of them. Now then..."

"Dear Flo Bel," Mallory said and bent to touch her aunt's soft, fragrant, barely wrinkled cheek. Flo Bel was really ultra-modern in that she preferred Uncle Peter's name for her, rather than a stilted Aunt Florence.

"It's all right, Mallory. In fact, it's better than all right." Flo Bel's thoughtful little frown returned. "I hadn't planned it this way..."

There was something puzzling in the way she said it. Mallory asked, after a moment, "You mean the wedding?"

"No. That is, well—yes, of course. Naturally I was speaking of your wedding. But—never mind. When Gorham has brought the trunks down, send him to Brown's for a hansom. I'll send the notes around at once. We haven't much time."

As Flo Bel continued speaking, Mallory paused at the door, caught by a serious and reflective note in her aunt's voice. "I wonder," Flo Bel said, "why young Scott Suydam didn't want to talk about Richard's accident. Did you notice that?"

"I don't know—that is, yes, in a way. It seemed to me he might not be telling—oh, something or other. It didn't matter. I was thinking mainly about him—Mr. Suydam, I mean."

Flo Bel gave her a swift and bright glance. "Thinking about him? I grant you he's attractive, but remember he's

12

your husband's—that is, your husband-to-be—best friend. Richard sent him to bring you to San Francisco."

"Oh, I know. Good heavens, I certainly was not thinking of Mr. Suydam in any special way!"

"Well, don't," said Flo Bel. "Now get to sorting and packing." She reached for a stack of what remained of the heavy, rich Bookever notepaper.

The two days, their last days probably in the Bookever house, went as swiftly as a dream. Flo Bel had already put in motion plans to sell the house immediately after Mallory's marriage. She had to sell it; there were no more mortgages to be had. There was nothing more to be sold. Flo Bel's jewels had gone; the famous Bookever collection of paintings and sculpture had been sold; the immense Bookever silver had been sold—all the huge trays and tureens, initialed flat silver, everything. So much of it had been discreetly disposed of that Flo Bel and Mallory had been reduced to eating from plated silver, Flo Bel hating it, Mallory not disturbed by any difference. In fact, everything salable in the great house had been sold except Flo Bel herself and Mallory.

Mallory caught back that ungrateful and, indeed, wicked reflection. She was not being sold to Richard Welbeck—what a notion!

She sorted, shook out dresses, petticoats, lacy underclothes, folded and packed and packed.

The florists who had been consulted about the wedding had made arrangements for a design of tropical shrubbery and flowers to cover the bare spaces on the walls, once occupied by paintings which, for the most part, had gone to private collectors, the majority of them all too willing, even eager, to seize some of the Bookever collection. The wines had gone to equally avid buyers. "They'll boast," Flo Bel had said once in a rare moment of bitterness. "They'll say oh yes, fine old Madeira, came from Peter Bookever's cellar. Poor old Bookever."

The Panic of 1893 had taken its immediate toll of bankruptcy and economic collapse. It had also, gradually, taken a further toll of some of its victims.

Mallory's father had been one of the first bankers to take the blow. Her mother had died a year or two previous to the

13

panic, and clearly, her father hadn't felt like starting again without his wife. In any event, he had quietly handed over all his records to the lawyers, sent a note tō Flo Bel asking her to see to his daughter Mallory, then six years old, gone secretly to the hunting lodge in the Poconos, which, with all his real property, was to be taken over in his bankruptcy, and there, in the woods, had had an "accident" with a gun. It was not surprising, Mallory reflected, folding up a creamy yellow ball gown in carefully saved tissue paper, no, not surprising that Flo Bel had felt sensitive to that word—accident. Mallory herself could remember very little of the event that had so strongly affected her life.

It was all that Mallory knew—at least, all she had been told; she suspected the truth, but only gradually as she reached her teens did the facts of the tragedy reveal themselves to her. By that time Flo Bel and Uncle Peter had taken the place of very indulgent parents; indeed, at Uncle Peter's insistence, they had legally adopted her and given her their name. She had had a very happy and snug childhood, except for an occasional but brief difference of opinion with Flo Bel. She had only the faintest memory of her real father.

But then the Panic of 1893 reached out its long-lived tentacles again; men Peter Bookever had trusted proved not to be trustworthy. Too many of them were trying in every possible way to retrieve their own lost fortunes, but most failed, even after the Morgan-Belmont agreement to supply needed gold to the government. The economics of the nation still seemed to teeter, barely on the edge of a further debacle. Mallory herself heard only snatches of conversation at the family dinner table; she did realize that rather often, suddenly, men were coming at night, talking, talking behind the closed mahogany doors of Uncle Peter's big library and study.

She was too young to recognize just what desperate attempts Peter Bookever had made to stave off coming disaster, that he had tried this venture and that; had gambled wildly, in fact. Then one morning he did not arise at his usual hour; he did not ring for Gorham. Suddenly there were doctors, the servants were in a tumult and Flo Bel came to her and told her, simply, that Uncle Peter had died in the night. An overstrained heart, she said, her lovely face very white below its flaming crown of hair.

But after it was all over, after the visits, the smell of tuberoses and lilies, the entire, sad experience was in the past, Flo Bel told her how all of Peter's efforts had failed, that he had trusted perhaps too many people. And finally, that he had mortgaged the enormous and lovely house, and almost everything else he could mortgage, and died a bankrupt. So, Flo Bel said sternly, they must go on as best they could, but they must give no hint of the actual extent of the financial disaster. Mallory was to continue her schooling at Miss Curely's; then they would see. Somehow Flo Bel had seen.

It was during that time that Mallory began to admire Flo Bel so completely that she found it easy to fall in with all of her plans. She might rebel sometimes, inwardly, but only a glance at Flo Bel's fragile-seeming, yet firm and beautiful face was enough to subdue any incipient revolt against her aunt's expressed desires. She told herself always that she must be grateful, unendingly grateful, to Flo Bel, and indeed she had every reason for that gratitude and obedience. Sometimes, though, in her heart, she questioned Flo Bel's decisions, but she held herself firmly in rein.

Flo Bel wouldn't give up the debut for Mallory; it was important. She wouldn't give up anything of outward show. Yet surely their most intimate friends must have seen what was happening—had to be aware of the gradual disappearance of paintings, rugs, crystal, silver, Flo Bel's jewels—the Fragonard panels that had been among the last to go.

And then—then Richard Welbeck had come to New York, met Mallory and liked her. He had asked permission to call. He had taken her for rides in one of the new electric motors that were now seen frequently, traveling at the whizzing pace of fifteen miles an hour once they got past the sparsely built-up streets in the Seventies and Eighties. There was even a sudden and exciting rush of gasoline-driven carriages that the daring young men called gas buggies, dashing recklessly and rather odorously along the avenues. The ladies perched beside the goggled driver in a small seat in front;

15

the ladies were goggled, too, and wore long coats, called dusters, and enormous chiffon veils tied over their hats.

It was all suddenly very new and pleasing. Even Flo Bel liked the novelty of modern ways and permitted a telephone to be installed in the pantry. This location very soon became rather a nuisance, for Gorham was usually to be found there in his shirt sleeves and apron, with a pipe and ashtray, cooking or washing dishes, or directing, with some of his former dignified-butler poise, the slapdash cleaning women who turned up at intervals. Mallory began to suspect Gorham himself paid them out of his own pocket.

Gorham now did everything. He had a variety of coats: one for marketing, a white one for doing what chores he could around the house, a neat black alpaca, an old black coat for formal wear—but this soon disappeared, since dinner parties, too, had disappeared from the pattern of the days. Sometime, somehow Mallory became aware of the fact that in a moment of pressure and desperation Flo Bel had borrowed part of Gorham's savings. Gorham never reminded her of it; he was too polite, and indeed too strongly attached to his place, if not to Flo Bel or the memory of Peter Bookever. Folding up a lacy, beribboned peignoir—expensive, all too expensive, and probably not paid for—Mallory wondered what, now, Gorham would do.

The engagement ring Richard had put upon her finger flashed in brilliance of sapphire and diamonds. She wished she could sell that, too, but of course it was impossible—it was a gift from the man she was to marry.

Richard's courtship had been wonderfully gentle, kind and considerate—also, she thought rather unexpectedly, extraordinarily respectful. Not for him the ardors and caresses the girls at school had read about in novels secretly obtained and secretly passed from hand to hand. And there were confidences, too, in dressing rooms while adjusting hair and flowers and bows before advancing, with all the mien of properly brought up young ladies, into a reception, or a ball or a wonderful buffet supper after the opera—where young gentlemen herded, between the acts, into the boxes wherever young ladies sat and smiled and waited demurely.

No, that was not Richard's style, but he did—well, he liked her, Mallory told herself defiantly, and she liked him.

So she was not simply marrying him for his money. It merely happened that Richard, with his good looks, his charm, his kindness, his...oh, he had many admirable attributes—with all that, he was a catch. Without money he'd still have been a most desirable husband. Perhaps not quite as desirable, she admitted candidly, if one looked at it coldly, as having so much money made him, but certainly very desirable and she was fond of him, was probably in love with him.

His letters clearly were rather stilted and her replies were on the formal side, for it didn't do, ever, for a maiden to express herself with any kind of intensity. Flo Bel had told her firmly: Never put anything in a letter you wouldn't wish your worst enemy to read. Mallory hadn't, it was true, felt overwhelming ardor, so it was easy to comply with the rules for polite behavior. Richard had her warm, grateful friendship; he had appeared like a genie to rescue Flo Bel and herself. She liked him and admired him, and desire would surely come when she was his wife, living in close association with him, sharing his life.

Mallory left her trunk for Gorham to close and went to Flo Bel's room—once so luxurious in its gentle rose silks, now worn and shabby but very, very neat. She chose carefully from a rather scanty wardrobe; lately, if Flo Bel spent money, it was for Mallory.

The two days passed with such frantic speed that afterward Mallory could barely remember them. Write, send messages, accept flowers with Richard's card, obviously ordered by Scott Suydam; receive the friends who would have been her bridesmaids, all of them thrilled at the exciting prospect of her crossing an entire continent to meet Richard and be married in what must be a most exciting and very rich city; receive, also, older friends of Flo Bel's who were not so thrilled—indeed, there were one or two heads shaken and lips pursed. Wouldn't it have been easier to wait until Richard Welbeck was able to make the journey to New York? Flo Bel said no so firmly that the suggestions were tacitly withdrawn.

Last-minute shopping for small things, such as chiffon scarfs to be wound turban-wise around their heads. The trains, everyone said, were full of the soot which belched from the engine. Flo Bel remarked with dignity that of course Richard's private car would be attached at the end of the train, so there would be little soot. One of her friends shook her head, too, about that, and commented realistically that there might be considerable sway in the private car. "Better take some seasick remedy," she said.

Flo Bel laughed, but saw to it that the last of Uncle Peter's old brandy was packed in a carryall, along with raincoats. Someone had said that it rained very often in San Francisco. Flo Bel had replied haughtily that of course Richard's motor, a new Daimler ordered from England for his wedding, would be sent to meet them, but Mallory noticed that she packed the raincoats just the same.

Then, suddenly, it was time to leave. They were to board the train, gloriously if sometimes optimistically called an express from New York to Chicago, the already glamorous Twentieth Century.

After a polite telephone call which Gorham took in the pantry and relayed to them, Scott Suydam came to escort them, via one of Brown's hansoms, although it was now a rather dangerous trip amid all the motor traffic, down to the Welbeck private car.

Around the railway station it was immensely crowded; unshaded electric bulbs flared with glaring lights everywhere. Gorham was already there, seeing to the trunks. Gorham, it developed, had locked up the house, left the keys with a banker and was going to San Francisco with them.

The car stood at the end of the train; there was a tumult of baggage carts, noise, commotion, people, and all at once Scott Suydam was at Mallory's elbow assisting her up the steps to the long gleaming railway car. She saw its name, *Dolores,* pricked out elegantly in gold; it was the name of Richard's cousin.

The date was April 11, 1906. San Francisco stood on its hills, sloping down to the Bay and the blue ocean, overlooking the misty hills of the southern peninsula, and Marin County

18

across the Golden Gate, all of it calm and lovely. Its handsome mansions were solid and firm, the shacks along Fisherman's Wharf were solid too, warm and friendly, the Ferry Building like a sturdy sentinel. The gracious patterns of life that gold had brought it, gold and trading and furs from Alaska, and tea and jade and porcelains and silks from the Orient—all this was serene, steady, firm and generous. April 11, 1906.

Two

The car was the very height of elegance. There was, first, a kind of railed veranda, or balcony, which Scott called the observation platform and where two strange people stood, bowing and bowing. Mallory had seen almost nothing of Scott Suydam during those two hurried days, and he had not happened to mention that Richard had sent two servants to attend them on the journey; but if she had given it a thought, she'd have known that Richard would provide just such a thoughtful courtesy. However, it gave her a tiny surprise to discover that both the servants, bowing and smiling, and bowing and smiling, were Chinese, dressed in loose black jackets fastened at the neck, and loose trousers. One was a girl, her face lovely above the beautifully embroidered silk jacket; her black shining hair was coiled up neatly on her head and her eyes were lively with curiosity.

"Su Lin," said Scott.

Su Lin bowed again and giggled a little, then looked shrewdly at Mallory's hat and suit and at Flo Bel.

"Kai Sing," said Scott.

He bowed again; his yellow face was round, very bland and smiling, punctuated with bright black eyes.

Flo Bel murmured something polite. Scott led the way into the car itself—a wilderness of thick red carpets, red damask chairs, mahogany panels, mahogany tables, brass chandeliers and table lamps with painted glass bowls, and a faint pervading odor which Mallory learned later was sandalwood.

They had entered, it seemed, the lounge. From it a narrow passage led beside a row of windows, past a small galley glittering with silver and china and crystal, its tiny shelves equipped with fiddles, barriers to keep the china from sliding, which Flo Bel eyed rather sharply, and then on to a tiny washroom and three excellent if tiny compartments; these were really staterooms with berths, now neatly made up under red embroidered covers. There were tiny dressing shelves, places for hand luggage and mirrors. It was all like a richly equipped and charming dollhouse—or, as Flo Bel said, like a steamer. "Very nice, very comfortable." She said it clearly, probably so Scott Suydam could hear. There were flowers on the shelves of two of the bedrooms, and Flo Bel said, again clearly, "How like Richard to remember flowers."

Scott Suydam looked slightly uncomfortable at that. Mallory instantly guessed that he and not Richard was responsible for the flowers.

Su Lin, bowing again, asked in perfectly good English if she might unpack. Somehow Mallory had expected anything but that from her—Chinese or, at least, pidgin English.

Flo Bel thanked her. "Yes, certainly."

Gorham had discreetly disappeared. Scott Suydam explained. "The servants and your butler have been placed in the car ahead of us. I think they'll be comfortable there. Now then..." He pulled a watch from his immaculate waistcoat and looked at it. Away off, far in the distance it seemed to Mallory, the engine hooted several times and puffed and hooted and the train began to move. Flo Bel clutched at a table and then sat down, composing herself in one of the huge upholstered chairs. Everything appeared to be bolted down, which struck a rather ominous note. Still, it was all very elegant, very luxurious and, indeed, very exciting. A private car! Richard Welbeck's private car! Richard Welbeck's friend and two servants sent to escort his bride on the long journey, in the most modern and luxurious manner, across a wide continent!

Mallory didn't realize, just then, how very wide the continent was.

The windows of the lounge and of the staterooms and galley, too, were on what Scott described as at the port side. Flo Bel understood him at once and said, "Posh. Port side out, starboard home. Very nice."

Scott Suydam gave her the first twinkle of a smile Mallory had yet seen. "You are accustomed to the Oriental trade."

Flo Bel's eyelids lowered for a second; then she smiled and lifted graceful shoulders. "Oh, no, not really. My husband had many interests, but the Orient—well, yes, perhaps. I didn't know the full extent of his interests. I must have heard the expression somewhere. Dear me, there are the Palisades."

They were chugging somewhat laboriously along the Hudson, but there was a magnificent view of the Palisades. Mallory said. "So...so high!"

"You've never come this far north?" Scott Suydam said. He was probably braced to carry on a semblance of light conversation all the way to the West Coast. Rather a strain, Mallory thought. He continued, however, "Wait till you see the mountains. Oh, there's no need for alarm. They put on an extra engine, I think some place in western Nebraska or Colorado. Have you selected your staterooms?"

Mallory replied, "Yes, thank you."

"It wasn't difficult." Flo Bel smiled briefly. "The lilies of the valley were certainly for the bride. But I am most grateful for the roses."

So she, too, had guessed who had provided the flowers. Scott's face grew a little firmer. "Good. I hope the servants will be efficient. I'm sure they will be. Kai Sing works in the Welbeck house. Su Lin is his daughter. Dolores sent them."

"Dolores?" Mallory said. "Richard's cousin? The train is. named for her?"

He flicked one glance at her and said yes. Su Lin bobbed at the entrance of the narrow aisle. "If Missy like to see how I arrange—"

Missy would, and rose.

Su Lin had accomplished a perfect arrangement; she had even placed the photograph of Richard, framed in silver, upon the tiny shelf beside the bunk. Mallory glanced at it, almost as if hoping for reassurance. But, she thought, there was no need for reassurance—everything Richard did and planned

21

was sure to be perfect. Su Lin, however, dispelled one notion of Richard's all-embracing forethought. "Missy—I mean Missy Dolores—made all the plans. She said nothing about your mother. I hope I have made sufficient arrangements for her."

"Oh, I'm sure you have." Mallory was already impressed by Su Lin's efficiency, as well as by her fluency in the English language. A curious question, however, struck her. "You mean Miss—" (What *was* Dolores' married name? Richard had mentioned her a few times; she knew that his cousin Dolores was married, but her name? No, she couldn't remember it if she had ever heard it.) She went on, "—Miss Dolores made all the arrangements for the journey?"

"Oh, yes, Missy. Mister Richard was not well enough to see to the details."

"Oh." So it was Dolores, not Richard, who had not seen fit to invite Flo Bel to accompany his bride. But perhaps conventions in a Western locality, so newly emerged as a city, were not as rigid as those in New York.

No, she reasoned, that would be wrong. She was not a fool; a newly rich, a magically but suddenly luxurious, city might go even further in insisting upon the proprieties than an already established city certain of itself and all its mores. Surely she had heard tales of miners' wives unexpectedly becoming roaring rich and sending for Paris gowns, jewels, everything.

Since San Francisco was to be her home, she repressed these unimportant but denigrating speculations. Su Lin smiled and nodded and bowed herself silently away.

Mallory sat down at the small dressing shelf and gazed at Richard's photograph. Unfortunately, it was stiff and posed; it showed none of Richard's pleasant charm, his rather boyish warmth.

She looked up at her own image in the mirror above the shelf. The car jolted a little as they crossed tracks, which proved to be, when she looked out the window and found a sign, a place called Harmon. There was nothing to be seen but the sign and tracks. She went back to the mirror, half smiling as she recalled Su Lin's conclusion that Flo Bel was her mother, for indeed many people had taken them to be mother and daughter, which was, Mallory could not but know, a compliment to her own looks. Her hair was a deep red, with waves which she could not quite suppress although she wore it smoothly brushed up into a pompadour and in the latest fashion, a kind of loop on the top of her head called a Psyche knot. It added to her age, perhaps, but it was becoming. She did resemble Flo Bel, for which she was thankful.

Long-time friends of Flo Bel's, most of whom had also known her mother, had always said that Flo Bel and Mallory's mother might have been twins, they were so similar. They were, of course, not twins—Flo Bel was two years younger than her sister—but they did look amazingly alike. There was a portrait, life-size not a kit-kat—was it a Sargent? Yes, John Sargent, a young artist who was now very famous and sought after—he had painted the two sisters together, standing and holding hands in a rather affected pose, but looking directly into the beholder's eyes. The portrait had later become valuable, but Flo Bel had refused all offers for it until almost the very last. Actually, it had gone then to help pay for Mallory's debut. Flo Bel had watched it being packed carefully and carted away, a look on her face which made Mallory want to put her arms around her aunt and say, "Go ahead. Cry..."

Flo Bel would have detested that. But she did say, "That's the first thing I'll buy back as soon as I get—" She broke off, turned away and finished nonchalantly, "As soon as possible."

Flo Bel had hated her name—it was Florence Christabel, quickly shortened to Flo Bel. She said it sounded like a chorus girl, although Flo Bel's knowledge of what a chorus girl might be was limited to hearsay. All they did, Mallory herself had been assured by one of her more sophisticated friends, was stand around on the stage twirling parasols and looking very statuesque. Sometimes one of them unbent so far as to nod or smile at some gentleman in the front row.

Mallory was not fond of her own name, but it had been her mother's maiden name. Now she tried to imagine her new name, as she had many times: Mallory Welbeck. Mrs. Richard Welbeck.

The slippered, softly moving Chinese (Kai Sing?) bowed at the door and told her tea was served.

It was a delicious tea. Dolores had planned well in the commissary department. But Flo Bel's lips tightened when she picked up a spoon. It was sterling silver, and it was engraved *Dolores*.

Scott apparently noted Flo Bel's disapproving look and said, rather quickly, that of course Dolores was Richard's only relative. Naturally, they had been very close.

"Naturally," said Flo Bel after a moment.

Dinner was to be served at eight o'clock. Flo Bel retired to her own stateroom; the only chink in Flo Bel's armor of reticence and dignity of which Mallory was aware was a tendency toward seasickness, which, however, Flo Bel referred to as *mal de mer* and passed over lightly. Her trips to Europe had been undertaken with courage, although every time when she returned and saw Mallory at school or brought the girl home to the lovely big Bookever house, she had said firmly that she would never put a foot on a steamer again. Of course she had, though, but not after Uncle Peter died. Nothing after that had been the same.

Scott Suydam disappeared, too, with a muttered excuse of seeing that Gorham was comfortable.

Mallory retired to her own stateroom and lay on the bunk, turned so her head was cushioned and she could watch the landscape. She almost fell asleep thinking of the famous, fabulous city she was about to visit.

Visit? That brought her awake again. Why, she was going to live there! It was to be her home.

Idly she watched the chill, purple April dusk settling over low hills. Lights twinkled from houses, giving the view a touch of warm hominess. Flo Bel did not emerge for dinner, but sipped a cup of soup with determination when Mallory brought it to her.

"Oh, no. I'm quite all right. It's merely the...the motion of the car. I'll get over it." She finished defiantly, "I always did. Even in a storm at sea." She then closed her eyes and leaned back.

Thus Scott Suydam and Mallory had dinner together, with rose-shaded lamps on the table and in sconces along the mahogany-paneled walls. The food was delicious; there was a room-warm wine, a burgundy, not too heavy, not too light. Uncle Peter had known about wines; he had had, everyone said, and it was true, a very fine cellar. Mallory knew it was fine mainly because she knew the price it had fetched.

As Richard's wife she need never again even think about prices.

The Chinese, bowing, smiling, silent and swiftly efficient, served dinner in courses on pale-green china that looked Chinese and which Scott assured her was. "Celadon," he said briefly. "Too good for the racketing around of a railway, but Richard insisted upon it when he and"—he checked himself and finished—"ordered other things for the car."

He had intended to say when Richard and Dolores ordered things for the car; Mallory was swiftly visited by that conclusion. But certainly there was no reason for Scott not to say so. He went on, rather quickly, "Not that there is much danger of rattling around in this car. It is handsomely and sturdily made. Of course, all the railway cars are made of wood and that may eventually prove to be a mistake. Steel, now—well, that's in the future. I'm sorry your aunt is not well."

"Don't tell her that!"

"Oh, I see what you mean. Yes, she strikes me as being an extremely independent lady." As Mallory bent over a strange fruity dessert, he said, "Mainly lychee nuts. Prepared—I don't know how, but good."

Mallory agreed and Kai Sing bowed and smiled at something Scott Suydam said to him in, to Mallory, strange and incomprehensible syllables.

"You speak Chinese?" she couldn't help asking.

"A little. I've lived in San Francisco all my life. All right, Kai Sing. We'll have coffee now, please."

The meal was over when Mallory discovered, with almost a leap of pleasure, Gorham, in full butler's regalia, standing with his arms folded, watching the action of his Chinese peer. But nobody, *nobody,* could actually be a peer to Gorham.

There were liqueurs served with the coffee. Kai Sing, watched austerely by Gorham, silently cleared the small table. Then they both left the lounge, and Scott Suydam, fidgeting a little, got out a cigar, looked at it, looked at Mallory and said he was afraid the smell of tobacco might disturb Mrs. Bookever.

"Well, yes, it might. Could you...could we get a breath of air on that...that balcony?"

"The observation platform? Why, yes. But you must get a wrap. The air is cool and the speed of the train makes for a certain breeze."

Flo Bel's door was closed. Mallory groped in the tiny built-in cupboard in her own stateroom. Su Lin had been there, turned down the bed (the bunk, whatever they called it), left fresh towels, plumped up the pillows and laid out nightgown and dressing gown. Slippers were properly placed in dancing position beside the bunk.

Mallory got out the tailored woolen coat, pale beige and long, which she had worn over her suit to the train.

Their clothes had been a source of considerable if hurried debate between Flo Bel and Mallory. What did one wear in San Francisco? More important, or at least more urgent just then, what did one wear on a train?

Suits, Flo Bel had decided. No question of it. San Francisco ladies wore suits. Somehow, during Mallory's engagement to Richard, Flo Bel had acquired bits of lore about San Francisco. She had even begun to interlard her conversation with odd bits of West Coast idiom; she smiled at this, herself, obviously enclosing such words as "strike it rich" or "pay dirt" or "down to cases" in quotation marks. In the course of her seeking for knowledge about the city which was to be Mallory's home, she had even explored the dress and customs of its population. The temperature in the winter averaged fifty; rains or fog were frequent and sudden. So the answer for street—or train—wear was clearly suits. Flo Bel's suit was, of course, black. It was extremely lucky, Mallory felt, that styles just then were flattering to a woman's figure; there was none of the bunchiness and overornamentation of a few years earlier. Her beige suit had a long, full skirt over a taffeta petticoat; the jacket was short, cut off just below the neatly pulled-in waistline, and below it the skirt billowed out, reducing the already slim waistline. A ruffly blouse went with the charming jacket, buttoned so only pleasant frills of

26

white showed at one's throat, also in a flattering manner. She was never sure that she really liked the huge and somewhat over-plumed hat that went with the suit, but she needn't keep the hat on.

They wouldn't need furs. Flo Bel had looked long at her once-luxurious Russian sable coat and shaken her head. "No. Hardly a guard hair left. Still, I had intended to wear it again next winter. Now I'll pack it away in mothballs. Your little summer ermine—no," she decided. "Too worn. Better no fur than shabby furs. We'll take woolen coats."

These woolen coats, like the suits, had been swiftly but carefully chosen; Mallory was not sure that the bills had been paid. However, Mrs. Peter Bookever's custom was not to be entirely dismissed, at least for another year or two. Certainly word of Mallory's engagement to Richard Welbeck of the Welbeck fortune had gone the rounds of tradesmen as rapidly—if not more rapidly, really—as among their own circle of friends. Credit was quickly prolonged. What a relief it would be, Mallory thought, as she had thought before then, to be able to pay bills. The exquisite luxury of that! All thanks to Richard—who, of course, didn't know about the bills. Unless he had guessed. Or unless some eager, if not particularly friendly, acquaintance had taken pains to inform him of the fact.

How lucky it was that she was genuinely fond of Richard!

She took a pale-pink motoring veil from the neatly folded little stack of belongings which Su Lin had unpacked, and tied it over her head, tucking its long floating ends into her coat collar.

Scott Suydam was waiting in the lounge. He held open the heavy door from the lounge to the vestibule—no, he had called it an observation platform.

Someone had placed small chairs there, very close to the car itself. It was windy, and the occasional whiff of smoke from the distant engine fell upon her. He gestured to the chairs. "Better keep your veil close. Sometimes there's a bit of cinder—" He had to shout over the din of the rattling train. The car did sway.

He sat down on the other chair. There was a shaft of light coming from the lounge and in it she saw his face change.

It had been, up to then, serious, almost grave; certainly not unfriendly, but not friendly either. She would almost have called it wary and guarded. But now he smiled a little and shouted jerkily, "The last car—does leap about—sorry your aunt is bothered by the motion. Reminds me—game called crack the whip—last one on the end got a real whirl—"

His words came in snatches above the rush of wind and clatter and jounce of the train.

Crack the whip. She remembered that game from very early schooldays. Children lined up, each taking another's hand; then the leading child ran, the others all ran, suddenly the leader stopped. The others had a chance to check themselves, but the child on the end had built up too much momentum, and unless very knowledgeable and very adroit, took a tumble—to the hearty glee of those who had contrived to remain on their feet. Perhaps the West Coast was not so different from the East in its customs.

"You've known Richard a long time," she shouted.

His face, still in that shaft of light from the lounge, instantly resumed its serious expression. "Oh, yes. Since we were children."

The train chugged and rattled on. "You must know his cousin, then, Dolores."

He drew back completely into the shadow. "Yes, certainly."

"I don't know her married name. Richard didn't tell me."

The answer came briefly from the shadow. "Beaton. Mrs. Henry Beaton."

"Oh."

A farmhouse went past them, lights showing briefly. How very fast they were going!

A strong whiff of smoke drifted back to them. She was probably getting covered with soot and grime. She drew her veil more tightly over her hair, for she couldn't imagine how she could get it washed before they reached San Francisco; oh, no, that would be simple. Su Lin would certainly help her if assistance were needed.

After a while she ventured again. "It was kind of...of Dolores to take so much trouble arranging for this trip."

This brought no response. Perhaps she was showing herself too inquisitive about Dolores. But Dolores was Richard's cousin, his only relative; Dolores would soon be legally her cousin too. Presently she plowed on. "Of course, she must have simply forgotten my aunt."

This brought a quick answer—quick, but jerky again due to the train's rounding a curve. "Oh, yes. Everything was hurried. Richard undoubtedly forgot—he was in great pain and left things to Dolores. She has always seen to things for Richard. Older— And yes, in the decision to ask you to come to San Francisco for your marriage, and the hurried preparations—everything was done hastily."

The train straightened itself out—on the very verge, Mallory felt, of going around in a complete circle, if not crashing down along the roadside in its own frantic efforts.

She sat back, relieved, in her chair. He said, unexpectedly, "Don't be frightened. This is all very safe, you know."

"No, I—that is, yes. I know." She got her breath and tucked in a flying end of her scarf. Something had got into her this night—some little demon of mischief perhaps, the excitement of travel, even the burgundy for dinner and sitting out in the windy darkness over the furious rush of the train's wheels. She turned to see his face. "There were flowers for my aunt, too. Dolores must have known that Flo Bel would be here."

There was another moment of silence on his part. Then he said, in a very casual way, "I sent her a telegram. She knows, and flowers were suggested."

Suggested by you, Mallory thought, and then, Dear me, how suspicious I am becoming! And how many questions I am asking! But I've got to know many things about this new life I am engaging upon, and the man sitting in the shadow, near me yet not really near me, could supply some of the answers. If he so chose.

She said, groping, "I suppose Richard's cousin has been of great help to him since his accident."

He did seem to jerk around toward her at that. However, he said, smoothly, "Of course. She and her husband make their home with Richard."

"They—*what!*"

"I thought Richard had told you. He couldn't have been very happy, living alone in that great house his father left

29

him. And naturally, his cousin—Dolores, I mean—felt it was her home. She had lived there since she was a child. After her marriage, Henry, her husband, and Dolores both settled down with Richard. The sensible thing to do. Dolores is a wonderful hostess. Enjoys dinner parties. Balls, even. The house has its own ballroom."

"Oh, dear! So...so splendid!"

Even in New York there were few private houses supplied with ballrooms of their own, and these were usually owned by elderly society matriarchs, only one or two by young married couples. Such a ballroom had been lent Flo Bel for Mallory's own debut: little gilded chairs along the walls, flowers banked everywhere, but especially obscuring the orchestra; also, sometimes partially obscuring a young unmarried couple, interested in flirtation if not in marriage. As a rule, in that governed few, it was marriage. Why, she thought suddenly, Richard asked me to marry him in Mrs. Lowell's conservatory; we were sitting near something or other which sent up a sweet, almost overpowering fragrance—freesia? Perhaps. She remembered only his formal statement of intent, so to speak, and her prompt—possibly too prompt—acceptance. But then, she had known his proposal was to come; Flo Bel had informed her.

She said now, "I haven't had any experience in giving balls."

After a second or two he said, "Dolores will help you."

Dolores again. She began to wonder if perhaps she would get a little too much of Dolores, sometimes.

He said, suddenly, "I hope you don't mind the Chinese servants. They are very good, you know."

"Yes, I—that is, I'll get used to them. They seem very neat and quiet and—efficient."

Selected by Dolores, she reflected, rather troubled. Suppose she did not prove to be as good a housekeeper—and trainer of servants—as Dolores? "Are there many Chinese in San Francisco?"

"Oh, yes." She felt him give her a close look through the shadows. "Always have been, at least as long as I can remember. The Boxer Rebellion, of course, sent many families here. But even before that, yes, we have always had Chinese."

"The Boxer Rebellion?"

"Long over now."

She groped back and regretted that she had given so little time to historical events and so much to French verbs. "Wasn't the old Empress said to have been on the side of the Boxers?"

"Secretly. Oh, everything has been said of the old Empress. She's still alive, you know, giving presents to all, and apologizing for what she calls a sad mistake." He went on, making conversation, yes, but also obviously trying in an impersonal yet friendly way to inform her about the city in which she was to live. "For a long time people in San Francisco have disliked the Chinese population, particularly when it began to increase. They don't like Chinatown. There are rumors—quite ridiculous rumors about Chinatown—"

"Chinatown." She had heard of Chinatown.

"The section of the city where, naturally, the Chinese live together, among their own people. But I do assure you, if any—oh, opium dens or secret underground passages exist, I don't know of them."

"Underground—for storage?"

"Well, no. People say that girls were brought in, sold as slaves—perhaps that happened at one time. Also, there still exists a certain amount of smuggling, I believe, and it is difficult to stop the process of getting sailors."

"Shanghaied?" She had heard that word, too.

He nodded, with the flicker of a glance in her direction. "Oh, yes, that did go on. Still does, I suppose. In fact, I know, but it is not fair to say one knows something unless one has seen it. I myself have never seen anyone shanghaied. But then, I wouldn't. I've spent most of my life either at school or—now—at work."

"Su Lin speaks excellent English."

"She was born in San Francisco. Her father was an immigrant, but he sent her to a good school somewhere down in the Peninsula. A Catholic school for girls. Su Lin is a very nice child." He thought for a moment, then said, "Lately, it seems the Chinese government has been encouraging people to come to the United States and learn our ways. The young, at least. You'll find that most of the servants are Chinese.

Some Japanese. Some Mexicans. Many Italians. San Francisco is quite a city." This time his voice was warm with pride and affection.

"It may take me some time to learn all these things."

He withdrew again into an impersonal politeness. "I don't think so."

"I do," she said glumly, to which he made no response at all.

It was not quiet, there was a noise and clatter all around them, but curiously there was a strong sense of silence which, for no reason Mallory felt, still must be filled, so she continued to resort to light conversation. "I hope your business in New York was satisfactorily settled."

"I think so. I'm not sure. I was arranging for some cargoes for New York."

"Cargoes?"

"For my ships. The Suydam line. Cargo ships, mainly for the Oriental trade."

He paused, then added, "I didn't begin the firm. My grandfather started it in a small way. My father built up the coastal trade, then the Oriental trade. He left the business to me."

"How exciting!"

She felt a rather skeptical glance in her direction. "If you like hard work. It is not at all romantic, you know. Trading, fixing prices, dealing with men—ship captains, supercargoes, crews, business contracts. We still have only five ships. Small, but good ones. And good men, for the most part, to sail them."

"To the Orient," she said softly. "It may not be romantic, but it sounds—oh, fabulous. Hong Kong? Singapore?"

"Pekin." He pronounced it Pekin to rhyme with reckon, not Peking as she had, but scantily, been taught. "That is, it was formerly Pekin. Now, since Hong Kong is a British Crown Colony and will be for nearly a hundred years—give or take a few—it has been easier to trade with Hong Kong; nearer, certainly. Pekin is a long sea journey, and even then, is a hundred miles or so from the seaport."

She thought that over. "But you were in New York—"

"Oh, yes. My ships carry all sorts of things, but our most lucrative trade is in silks and tea. Arnold Constable gave me a very..." He paused for a moment, and went on, "Yes, a good agreement. It means shipping across the continent by train just now. But as soon as the Canal is actually built, it will facilitate using my own ships."

"The Panama Canal is really to be built, then?"

"The plan is to start the construction next year. Of course, nobody knows just how long that will take. But it can't take forever—I hope," he said rather pessimistically. "Now we must go in. You must be getting cold."

She wasn't, really, but when a gentleman hints goodnight, one must take the hint instantly and politely. "Yes, I think I am." She rose.

Scott Suydam held open the heavy door into the lighted lounge. As she passed him the train suddenly lurched and jerked around a curve and threw her into his arms.

Three

He had to hold her for a moment until the train straightened out, until he could get his own balance and until she could clutch at a nearby chair. His cheek had barely brushed her own. He, too, grasped a chair, steadying himself. Then he said, very formally, "Sorry about that. You'd better take my arm. The Twentieth Century made a record run of eighteen hours from New York to Chicago—I think that was about four years ago. It is a very good train, but we still have to be careful on the turns, and things can go wrong now and then. There may be some long waits during the night. If we are delayed for any reason at all, think nothing of it. Goodnight," he said firmly, and didn't quite thrust her into her stateroom but it felt like thrusting. The narrow door closed firmly too.

She waited a moment and then sank down on the bed, ruffling up her night clothes and the neatly folded-back linens and blankets and silken cover. Richard's photograph eyed her rather reproachfully. On an impulse which she did not define, she took it in her hands and put it carefully in a drawer.

Scott had been obliged to hold her closely; he couldn't have done anything else. His cheek had been warm and he couldn't have helped brushing hers lightly, yet a kind of tingle seemed to remain, so she put up her hand and touched her cheek. It was rather warm, too, but otherwise just her own face.

She brought her hand down, and in the glow from the small table lamp, Richard's ring twinkled at her. She ought to return Richard's photograph to the shelf so she could see it. She didn't.

Richard's decorous embraces had never quite stirred her so her heart beat as fast as it was beating now.

Well! Stop it this minute! She wasn't Richard's wife yet, but it was so well established a promise that she was bound to him and thus bound to have no quickened pulse, no feeling at all concerning another man. So forget it! Sheer accident! No meaning! Go to bed.

The engine, far up ahead, gave a long whistle, a mournful sound streaming out into the night. Suddenly the train came to an unexpected, jarring halt.

For a long time there was no further motion. Then someone knocked lightly at her door. She snatched her old red dressing gown and opened the door. Scott Suydam said, apologetically, "I'm sorry. I hope you weren't asleep. I thought I'd better explain. You see, the train—some car ahead has developed a hot box. So we may have to struggle along for some time."

She wouldn't ask what a hot box was; she had already displayed far too much ignorance to Scott Suydam. He said, "We may have to keep stopping during the night. I've talked to the conductor. They may have to wait, you see, for other trains to pass. I am sorry."

"It doesn't matter. But thank you."

He nodded, said goodnight again and went away.

The train went on; the train stopped and waited endlessly, probably on some siding, as other trains rumbled along past it. Finally it resumed, it seemed to Mallory, a rather cautious

34

speed, before it stopped again. It became a hypnotic kind of monotony, and Mallory at last slept.

Eventually morning came, with Su Lin bringing in a tiny cup of tea and the train resuming its pace, but still rather cautiously, over smoother land.

It was a quiet day. The tinkle of china and silver from the galley was now easily heard, since the train no longer puffed so resolutely around hills and curves. The two meals provided that long day were delicate and handsomely served. Even Gorham seemed satisfied, and ceased to stand sentinel over every move that Kai Sing made. Once when Scott went up ahead to see that Gorham and Kai Sing were quite comfortably taken care of, he returned, grinning. Flo Bel gave him a questioning glance. He nodded. "It's all right. A couple of travelers have joined Kai Sing, and your Gorham has been playing poker with them, but I rather fear he has taken most of the stakes."

Flo Bel tapped her slender hand on the arm of her chair. "I hope that Oriental is not impulsive."

"You mean a knife or two." Scott chuckled. "Kai Sing? Never! He may not like to lose. Who does? But he is very peaceable. All our Chinese are. As a rule," he added.

Mallory said, "As a rule?"

All at once, it seemed to her, he became remote and very polite. "One hears stories but pays no attention to them. I told you last night. They are in fact very good citizens."

"Well, but—aren't there such things as tong wars?"

"At one time. Nothing that could trouble you." Scott sat down and opened a magazine that had lain on a table.

Mallory craned her neck to see what it was. He felt her scrutiny and obligingly held the magazine nearer. It was the latest issue of *Harper's Weekly*.

Flo Bel began to question him before dinner, when Kai Sing brought in small glasses on a silver tray. Mallory took one rather quickly, for she was afraid Flo Bel would object; in New York, young girls were not supposed to drink anything but a discreet glass of sherry during a long dinner. This drink tasted like nothing she had ever had before, not precisely good, but icy cold and rather tart.

35

"Gin," said Scott, eyeing her and explaining, "with a dash of vermouth. Like it?"

"Yes." She tilted the glass up to her lips again.

Her aunt had no qualms and sipped at her glass. Her eyebrows lifted slightly at the unfamiliar taste.

"Gin is not really considered a gentlemen's drink," Scott said conversationally, yet Mallory had a notion that he was amused at their reserved manner. "If you prefer sherry—"

"No!" Mallory said. "I'm tired of sherry."

Scott gave a quick nod, then resumed an air of detachment.

Possibly under the influence of the unusual drink or possibly because so many questions had been stirring around in her mind, Flo Bel began to question him. "About Richard's accident..."

Scott's face seemed to freeze.

"Were Richard's cousin and her husband actually in the house when it happened?"

"Yes," Scott said shortly.

"How very fortunate!"

"Very," said Scott. "But as you know, they live there."

"I've forgotten. Did Richard say how long his cousin and her husband had lived with him, Mallory?"

"Why, I—well, I don't remember. Actually, I don't remember that he ever told me they lived with him."

Scott said at once, "Probably he thought you knew. It's been so long. Dolores came into his father's care when her father died. Naturally, after her marriage she and her husband remained. His father had died and Richard couldn't live in that big house alone."

"Naturally," Flo Bel said, just a little too sweetly.

Mallory gave her a quickly suspicious glance. When Flo Bel spoke so sweetly it was well to watch out. "Do they intend to stay on, after Richard's marriage?"

This took Scott aback a little. "Why, I—really, I don't know." He rallied. "I rather think that Richard feels Dolores might be of help to...to Miss Bookever—"

"Oh, for goodness sake!" Mallory surprised herself. "Use my name. I mean—"

"That is your name," Flo Bel said coldly. "You were legally adopted."

"Yes, yes, darling. Yes. But—well, Mr. Suydam is Richard's best friend and..."

"Certainly," said Scott. "Thank you—Mallory."

Flo Bel had to let it go at that, and indeed it was not important. No more important, Mallory reflected, than a moment when the train lurched around a curve and flung her into Scott's arms and he held her there—and since then, quite clearly and properly, had forgotten all about it. She finished her drink, decided to ask for another and did.

Scott nodded toward the galley, that was all, and Kai Sing came swiftly forward and replenished her glass. Mallory felt an icy beam of disapproval from Flo Bel but preferred to ignore it. It was a really pleasant drink, once one got used to it.

Flo Bel resumed her not very adroit inquiry. "How very fortunate they were in the house when Richard's accident occurred. It might have been tragic indeed if no one had been there. Of course, the servants—"

"Oh, yes, someone would have found him," Scott said, rather hastily. "There was Grenay—I mean Mr. Grenay, the lawyer—in the house at the time, too. And I came in just after the doctor."

"So kind of Richard to send two servants—besides his best friend—to ensure his bride's comfort on this long journey." Flo Bel looked at her empty glass, and to Mallory's utter astonishment, accepted another as Kai Sing, again at a nod from Scott, brought it to her. "Of course, I'm sure there is no lack of servants—Richard and his cousin and her husband..."

Scott seemed to think it over before he replied rather carefully, "Su Lin is newly engaged."

"By Richard's cousin?" said Flo Bel.

There was a pause. Then Scott said, flatly, "Yes. I suppose so."

"Yes, naturally. Very kind, I'm sure. Now how *did* the accident happen?" Flo Bel twirled her glass with a rather elaborate nonchalance.

It was, by then, a persistent inquiry. Could Flo Bel possibly— Oh, no! Mallory decided that a swift and extremely unpleasant notion that had come to her from some quality in her aunt's voice had to be sheer fantasy. An accident cannot be made to happen.

Scott Suydam had picked up something unsaid in Flo Bel's tone, too. He replied, distinctly, "It was a most unfortunate accident just at this time. One of those things than can happen to anybody."

"Yes, certainly. You didn't tell us how it happened." Flo Bel could be extremely, sweetly determined.

"You did tell us," Mallory said boldly. "He fell on the stairs."

"Yes, of course." Flo Bel nodded with dignity. "But *how* did it happen?"

"He—well—he just tripped and fell." Scott rose and looked out the window. The train seemed to be slowing down again.

"What tripped him?" Flo Bel was so insistent that again the monstrous notion flitted across Mallory's mind. Surely Flo Bel did not think that somebody contrived to bring about that fall. What purpose could that serve?

It might have killed Richard, but nobody wanted to kill Richard. It might have prevented his marriage. But no, that was wrong; he had sent his private car to bring her to him and their wedding, and Dolores had made all possible arrangements for their comfort. Mallory couldn't control her thoughts, certainly, but she could try to be rational. The train jerked to a stop.

Scott Suydam said, again, "He just tripped and fell. This must be Gary at last. I'll see if I can get some newspapers. We'll be in Chicago very soon."

With that and with, really, the effect of an escape, he pulled open the heavy door to the observation platform and disappeared.

"Dear me!" Flo Bel emptied her second glass. Then she blinked once at Mallory. "A very strong drink, isn't it? I hadn't realized—"

"Strong enough for you to suggest to him that somebody tried to hurt Richard."

"Now, Mallory— Well, perhaps I did, but one must be sure of...a number of things." Flo Bel hesitated, glanced rather warily at the empty glass in her hand and said firmly, "A very strong drink. Don't take any more of it, Mallory."

"I already have. I feel all right. In fact, simply great!"

"Mallory!" It was a reproof. But then Flo Bel's eyes grew serious. She said thoughtfully, after a moment, "I'm not sure I'm going to like this Dolores. We—I mean you will have to get her out of the house as soon as you can. Two," said Flo Bel with dignity, "is company, three is a crowd. I should say four. Especially a cousin and her husband. I'm going back to my room."

She went with unimpaired dignity but clung to the back of the chair and settee as she moved. Mallory thought charitably that she had never seen Flo Bel with one too many drinks under her handsome belt, or indeed even slightly cheered by wine. But she had eaten almost nothing since they had started. An empty stomach—yes, Mallory had heard Uncle Peter mention the effects of drink upon an empty stomach. She herself felt great, really, as she had said, yet rather in the need of fresh air. She hesitated, thinking perhaps she would need a wrap; she decided against it, pulled hard at the heavy door and was all at once out into the air. It wasn't really fresh air; it seemed to be laden with train smoke and soot. She gulped once or twice and advanced to lean against the fancifully decorated wrought-iron railing. Here she and Scott had sat and talked; an unrevealing talk, but a talk nevertheless. And just there, behind her, as they entered the lounge, the now quiet yet still puffing train had swerved around a curve and shot her into Scott's arms. Well, she wouldn't remember that.

The gate, leading to three steps which in turn went down to a dusky streak of pavement, was now open, as Scott apparently had left it. She gulped in more sooty air. Somebody, Scott perhaps, in the desultory conversations which had sprung up between them occasionally that day, had spoken of the steel mills at Gary.

She wondered what Chicago would be like and hoped they could see something of that powerful city.

She went to the open gate, and could see only moving lights; there was the noise of train crews, distant voices. Scott ought to be returning. She had no idea how long the train would stay there; indeed, during the journey and many long stops thus far, there had been no way of knowing when the

train would resume its jolting way. Off in the distance someone shouted hoarsely—and two strong hands shot out of the
dusk below her, grasped her ankles and pulled.

Four

She reached out toward the railing and clutched it as hard
as she could, and then, instinctively and violently, tried to
kick with the feet which were being dragged as if those two
strong hands were determined to force her down.

Under the train, she thought coldly, for the train gave its
usual premonitory jerk and puff that meant it was about to
start again.

There was another jerk, the grip on her ankles tightened;
she kicked wildly and then heard someone screaming, wildly
too. Why, that's me, she thought, and screamed and kicked
and the door behind her must have swung open, for suddenly
someone plunged out toward her, caught her firmly, shouted,
"Stop that screaming!" and...and the hands gripping her
ankles and pulling with such ugly power relaxed, were gone,
and there was only the sound of footsteps pounding away
somewhere into the heavy dusk.

"You all right?" Scott Suydam shouted in her ear, pulling
her erect.

She got her breath and stopped screaming.

He gave her a quick shake, holding her shoulders; in the
dim light from the lounge his face was ghostly white. "Are
you all right?" he shouted again above the increasing rattle
and jolt of the train.

"No! No, I'm not all right! That man—somebody—"

He drew her swiftly into the lounge, dropped her down on
a chair, gave her a quick, searching look and said, "Where
are you hurt?"

"I'm not hurt! But he tried to kill me!"

"He— Stay there! Don't move." He left her and ran into the tiny passage, toward the front of the car.

But I *am* hurt, she reflected dismally, rubbing her bruised ankles. More than that, I'm terrified.

Who would act so boldly, so swiftly, taking advantage of her exposed position, the fact that she was alone on the little ornate platform?

Could that person with those strong and, yes, murderous hands have been watching for just such an opportunity and seized upon it?

Well, but then—why?

Flo Bel came into the lounge, stopped when she saw Mallory, looked surprised; at least, she lifted one of her exquisite eyebrows. "Mallory! Heavenly days! Go and brush your hair at once! Wash your face!"

Scott Suydam came back along the passage. He had been running and his breath was coming quickly. But he paused when he saw Flo Bel, then in a deliberately controlled manner, strolled across the lounge, or would have strolled if the car had not given one of its convulsive jerks so he had to grasp at a chair.

Flo Bel, under the compulsion of motion, sank down into another chair. "Mallory, what *have* you been doing!"

Scott answered, "It's all right, Mrs. Bookever. That is, it's not all right at all, but I think no real harm was done. Did he get your handbag, Mallory?"

She shook her head numbly.

"Jewelry?" Scott insisted.

"No. Or, wait a minute— No." She lifted her left hand. The beautiful glitter of Richard's ring was still there. So were the bruises and scratches on her ankles.

"But he grabbed my ankles. He tried to drag me off the train. Just as it started moving..." Her voice sounded breathless, shaken, trembling.

Flo Bel sat even straighter than was her usual pose. A kind of cold flash came over her face, a blink, like white lightning. "*Who* did this?" she demanded icily, turning to Scott.

He replied. "Some thug. Some tramp. Some thief. They do hang around stations sometimes. A private car almost invites an attempt at stealing. I suppose he saw Mallory and—just grabbed."

"I'd have gone under the train." Mallory heard the quaver in her own voice, but she had a right to quaver, hadn't she?

Scott said, "He didn't get you. He didn't get any money or jewelry."

Mallory was not in the mood for sensible reassurance. "It wasn't you he tried to pull out like that!" She was angry and still frightened. Perhaps she hoped for consoling words. If so, she was disappointed.

"Well, I'm thankful to say no harm was done." This time Scott looked at her legs. "Your aunt is quite right. Your face and hands and stockings, shoes, ankles— Su Lin is in the galley. She may have some sort of salve or...or something."

Mallory had been so thoroughly terrified that his controlled manner only infuriated her. "I'd rather have a drink."

Flo Bel continued to sit very straight and still.

"I'll get it. Sherry..."

"That other drink. Gin and whatever it was," Mallory said.

Scott did not smile, but his mouth did twitch slightly at the corners. He called over his shoulder, "Kai Sing."

Kai Sing appeared like magic from the small aisle. Scott spoke to him quickly in Chinese. Kai Sing bowed, did not even glance at Mallory and vanished. But she felt that his narrow Oriental gaze had taken in the whole picture, even the silver buckle gone, she then saw, from one shoe.

The drink came, like magic too; he must have had it already prepared. Flo Bel did say, but without conviction, "Now, Mallory, it is a very strong drink..."

Mallory sipped it, but this time cautiously.

"Mallory!" Flo Bel cried. "Your shoe! The buckle is gone."

"I kicked, I told you. I held on to the railing and kicked and kicked."

"I hope you hit him." Scott was suddenly grim, and she could see that he was very angry beneath his cool manner. "Here, let me help you to your stateroom." He took her arm.

Su Lin looked up as they passed the galley, and her round, placid face turned a little waxen as Scott spoke to her in soft, incomprehensible syllables, then she quickly followed them.

Mallory allowed herself to collapse on the bunk. She still

42

held her glass, and unexpectedly Scott reached out and took it from her. "Your aunt is right. It really is rather strong. Dinner will be served soon, I believe. Su Lin will see to your ankles."

"Did that...that man get away?" she asked.

Scott nodded. "Seems so. I found nobody suspicious. Trainmen had seen nobody except the usual baggage handlers, passengers getting off, train crew." He looked down at her, serious, intent, obviously still angry; then in an absent way he lifted her glass to his own lips and downed its contents.

She couldn't help a feeble smile. "Strong drink," she reminded him.

He glanced at the empty glass, smiling briefly, and went away, closing the narrow door firmly behind him. The train picked up speed.

Su Lin uttered some shocked and commiserating murmur and knelt. She pulled off Mallory's shoes and torn stockings, vanished, returned quietly with some kind of liniment, a little pot of it. First, murmuring again, this time as if in apology, she cleaned Mallory's ankles gently with warm water and a sponge, dried them as gently with a towel, applied a mild salve and then sat back expectantly for directions.

The skirt Mallory had worn was stained with sooty smears. Her hands were black too. She motioned for more water, rose, rather painfully, and washed her hands and face. Su Lin took her once-white blouse.

Mallory turned to the tiny built-in mahogany cupboard. Clearly she must change. She took out another blouse, hesitated, then removed the soft green tea gown which she had packed in the valise for a possible emergency. She had been struck by a notion that they might arrive at Richard's house, meet him, be given dinner or tea or whatever was suitable to the time of day, and that the trunks might not be delivered in time to change. The green dress and the kid slippers, covered with something that looked like bronze, would not only be a grateful change from a traveling suit but would be a more flattering introduction to Richard's home—and certainly more pleasing to Richard's eyes than a travel-worn suit.

Su Lin's face beamed. The dress was of the latest fashion, designed for her trousseau. Mallory had already worn it once or twice at tea parties arranged in her honor. She looked with frank satisfaction at as much as she could see of herself in the small mirror. In front, the dress had a white lace guimpe which went almost to her throat and had a white delicate lace frill around the neck. The sleeves were full to the elbow, then finished in tight white lace to her wrists, ending with a lace frill, flattering to anybody's hands, especially one decorated with an enormous sapphire and diamond ring that flashed cheerfully in the light. There were adroitly situated tucks around the top of the dress and an even more ingenious belt, for it came down in a V in the front, accenting her slender waist; the long, full skirt billowed out so her hips seemed very graceful. She was far too elegantly dressed for dinner on a train, yet she could not bring herself to wear the beige skirt until it had been suitably cleaned; she knew she could leave that to Su Lin.

She brushed up her hair into its usual pompadour, and felt so far restored that she used a dab of perfume on her ear lobes; she had purchased that secretly, for she felt that Flo Bel would not approve.

Su Lin gave her an encouraging, almost a congratulatory and proud bow as she opened the door and went out into the aisle and into the lounge. When she passed the galley she had a quick glimpse of shining copper, and Kai Sing wielding a huge, extraordinarily sharp-looking knife as he cut what appeared to be a melee of vegetables into tiny pieces.

Flo Bel gave her a startled glance, but then nodded and said, "Of course. You couldn't wear that skirt." Then the train gave a lurch, and she clung to the arm of her chair and turned rather pale.

It seemed to Mallory that Scott had an approving look in his eyes. But by now all of them were slightly under the influence of the unusual drink to which Scott had introduced them. Fortunately for Flo Bel, the train had halted again for some mysterious reason. Soup came and a mixture of fish and tiny crisp pieces of some vegetables which Mallory could not identify. As the train obligingly continued its pause both Flo Bel and Scott seemed tacitly to agree to discuss no further the ugly experience Mallory had had. She, too, tried to push it to the back of her mind, but she couldn't—she still felt the strong determined hands on her ankles. She made herself listen to Flo Bel's charming but persistent voice.

When Flo Bel wished to do so she could be as adroit at extracting information from anybody as Uncle Peter had been adroit at opening one of his fine wines. Would Mr. Suydam's wife be at the train to meet them?

"Scott," he said. "If you please. You may as well, you know. You'll see me often in San Francisco."

Of course; he and Richard were such close friends. And his—that is, Scott's wife would probably be one of their close friends, too.

"I don't think my wife will meet us," said Scott, his lips twitching a little.

A fish course arrived and Scott offered the information that it was Lake Superior white fish, taken on at Gary along with ice and a few other fresh foods.

Not to be distracted, Flo Bel returned to her gentle attack. "I have understood that owing to the amazing flow of wealth from the gold mines and other sources, San Franciscans have some unusual additions to society."

Scott took it without a flicker of an eyelash and agreed. Oh, yes, there were various odd stories, odd but interesting.

Flo Bel pursued it. "Didn't I hear somewhere that one of the influential matrons had once been a cook in a mining camp?"

Scott agreed cheerfully; then seemed to take the bull by the horns—although likening Flo Bel, with her fragile, feminine charm, to a rampaging bull was preposterous. Scott told them, cheerfully, almost proudly it seemed to Mallory, that there was indeed a former cook from a mining camp—also, he understood, one or two former laundresses.

"Most admirable women, I'm sure," said Flo Bel with an annoying loftiness.

Scott had a glint in his eyes by then. He assured Flo Bel that San Francisco was indeed a metropolitan city; he added that it had almost as colorful a history as New York City.

This silenced Flo Bel for the moment, but she returned to her delicate yet pointed inquiries. "I believe you said that you arrived just after the doctor. I mean, of course, when Richard's accident occurred."

Scott waited a moment. Then he said, tersely, "My home— my father's and grandfather's home—is not far from the Welbeck mansion. I am a native San Franciscan." He smiled a little but his eyes did not smile. "Indeed, few people could be more completely native. My grandfather came out from New York—Rhinebeck. Married a lovely Spanish lady. My house had been built by Spaniards. Casa Madrone."

Flo Bel lifted her eyebrows politely. Scott explained with a kind of hard-held patience. "The madrone is a shrub," he said, "so heavy and big it's almost like a tree. There are many ancient madrones all around the house, so old that they have big silver trunks, heavy foliage." His voice had changed a little; it was both respectful and gentle. "It is a very old house, but very solid and well built. There are huge eucalyptus trees around it too; but the name Casa Madrone seemed to fasten itself upon the place—oh, many years ago. I was born there. I live there now."

"Oh," said Flo Bel without much interest.

"But about Richard—I came to see Richard the night of the accident. Everything was confused. Richard, lying at the foot of the stairs. Dolores, trying to do something, anything. I believe it was Kai Sing who had taken things in hand and made the rest of them leave Richard as he was until the doctor arrived. They sent the coachman, Murphy, for the doctor. He put splints on Richard's leg then and there. Murphy and I carried him to his room." He leaned back, eyeing Flo Bel as if he wanted to say, Is there anything else you want to know?

But Flo Bel said, rather apologetically, "I'm sorry. I didn't mean to insist. I can see that it was an accident and—"

Scott broke in abruptly and rudely, "What else could it have been?" He rose, for the train had resumed its joggling, now hasty way; the china and glasses jingled. Scott said briefly that they were running into Chicago and he was afraid the car would be shunted around some; indeed, it must be shifted to a different station and they mustn't mind it. In the meantime he would try to get a *Chicago Tribune*. "It's a morning paper. But I may be able..." He paused to pull thick

46

red velvet curtains across the windows. "I expect you'd like to get out and walk, but—"

"Mallory?" Flo Bel cried. "In those slippers?"

"No. No, of course not. However—do please stay right here. Don't even go out on the platform." He looked directly and gravely at Mallory.

"I wouldn't dream of it," she cried.

However, it did not satisfy Scott. He took both Mallory's hands in a warm, firm grasp, startling her, it seemed so intimate. "I don't want to frighten you. But there was a strike not long ago, here in Chicago, a very unpleasant business, from what I hear. There may still be some rather rough men hanging around. Perhaps in Gary— But in any event, neither of you could get much exercise here. The car will be moved over switches, and all that. The train sheds are dark and there are baggage trucks, trainmen, soot, smoke— No, you both really must stay right here." He seemed suddenly to realize he was holding Mallory's hands and released them gently. Mallory felt rather than saw Flo Bel's eyebrows lift. Scott said, unevenly, "You see, I don't want to lose you."

"I told you," Mallory said. "Nothing could induce me to leave the car even as far as the platform."

Scott turned away abruptly and went out along the passageway, rather than by way of the platform.

Flo Bel permitted her eyebrows to resume their usual curve and said practically, nodding toward the door to the platform, "I suppose he has locked that door."

Mallory tried the door. Flo Bel was right. "So whether we like it or not, we are boxed up here," she said shortly. "I'm perfectly sure he has given orders to Su Lin and Kai Sing not to let us leave."

"Sensible," said Flo Bel. "Mallory, who was the man in that station, Gary? You must have seen him."

"No, I didn't. I couldn't have seen him."

"But even in the dark—"

"It wasn't quite dark. Almost."

"Tell me exactly how it happened."

"I don't know—that is, all I know is that I was standing at the railing, holding on to it actually." A kind of chill went up her back. "Luckily, really. But the little gate, the gate that opens so you can go down the steps, was open. I just felt two hands come out and catch my ankles and pull and I—all I could do was hang on to the railing and scream. And kick."

Flo Bel thought for a moment. "Do you think you struck him?"

"I hope so," Mallory said viciously. "I hope I hit him so hard he'll never try that again!"

There was a long pause. Then Flo Bel said again, "Why didn't you see him?"

"How *could* I see him? I was looking down the track behind us—what I could see of it, a few lanterns, that was all. Then when he grabbed my ankles I just held the railing until Scott came."

"Yes, of course. I'm thankful you showed that much good sense. Indeed, I am very thankful young Suydam came as he did. But don't be too grateful. Make sure you do not forget that you are to marry Richard."

Mallory became a little stately herself. "I'm not likely to forget that. With a sudden quirk of mischief she remembered the old story of the mother who told her children not to put beans up their noses, a notion which had never before entered the children's minds. However, she told herself sharply, she was not a child.

The car gave a jerk, and started jogging backward. Flo Bel sighed, turned slightly green, rose unsteadily and went, without another word, into the passage. Mallory heard the door to her stateroom close. The car jerked again, stopped, waited for some mysterious signal, started again.

The switching process seemed to go on forever while she sat alone in the plush and splendor, looking idly at her bronzed slippers and determining not to brood about the brutal strength which had so nearly drawn her from a moving train. Under it— Oh, no, that couldn't have happened to her! No. Think of it as merely an accident, over with, to be forgotten.

But she didn't, couldn't put it out of her mind.

The lamps blinked and went out, leaving her for a moment or two in a darkness which was threaded through by beams of lights through the slits of openings in the red curtains. Station lights, workmen's lights, something. During one of the conversations that had gone on, occasionally, she had heard Scott tell Flo Bel that the car had its own electricity system and generator. After more jerking and shunting the lights came on again—their rosy shades filtering the stunning brilliance of the filaments within the glass bulbs.

After considerable pounding and numerous hoarse shouts from outside, the train began to move forward in a resolute way.

A moment or two later Scott came back—his coat collar turned up, his face rather grim. There was no mistaking the look of something very like relief when he saw her there, exactly as he had left her. He had some newspapers under his arm. He sat down and stretched out long legs. "Whew! I've been through every car—that is, I mean I wanted to make sure that Kai Sing and, of course, your butler were comfortably settled. In the next car again. It took a little managing."

"That was kind of you."

"Only some running around outside. It's damn cold. I mean—very cold."

Mallory heard a slight giggle in her own throat. "I've heard the word damn before. In fact, I've used it."

He gave her a long and oddly serious look. "You don't look as if— Oh, well, schoolgirls."

"I am not a schoolgirl."

"No, I mean— Oh, never mind. Now then, I promised Richard to see you safely to San Francisco. I'll have to ask your help. That thing at Gary—"

"I'll never take a chance like that again."

"Don't—"

Suddenly she felt that it would not be a good idea for her to sit here in the cozy intimacy of the lounge. That was due, certainly, to Flo Bel's shocking implication! She rose. "Thank you for everything."

"It was nothing."

"Saving my life means something to me."

He rose. His eyes took on a grave and intent look; then he moved toward the aisle. He said something over his shoulder. She couldn't be sure what it was; it sounded like "to me, too."

49

Naturally, if he were to deliver his cargo intact to Richard...

He said goodnight then, clearly.

In her tiny stateroom, she removed the dress and slippers and then sat in her ruffled corset cover and long taffeta petticoat, selected for its color and it pleasant rustle when she moved.

It had been a frightening evening. And even now she shuddered as she remembered, too clearly, the moment of terror, hanging for dear life to the railing. But she must not brood about it. It was a tramp, or an out-of-work laborer, thinking to rob her of jewels or money.

She went to bed.

The first time the train came to a halt at some station, Flo Bel knocked on the door politely and came in. She had a small bottle in her hand.

"Chloral hydrate," she said. "Where's a glass? Oh, here! I was given this by the doctor after your uncle died. I used it only a time or two. I knew I had to face things, no use trying to procrastinate. But here—you had a dreadful experience. I'll just measure out what you can take." She tipped the bottle carefully, counting the drops that fell into the glass. "A little water in this. No more medicine, though, even if you can't sleep. It is very dangerous stuff. Goodnight, my dear."

She went away, taking the bottle with her and closing the door softly.

Mallory left the glass on the dressing shelf. She didn't expect to sleep, but the train had resumed an even motion and it lulled her into so deep a sleep that she was confused when she awoke just before daybreak, feeling sure that someone was in the room.

But it couldn't be. She struggled out of sleep, roused to turn on the lamp—and, of course, Flo Bel had not quite closed the door. It was swinging gently, making just a sharp enough click to awaken her. She rose, closed the door firmly and went back to bed.

Five

Morning came slowly. It proved to be a dull and misty day, not quite raining. Su Lin, softly knocking at the door, again roused Mallory, set down the cup of tea, asked Mallory's permission to open the curtain and did so; gray light streaked in. The hot tea was delicious. Over it Mallory idly watched Su Lin straighten the little room. She also happened to be watching as Su Lin picked up the glass with its sleeping draught untouched. Su Lin became very still. After a second or two she lifted the glass, sniffed at it, and swift as a plump, pretty little cat, turned to throw it out.

Something compelled Mallory to explain, "That was some sleeping medicine. My aunt gave it to me."

Su Lin, as motionless as a lovely little statue, didn't look at Mallory. Mallory said, unaccountably annoyed, "She thought I might need it after the...that..." The less said of the incident at Gary, the better. "But I didn't take it."

Still the girl didn't flicker an eyelash; her round face was lowered. Mallory was defeated. "It's all right to throw it out. Now, what shall I wear?"

The beige skirt had been neatly cleaned and pressed. Mallory looked down at the walking shoe from which the thug had snatched the buckle; it was very modern, for it had no buttons and was cut low, but instead of a silver buckle, now there were only torn threads. She looked away quickly, for again she could almost feel the two strong hands gripping her ankles, pulling and tugging her downward as the train started to move. And she realized her hands were still a little sore from grasping the railing that had saved her.

Better not talk of it and much better not think of it. She said, "It's raining."

Su Lin shook her pretty head; her face remained perfectly blank. "Not yet, Missy. Soon perhaps."

"You speak such good English, Su Lin."

Su Lin shook out the green dress and looked it up and down, probably for spots. "Oh, yes, Missy. I was born in San Francisco." She took out fresh towels. "There have always been many Chinese in San Francisco. I believe breakfast is about to be served."

"Thank you, Su Lin."

The train was rolling along easily now, over what seemed to be flat prairie land—or at least flat land, no sudden hills. Flo Bel was already in the lounge. Kai Sing was trotting swiftly in and out of the shining small galley. The fragrance of coffee was pleasant; eggs and bacon and fruit—all of it was on the small table, lighted with rosy lamps this dreary morning and sparkling with silver and china.

Flo Bel looked up from a cup of coffee. "There you are. You did sleep, then."

Scott was not to be seen. Mallory sank down in a chair which Kai Sing held for her, then smiled and bowed himself away. "Oh, yes, I slept."

Flo Bel put down her coffee cup. "But you really shouldn't have taken that bottle of sleeping medicine. I didn't hear you come in my room. How much did you take?"

"I didn't take any. Su Lin poured out what you gave me last night."

Flo Bel's pretty face was stony and sharp. "The bottle is gone!"

"The whole— But I didn't take it! Why should I? I didn't want it. Flo Bel, you said it was dangerous!"

"It is. Exceedingly dangerous." Her eyes narrowed, looking, however, at nothing. "This is very strange," she said flatly. "I wonder if that Chinese..."

At that instant Kai Sing came softly into the lounge. "Madam wishes more coffee?" he inquired.

"No, thank you," Flo Bel said stiffly.

She went to the lounge chair and sat down, gracefully, as usual. Kai Sing pattered softly about, fluffing up cushions, removing invisible flecks of soot, muttering apologies as he moved, his slippers soundless on the carpeted floor, his smile

bland and unrevealing. He had had his pigtail removed—
wasn't there a law to that effect? Mallory dimly remembered
something Richard had told her about forcing certain of the
Chinese to have their native long braids cut off and forbid-
ding American-born Chinese to grow them.

Flo Bel looked steadily out at the rainy, gray landscape
until Kai Sing had bowed and bowed and padded softly away,
taking the table and its china and silver with him. There
began again the slight tinkle of cleaning up, and preparations
probably for luncheon, from the galley.

Flo Bel said, at last, "I think this needs looking into. Someone took that bottle from my room. I left it on the little shelf
below the mirror. It is not there now."

"But surely you'd have heard someone come in during the
night." Yet suddenly and too clearly Mallory remembered
the impression she'd had that the door to her own room had
not been properly closed and had clicked a time or two sharply
enough to awaken her. But—no, no one could have entered.

Flo Bel said, "I'll get to the bottom of it. A bottle of chloral
hydrate is nothing to have roaming about."

It was nothing, a tiny bottle lost, somehow, during the
swaying and jolting of the car, nothing at all. Yet there was
a lingering, annoying uneasiness about the incident.

Scott came swinging in from the passageway. He said good
morning, asked if they had slept well and announced that
they would soon arrive in a place called Council Bluffs.

"Will we stop there?" Flo Bel asked.

"For a moment or two. Then we cross the river and stop
in Omaha." He sat down. "We are really making unusually
good time now after all those delays. Eventually we get an
extra engine. For the mountains," he added explanatorily.

There was something about Flo Bel's attitude that suggested to Mallory that her aunt was about to launch upon
another inquisition about Scott himself, Dolores, Richard,
anything and anybody Mallory was likely to encounter in
this new life. She said, hurriedly, "Council Bluffs. An odd
name..."

Scott looked at her. He had a good face, Mallory thought,
her mind off on a tangent, not precisely handsome, as Richard
was handsome, but— She sought for another word, couldn't

find it and said to herself, Good-looking. He seemed, indeed, almost military in his quiet and yet decisive way of speaking and even in the way he carried himself, good straight shoulders and a firm way of walking. "Oh, yes," he said. "Some of the Indian tribes had their council fires there, on the bluffs above the river. Long ago. But the name is still that. Omaha is an Indian name, too."

Mallory groped back into rather scattered memories of geography. Few of those, particularly lessons concerning the West, had seemed of any possible importance to her when she was in school. London, Paris, yes. The first time she'd heard a great deal about San Francisco was during Richard's visit to New York.

Scott leaned forward to peer out the window. "We are up in good time to see the river when we cross it."

Flo Bel asked, rather icily and without any apparent interest, "What river?"

Scott's eyes twinkled just a little; he replied politely, "The Missouri. The Platte flows through Nebraska and into the Missouri. The Missouri continues on and flows into the Mississippi. Then—"

"Thank you," Flo Bel said crisply. "To New Orleans and the Gulf. How interesting!"

The twinkle in Scott's eyes became a little more pronounced; as if he realized that, he leaned forward and again looked out the window.

Flo Bel waited a moment and then said, "By the way, is there any way in which anyone from the cars ahead of us can get into this car?"

Scott turned back. "Why, yes. Certainly. How did you think the servants came from their car here?"

Flo Bel did not look in the least dashed. "Yes, of course. I mean from all the other cars of the train."

Scott's twinkle vanished. "Yes," he said rather slowly, watching Flo Bel. "Su Lin and Kai Sing and your butler are in the next car, and then there are Pullman cars. And ahead of the Pullman cars, there are several day coaches. I've been all through the train."

"Looking for anyone who might have attacked Mallory," Flo Bel said softly.

Scott did not reply to that. Instead he said, suddenly, "Mrs. Bookever, what has gone wrong? I mean, aside from last night at Gary..."

Flo Bel hesitated. Mallory made a motion to speak, but Flo Bel lifted her white hand to silence her. "A bottle of chloral hydrate has disappeared during the night." She paused, then added, "It is a very dangerous drug."

Scott sat in complete stillness; he was so still that Mallory was reminded of Su Lin's frozen, quiet face when she had emptied the little glass.

Then he rose. "I'll inquire about it," he said and walked out of the car into the passageway.

Flo Bel bit her lip. Mallory cried, "Flo Bel, *he* couldn't find out what happened to that damn little bottle—"

"Don't swear."

"But he couldn't! Why stir up—"

"Inquiry? I think it wise."

"Trouble," Mallory continued. "Nobody took that bottle. It must have simply fallen and rolled off somewhere in your room."

"It is nowhere in my stateroom. I searched."

"Well, but—"

"I'll do what I think best. Mallory, can't you see that"— Flo Bel bit her lip again and said—"someone tried to pull you off the train last night. Now a bottle of very dangerous drug has vanished."

"But...but, Flo Bel!" Mallory grasped at rapidly vanishing sanity. And yet there had been an oddly uneasy tingle along her nerves. "Nobody is trying to hurt me."

"Someone tried to pull you off the train. Possibly under the wheels."

The train clicked on, more slowly. Freight yards and red lanterns loomed up through fog. Mallory's hands hurt; her nails were digging into her palms. She said, at last, "Flo Bel, that is not possible! It was a thief at Gary. There is no reason for...for anything so—"

"Suppose someone does not want you to marry Richard." Flo Bel leaned back in her chair and closed her eyes.

After a long time the train came to a jerking stop. Mallory said in a whisper, "Who?"

55

Flo Bel wouldn't even open her eyes. Her lips looked bluish gray. She did manage to give a kind of shrug, a mere vestige of the gesture. "Probably nobody. Probably it is only my fancy. But—" She opened her eyes and sat up, full of energy again. "But we'll see to it that nothing like that happens. At least, I'll see to it."

The omission of a name was too evident not to remark, "You don't think Scott Suydam—"

"I don't think anything!" Flo Bel snapped. "But remember, Richard is not in good health. Indeed, he may be worse than we are told. It is possible that someone—*anyone* who is interested in Richard's money might think it wise to prevent Richard's marriage."

"Scott wouldn't care whether or not Richard married!"

"I did not accuse this young Suydam. There are these two Chinese hirelings..."

Scott came back, frowning and troubled, yet he quite clearly was trying to assume an air of ease. He had questioned Su Lin and Kai Sing; neither of them knew anything at all about the bottle of chloral hydrate, and, he said firmly, he believed them. "Your man—Gorham—heard me talk to Kai Sing. He thought about it and finally said that it must have rolled under something."

"It didn't," Flo Bel said.

Kai Sing, a worried slant to his eyebrows, came with a gleaming silver pot refilled with coffee. The train started again. Glancing from the window, Mallory saw that they were moving slowly over a bridge. Gray water surged below them. She hoped, surprised at her own thoughts, that the bridge was quite safe. But of course it would be.

Flo Bel looked out the window also. She then said, as if convincing herself of the safety of the bridge, "The Southern Pacific is considered a very good railway."

"Yes," Scott said shortly.

"I believe Peter, my husband, was acquainted with Mr. Harriman." Clearly, for Flo Bel that settled any possible question of railway safety, for Mr. Harriman was the president and main authority in control of the railway.

Scott lifted his coffee cup and said mildly that Richard knew Mr. Harriman, too. "Also"—there was again a gleam of mischief in his dark-gray eyes—"Richard is a friend of most of the substantial men of San Francisco."

Unexpectedly—or perhaps not unexpectedly, for Flo Bel had certainly informed herself not only of Richard himself, but of much of San Francisco, she said, "You mean—the Floods? The Crockers? The Stanfords? The—"

"Yes," said Scott firmly. He turned to Mallory. "We'll soon be in Omaha."

But she was watching the roiling gray-brown currents of the river far below—and thinking of Su Lin and her suddenly frozen face when she lifted the glass with the chloral hydrate in it, sniffed and then, swiftly, poured it away. Too swiftly?

She wouldn't mention this fleeting incident to Flo Bel—or Scott, or anybody. But she would question Su Lin.

Then the river was gone; the gray and drearily misty railroad yards loomed up. The train stopped. The tinkle of the silver and china in the galley could be dimly heard. Scott rose. "When we get to a less crowded station I expect you will both wish to get some exercise. But just to please me, not now!"

"That man cannot be on the train," Mallory cried.

"Please stay here. The car may be shunted around again. I don't want to . . . to lose you. Remember, I promised Richard to bring you to him safely." Scott went out along the aisle.

The train was not shunted around very much; this time it started out smoothly. Flo Bel said, "Dear Mr. Harriman," quite as if Mr. Harriman were embodied by the engineer, the firemen, the brakemen, the porters in white jackets, of whom Mallory had caught glimpses as they assisted passengers leaving or entering the train. Even the waiters from the dining car ahead, strolling along or receiving packaged food supplies, were, in Flo Bel's view, benefits derived from Mr. Harriman.

Scott came back. "I've been through the entire train again. There's not a man I can envision trying to drag Mallory off the train. I think we can be quite easy in our minds."

"I'm sure I hope so," Flo Bel said acidly. "I'll feel easier when you find that bottle of chloral hydrate."

The relaxed, easy expression on Scott's face wiped itself out. "Yes." He gave Mallory a swift glance, as if to make sure she was still there. "I don't know what more to do about that. I can't search the luggage of all the passengers on the train. I saw no one—well, no one I know."

Flo Bel was onto him like a knife. "Someone you know? Do you mean that you might know someone who just might use that dangerous medicine for...for a very terrible purpose?"

"You mean for Mallory." Scott, Mallory was learning, seldom had to have i's dotted or t's crossed.

"She *was* attacked."

"But that— No," he said forcefully, "the missing bottle will turn up. I'll talk to Kai Sing about it again. And Su Lin, of course—"

"These Chinese," said Flo Bel.

"I trust them," Scott said positively.

But he went out toward the galley and then must have gone up to the Pullman car ahead, where Kai Sing had now retired until lunchtime.

After a long time, barely in time for lunch, he returned. Gorham came with him.

Gorham, however, looked a little preoccupied. He knew nothing about the bottle of chloral hydrate. Kai Sing knew nothing. Scott had inquired, drawing each of them aside from the poker game, which, it developed, was continuing.

Gorham was calm. "Madam must have simply lost it, dropped it somewhere," he said. "Easy to do on such a rapid and sometimes rather jerky train. However, if Madam wishes, I'll take a look around."

Madam indicated she so wished. Indeed, she followed Gorham as he went to explore her stateroom. Mallory was aware of a rather low-voiced conversation going on before Gorham emerged.

Flo Bel had told him of the Gary incident. "Really, Miss Mallory," he told her disapprovingly. "You shouldn't go out of the car at wayside stations—not in these times. Lucky he didn't get your handbag."

"Or me," Mallory said tartly.

Gorham considered that, but still in a rather preoccupied way. He nodded. "Or you, certainly. However, I really think it was merely some thief."

He had gone quietly and with superb aplomb, when Flo Bel emerged from her stateroom. She was obviously ruffled. "That Gorham! I can tell! He used to go with my husband and me on our trips to Europe. He valeted Peter—or was supposed to. Once he gets into a card game, Gorham is a different man. There's kind of a look about him—"

"A gleam in his eye?" Scott suggested.

Flo Bel nodded, still with indignation. "But he is a very good man, just the same. When he is not really intoxicated—that is the only word for it—by a card game!"

Scott grinned. "He is very busy raking in poker money from Kai Sing and two traveling salesmen. They're not supposed to gamble for money, of course. But no conductor is going to stop an employee or guest of Richard's."

Flo Bel looked annoyed, yet also rather pleased, at Gorham's poker talents.

It was a long, quiet afternoon, soothing really, in the smoothly riding train amid great vistas, later, of farmlands, trees, wild pastures, sometimes cattle grazing within fenced acres.

Su Lin did not appear until tea time. Mallory was already in her stateroom when the girl knocked on the door, and at Mallory's word, entered softly.

Su Lin knew nothing at all about a missing bottle of medicine.

Mallory became insistent. "But this morning, early—that glass. You looked at it and sniffed at it and then—"

"Then I threw it away," Su Lin said gently. "I saw that Missy did not require it. Shall I put out the lovely dress you wore last night? So very becoming, and beautifully made." She opened the tiny wardrobe, extracted and shook out the jade-green folds.

"Su Lin, I really do want to find that bottle, you know."

"Yes, Missy."

"So please help me do it."

Su Lin's round face could have been made of pale-yellow wax. "Certainly, Missy."

Mallory felt in her heart that Su Lin would do nothing of the kind.

Six

But her attitude was understandable. Almost certainly, from what, by now, Mallory had learned of San Francisco and its Chinese population, not many Chinese were really welcome, not many Chinese were given much credit for honesty and loyalty. It would be quite natural for Su Lin, born and brought up in what must have seemed an inimical atmosphere, to avoid anything at all that might be, say, unpleasant. Or indeed, that might rebound upon her.

But the bottle *had* disappeared, no question of that. Hands *had* come out of the dusk and tried to drag her down and down just as the train started to move. Su Lin *had* had a strangely fixed expression on her bland face when she sniffed the glass of water—with, supposedly, only the few drops of chloral hydrate which Flo Bel had poured into it. Su Lin *had* disposed of it with neat, thorough rapidity.

There was no use in trying to question Su Lin further.

But thinking hard, as Su Lin assisted her in doing her hair and sliding into the flattering green dress, Mallory came to an odd and firm conclusion. She would drink only what everyone else drank; she would eat only what Flo Bel and Scott ate. Nothing would induce her to touch a drop that the others did not also taste.

But what a fantastic, unbelievable scheme that was! All the same, she had only to remember those ugly, grasping hands to decide that perhaps—just perhaps—Flo Bel's incredibly, yet unpleasantly, logical notion of danger to her, danger from someone who wished to prevent her marriage to Richard, just might be right. The grasp of the two hands coming out of the dusk was a cogent argument for Flo Bel's suggestion.

Flo Bel, too, had changed for dinner; she came rustling

out in black moiré touched with a white lace yoke. Black was very becoming to Flo Bel; probably she would wear it the rest of her life.

Even Scott Suydam looked dressed up: broadcloth instead of travel tweeds; his dark hair plastered neatly down with water. This time, however, gravely, yet with that distant twinkle Mallory was beginning to recognize, he served them sherry instead of the remarkable gin-and-vermouth mixture. Nobody mentioned the substitution. Flo Bel asked if the Omaha paper was a Democrat paper, and Scott said yes. "You've been reading its attack on the President."

Flo Bel lifted her graceful shoulder. "Uncalled for."

"They have to quarrel about something he does," Scott said equably. "But I think he is right. It wouldn't surprise me if he goes down in history for—well, for many things, but one phrase will never be forgotten."

Mallory had read the papers too. She said, quoting, "'Speak softly but carry a big stick!'"

"'*And* carry a big stick,'" Scott said, laughing at his own pedantry, but, she thought, with a brief gleam of admiration—whether for her memory or for the President, she couldn't know.

That night the train made very few stops, perhaps trying to justify its proud title of transcontinental express. That night the elegant private car rode smoothly. That night Mallory bolted the door to her stateroom.

The journey was long, yet in an odd way it seemed short, and was not, as Flo Bel remarked, monotonous. There was the always changing landscape; there was Scott Suydam, who unearthed a cribbage board from somewhere. Mallory had often played cribbage with Peter Bookever. She and Scott engaged in a long duel over the little wooden board and pegs. Flo Bel looked on—at first rather casually but later rather sharply as the two laughed, became hilarious over mistakes, fought over points and melds, and thoroughly enjoyed the game—and themselves. Scott was always first to bring Mallory's tea, taking it from Kai Sing's small hands and remembering she liked only milk, no sugar. Kai Sing could serve Flo Bel.

Occasionally, too, really quite often, they went out to the

61

observation platform; Kai Sing kept the chairs there dusted regularly. Flo Bel didn't like the wind and soot out there, but after a few times she joined them, taking the chair Scott politely offered her. Once she inquired more closely into Scott's family. His wife, she said, ought to have accompanied him on such a long trip; too bad she hadn't. For a moment his eyes squinted up against the wind, then he looked at her keenly as he said, shortly, that he was not married.

"Really?" Flo Bel arched her eyebrows. "How odd of Richard's cousin to send a young unmarried man to escort my niece on this long trip."

Scott watched the converging rails shining back of the train for a long moment before he said, dryly, that possibly Dolores and Richard were quite sure he would be an efficient escort.

This didn't please Flo Bel, and after a sudden motion of the train, she went rather unsteadily back into the lounge.

Scott laughed, for no apparent reason, and settled down in his chair again.

Once or twice Gorham turned up, wearing a rather saggy travel suit, probably an old discard of Peter Bookever's. He also had on a travel cap, which Flo Bel recognized and told Mallory later that it had belonged to her husband. "Peter used it all the time when we were traveling by steamer. That is, of course, on deck. Oh, well, there's been little enough pickings for Gorham lately."

Gorham, however, looked as pleased with himself as his long, lugubrious face could allow. He said nothing of Gary or chloral hydrate; he merely seemed to feel it his duty to visit the private car occasionally. Kai Sing, Mallory thought, began to look a little thoughtful, but still padded softly around, doing all the chores with quiet efficiency. It occurred to her that possibly the two traveling salesmen were having deep thoughts, too.

As they traveled through the mountains Flo Bel retired to her stateroom and would accept only an occasional cup of tea. Once, as Mallory watched the view from the wide windows she wondered, with a sense of astonishment, what she was doing in this elegant private car, traveling at such speed to a strange city where she was to live. Scott, across from her, was leafing absently through a magazine he had already scanned. For a moment the whole prospect seemed unlikely, untrue, nothing she, Mallory, had anything to do with. Richard Welbeck was a handsome, friendly stranger with a charming smile and perfect manners who had asked for marriage and been accepted.

Not many of the young men she had known had actually made what one could call definite signals in the direction of marriage. Realistically, Mallory could not have expected many serious attentions, once Flo Bel's and her own lack of money was widely known, or, if not known, for Flo Bel had kept up a brave face, certainly it was more than suspected. Few families of Mallory's acquaintance were really desirous of receiving a bankrupt's niece into their family circle. Without knowing it, Mallory had absorbed a realistic, if somewhat Victorian, approach to marriage.

There had been, naturally, a few young men who clearly admired her; one of them, plump George Van Piller, was as rich as Richard Welbeck. She had rather feared for a time that Flo Bel considered his possibility as a husband too favorably. But then Richard Welbeck had appeared, suitably armed with letters of introduction to friends of Flo Bel's, and quite suddenly her aunt had all but concentrated upon Richard. She had invited him to their home; she had insisted upon new ball gowns for Mallory, new dresses, new hats, which they could ill afford but which Mallory had worn with guilty pleasure. Flo Bel had had, Mallory knew, one or two conversations with Richard before he proposed marriage. Flo Bel had been frankly delighted.

Yet, thinking about it, it struck Mallory that despite Flo Bel's encouragement, she wasn't sure that her aunt really liked Richard.

Now, why did she think that? She could find no clues, no hints at all, during these few days of enforced idleness, to support that idea. Neither did Flo Bel really like Scott Suydam, but that, Mallory knew, had another reason: Scott was too attractive. Flo Bel might not truly like Richard Welbeck, but she was determined upon the marriage, and Scott Suydam just might threaten it. But how could he?

Certainly, Flo Bel knew that Richard Welbeck, with his

social background, was desirable as a husband, aside from his wealth. But it was important, too, that it didn't matter to him whether or not Mallory brought money with her. He had enough of his own, and he had no family to object to his choice of a wife.

He had the cousin, Dolores, yes. But she herself had married; probably she, too, had all the money she wanted, or needed.

Mallory couldn't honestly say that Flo Bel wanted her to marry money. But neither had Flo Bel acted quite as Mallory would have expected about her going to San Francisco. It would have been much more in keeping with Mallory's own knowledge of Flo Bel's character merely to postpone the wedding until Richard himself could come to New York.

Instead Flo Bel had insisted upon the trip to San Francisco, and accompanying her, especially, Mallory felt, because her escort was a young man. That was proper; that was logical. What wasn't logical or like Flo Bel was her immediate acquiescence to Richard's request. It had to be the ever-present pressure of debts.

Scott Suydam put down his magazine as she was considering this answer for Flo Bel's unusual behavior, and began to talk about anything that seemed to occur to him—the road, the mountains, the golden-spike railroad. "It wasn't really a golden spike," he said, smiling a little at Mallory's naïve surprise. "How could anything as soft as gold penetrate hard steel! No, but the spikes that joined the two railroads were covered with a layer of gold."

"Gold!"

"Ah, well, they used to say that San Francisco is paved with gold. Of course it isn't. But there is money there. Money—and music and the arts and anything a rich and splendid city wishes to possess. You'll like it all."

"There must be places where there are not such splendid houses."

"Oh, yes." He twirled the *Harper's Weekly*. "Chinatown and near the shore a section called the Barbary Coast."

"What is that?"

"The less you know of it the better," he said crossly, as if he wished he had not mentioned whatever the district was.

"Come, you'll have another magnificent view from the observation platform. Want to look?"

They went out again, sitting on the chairs Kai Sing kept in readiness, watching the tremendous stretches of mountains, and what Scott called mountain meadows, freshly green, seeming to rush past them. They didn't say much; oddly, after those hours of the pleasant give-and-take of conversation, a certain restraint seemed to have gripped both of them as they came nearer and nearer to San Francisco. The next day, before it could possibly happen, it was Sunday, the fifteenth—Easter Sunday.

Kai Sing, from his long-time knowledge of the Occidental observances, was the first to remember it. He produced flowers, huge white lilies, which, he said happily, had come from Mexico; he had kept them in a storage cupboard with chunks of ice all the way from Denver for this happy, happy day. He bowed and smiled. Su Lin bowed and smiled. Flo Bel unbent and bowed and smiled too, and Mallory felt tears in her eyes.

"Here we are!" She dabbed at her eyes. "Just imagine, only Kai Sing thought of Easter Sunday!"

Mallory enjoyed the fragrance of the lilies for only a few hours, because now, all at once, it seemed to her, they were rolling across the verdant, rich San Joaquin valley and approaching Oakland. Here they were to take a ferry across the Bay to San Francisco. It didn't seem possible, but this long—yet exciting—journey would soon be over.

But it was possible. Scott was in the lounge waiting for them. Su Lin, Kai Sing and Gorham were waiting, too. It was like a strangely stiff farewell party. Gorham's pocket was probably lined with money; he did look a little smug.

The ferry waited. They left the train, and Mallory, on an impulse, looked up and waved at the private car. Scott saw her and quickly looked away. Flo Bel did not see. Just as well, a tiny voice seemed to whisper in Mallory's ear. Indeed, there was no reason, no reason at all, for that childish, sentimental gesture. Waving farewell toward a car which had brought her across the country!

Now she was on the threshold of marriage and her new life. And it seemed to her that the train had brought her a very long distance, indeed, longer than she could define. She followed her aunt; the servants were somewhere with the luggage. Scott was waiting for them at the ferry. He found a seat in the sheltered cabin for Flo Bel.

He gave Mallory a long look and then said, abruptly, "You can see the city from the bow." She went with him along the deck to stand beside him, her gloved hands on a railing, looking westward. The water rippled below. The city loomed roseate, veiled in evening mist, against a gloriously dusky, barely darkening sky. There were lights dotted in mellow brilliance, everywhere. There were a few boats, rowboats, skiffs; out in the Bay steamers were berthed. Sea gulls swooped around the ferry, uttering harsh cries.

The ferry gave itself a kind of shake and began to thump its way quietly over the water.

A strong presentiment came from nowhere, striking into Mallory's being. This was a moment she would never forget.

The sky and the bleakly outlined city ahead, the rush of water below, the cries of the gulls, even the long-drawn-out hoot of a steamer, far out and now invisible in the Bay—all of it created a magic portent. Everything was clearer—the sounds, the softly veiled blues and grays of the evening, the thump of the ferry's engine, the feeling of the wooden railing under her hands. Her senses seem to surge into life as if she had never lived before that moment.

The faraway steamer hooted again, softly. Scott said, "That's the *Madrone Concita*. She was due to leave today."

"For Hong Kong?"

"Yes. And other ports. Depends upon her lading. I know what it was to be when I left to go to New York. It may have been changed a little."

"You have a number of men in your office?"

"Oh, yes. Not many, but enough. I can rely upon them. Mine is a small shipping line. Nothing like the Welbeck interests, but it's mine. My offices are just across the Bay, near the Ferry Building. I'll take you to see the wharf and my offices sometime—if you are interested."

It was a curiously perfunctory, almost constrained, conversation. She had brought the Easter lilies, clutched under one arm. The fragrance was very sweet.

Scott said, suddenly, "Perhaps you'd better drop the lilies

in the Bay. The stems are dripping on your skirt. Besides, I'm afraid they are almost gone."

They had wilted. But when she dropped them into the Bay it was with a sigh, as if they reminded her of some memory as fragrant as the lilies had been. They bobbed away on the darkening waters.

There was again the distant wail of the ship, farther away now, so it sounded like the mournful cry of a sea gull. Scott said, softly, "*Vaya con Dios.*"

"Go with God."

He looked swiftly at her. "Spanish?"

"No. Only that and—oh, *por favor* and *mucha gracias.* I can count a little, too."

His eyes hardened; he looked away. "Oh, yes. You can count."

It took her only a second to understand. "You mean the Welbeck—Richard's money."

"No. I don't think it means that much to you. I do think that your aunt—"

"She has a right to think of money. She's been wonderful. After Uncle Peter died—"

"Yes. I'm sure of that. She's not the kind to give up. But I don't think you are the kind to give up, either."

She turned to look at him, and he was looking at her.

So, she thought, as if from a great distance, this is what it is.

Scott's gaze darkened. For a time they stood together, with no words, nothing, yet communication.

When he moved, it was to reach blindly for her hands and to remove her gloves, very gently yet firmly. Richard's sapphire was like an observing eye. He did look down at her left hand. He brought both her hands near him, up to his body, so close she could feel his heart thudding. The ferry gave an imperative grunt of approaching arrival. He said, "I can feel your heart. Through your pulses, in your wrists. It's beating hard."

"So is yours," she whispered, not intending to speak.

"Richard sent me to bring him his bride. Safely."

"We know."

"Oh, yes. We know."

The ferry rumbled again, with authority. Scott said, "We're coming in to the pier. They'll be waiting for us."

He replaced her gloves; she thought he was going to kiss her hands, but he didn't; he put them gently back on the railing.

Gorham, behind them, said, respectfully, "Madam is asking for you, Miss Mallory."

There was the slightest little jar as the wide, bosomy ferry brought itself in to the pier.

The next moments were mainly confusion. Flo Bel erect and dignified, the servants laden with luggage, Scott, with a merely polite hand at her elbow, and Flo Bel, at his other side, made a small procession. There was the wooden platform of the pier. Then there was a carriage, two carriages, coachmen in uniforms, not the Daimler, after all.

She and Flo Bel and Scott were in the first carriage; there was a team of beautiful glossy bays; the coachman wore a small green cockade in his hat. The servants and the luggage were in a following carriage.

The streets became not magic, but streets, cobblestoned and bumpy. The lights were not magic lights now, merely the usual gaslights on tall black standards.

The air was moist; the smell of horse drifted back to them, that and a whiff or two of Flo Bel's expensive perfume, bought long ago and cherished for only special occasions, such as bringing her niece to her marriage and her new home. And her husband.

We know, she had said. Scott had said yes, we know.

Nothing was said of what they knew.

It was too clear. Too late, also. It was like the sudden thrust of a dagger.

Her wide hat toppled in a light breeze. She put up a hand to hold it to her pompadoured hair. Flo Bel said, "Tuck in your hair, Mallory. There's a wisp blowing across your cheek."

She looked up at Scott, seated opposite her in the carriage, and something in his direct dark gaze seemed to say, Let me tuck in your hair. Let me...

No, no, she must control her thoughts. She must control

68

even the hurried throb of her pulses, which had started up, there on the ferry, beside Scott.

The evening breeze freshened, yet was still moist against her face. Scott said, distantly now, "The tule fog is coming in. We'll soon be at Richard's home. This is Nob Hill. There are..." His voice faltered and stopped, as if he found his effort at being a guide too much for him.

Flo Bel took up the refrain, however, and leaned forward, then back with a particularly dignified pose. "Those enormous houses—dear me," she said.

The houses did seem enormous, and as far as Mallory could see in the increasing dusk, they were of different types of architecture, with towers, turrets, balconies, porte-cocheres, driveways, clipped shrubbery making shadows on the lawns surrounding them, lights from windows.

Flo Bel ought to feel at home here, Mallory thought remotely. The carriage swerved into a driveway. Here was another enormous house, lighted. There was a porte-cochere curving before a vast door—it was lighted too. The carriage drew up, gently. The horses puffed and snorted. Of course, they had been going uphill almost all the way. Mallory had not until then been aware of any hill. Nob Hill, Scott had said.

Scott helped Flo Bel descend; he gave a polite hand to Mallory but did not look at her.

A woman was standing in the doorway. She came down a marble step to greet them.

"I am Dolores." Her voice was sweet, very soft. "Mrs. Book-ever—my dear Mallory. I hope you had a pleasant journey."

They entered the house. Mallory had a confused impression of an enormous hall, marble floors, a high vaulted ceiling, a stairway railed in wrought iron, winding upward and giving access to galleries encircling the hall on three sides, also railed in delicately designed wrought iron and lined with paneled doors.

But her attention was held by Dolores, so small, so delicate, so beautifully dressed in a trailing gray tea gown flounced in lace. She said, smiling, so her lips made a neat crescent above a pointed chin, "Dear Mallory! May I show you both to your rooms? You'll want to see Richard at once.

69

But I told him you must have a chance to freshen up first, perhaps rest..." Her skirts rustled as she led them toward the stairway, Flo Bel first. She said cordially to Flo Bel, "How very thoughtful and kind of you to make this long trip! I hadn't quite the courage to ask you to come, too. It was all I could do to summon up the courage to give dear Mallory Richard's message. You are so very welcome, I can't tell you how pleased we all are. Now then— Oh, I see Su Lin has made her way to your room, dear Mallory. And then..."

Su Lin was standing in an open doorway, demurely, her eyes cast down. Behind her a pink marble fireplace held a gas log that cast a flickering glow over the room.

Mallory paused for a second in the doorway to glance down the long stairway, toward the hall below. Scott was standing in the doorway as if in the act of departing and two men were standing with him talking.

One was slim, neat, dressed carefully in a dark suit; his graying hair was parted neatly in the middle; his face was neat, too, and solemn.

The other man was taller, flushed in the face, rather paunchy although he couldn't have been over forty, if that; he had a bushy beard and a fat hand on Scott's arm.

Apparently he was inviting Scott to remain. For dinner? Scott was smiling and shaking his head—and unexpectedly shot one swift glance upward and met Mallory's eyes. He turned back to the men beside him, and Mallory moved quickly into the room waiting for her.

Dolores had put out a hand to guide Flo Bel in another direction; a great bracelet set with blue-green stones and many diamonds flashed on her wrist. She gave Mallory a look over her shoulder. "In a quarter of an hour, do you think? Dear Richard is so impatient."

Mallory found her voice, said, "Yes," as Dolores moved away.

She looked like Richard yet didn't look like him. Her hair was heavy and jet-black, not blond, like Richard's. Her face was as triangular as the face of a delicate little cat, wide through the jaws, very pointed as to chin. Her eyes were an odd pale-blue-green, like the stones in her bracelet, and so large that they showed white below the pupils. Like a fractious horse, Mallory thought unexpectedly, and ashamed, entered a luxurious bedroom, all pink damask and silk. A lavish bathroom connected with it. Steam and a scent of lilacs rose from a marble tub. "Miss Dolores thought you might like bath salts," said Su Lin in a quiet voice. There was also a lingering fragrance which Mallory remembered from the private car. Su Lin saw her sniff and smiled. "Sandalwood, Missy. San Francisco has much of the Orient."

Seven

Trunks stood in the room, miraculously, it seemed to Mallory, obviously delivered before her own arrival. Gorham and the two Chinese had also arrived first. Su Lin smiled again, noting her surprise. "We came a different way, Missy." Su Lin had already put out the jade-green dress and bronzed slippers.

"If you'll give me your keys, Missy, I can unpack while you are having dinner."

Her keys! Mallory looked with disbelief at the two trunks she had so carefully packed in New York, so far away, so very long ago. How could a few days seem now a great distance, almost a chasm between her life in New York and the life she now felt in all her pulses?

She must see Richard. She must renew their...their affection; certainly, her promises.

But it was half an hour at least before someone tapped very lightly on the door and Su Lin opened it. Dolores stood on the threshold. She seemed uncertain, yet also extremely self-possessed. Mallory was perfectly sure that her wide eyes had taken in every item Su Lin had unpacked, even the silver-backed brushes and hand mirror Uncle Peter had given her when she first went away to school.

71

Dolores trusted she was not hurrying Mallory. Mallory said no indeed.

Dolores would show her the way to Richard's room.

Mallory thanked her. Dear God, she thought, how cautiously polite we are! Like two strange cats eyeing each other on a fence.

She went with Dolores, along a wide, softly carpeted gallery which overlooked the vast hall below, and came to the open door of Richard's room. Richard was in a chair, his eyes bright, his handsome face all smiles.

"Mallory!" He opened his arms.

Dolores murmured something and swished away. Mallory went to Richard obediently. His arms were warm around her; it was like one of Uncle Peter's rare embraces, simply friendly and kind.

She wished with all her heart she had never experienced another kind of embrace when a speeding train had given her a sudden jolt.

She drew back. "Richard, you look—" She had started to say splendid, or very well, or something congratulatory, or at least encouraging about his recuperation. The words checked on her lips; he didn't look splendid, he didn't look well! There was something oddly pale and drowsy in his face. She said, "I'm glad to see you." That was perfectly true. She was glad to see him, but also... also, in her heart, she felt guilty.

He didn't look as she remembered him. He was still almost spectacularly handsome; his face was thin, but every feature was sharply delineated, his elegant high-bridged nose, his fine cheekbones, the deep hollows around his blue eyes—which, however, seemed misty. Even his wavy blond hair had a dull lifelessness. He wore a crimson silk dressing gown. One leg, encased in white plaster, was propped up on a cushioned divan.

"Darling," he said. "I couldn't postpone our wedding until I was able to go to New York. So Scott offered— It seemed a good idea. I simply didn't think of your aunt as chaperon. Scott is like a brother. I hope you had a good journey."

"Very good. Everything was done superbly."

"Lolo told me that she had seen to servants, everything."

72

Lolo. "You mean Dolores?"

"Of course. It's a family nickname. She has been looking forward to your coming."

I'll bet, Mallory thought instinctively and tersely, reverting to schoolgirl vocabulary. Yet Dolores—well, Lolo, if that was preferred—had indeed exerted herself to make the journey comfortable and their welcome a warm one.

"She has been very kind," she said truthfully.

"Dear Lolo, My favorite—well, my only family. Except, of course, her husband, Henry Beaton. I expect you haven't met him yet."

"No. At least—I saw two gentlemen downstairs in the doorway, talking to Scott."

Did a very slight flicker cross Richard's blue eyes? She added, "I mean Scott Suydam, of course. We agreed to use given names. He said I would see him often here in your home, Richard."

If there had been the slightest flicker of question in his eyes, it was gone at once. "Oh, yes. Scott has been my best friend since we were very young. But you know that." He still held one of her hands, the hand with the sapphire. He looked down at it, kissed it and said, "You haven't kissed me, Mallory."

"I...I will. Now." She leaned over and kissed him. His drawn face seemed chilly and a little moist.

She said, "You aren't too tired, are you?"

"Oh, a little, perhaps. Simply the pleasure of your coming. And of course, this is the first time they have let me out of bed. This confounded leg. And at such a time..."

"Can I—is there anything I can do?"

He laughed, the pleasant musical laugh that was a part of him. "Now I have Kai Sing back, he'll see to everything. And there's a new man. I think his name is Ching—Cheng—something. Oh, I'll be taken care of. Lolo said she had employed a new maid for you. Someone to accompany you here."

"Su Lin. Yes. She's a dear." His face seemed to stiffen a little as she spoke in such an affectionate way of a servant. "I mean, she is most efficient."

His face cleared, if indeed there had been a shade of change. "Oh, yes. Lolo is almost infallible about choosing

73

servants and training them. You said you saw Henry downstairs."

"I saw two men. One was rather...rather stout and had a beard."

He nodded. "Henry. Yes."

"The other one was slim, very—very neat."

He nodded. "Ernest Grenay. Lawyer once, but now sees to the Welbeck enterprises. He's a fine fellow. Most helpful. Sit down, darling, and let me look at you. I can't believe you are really here. All the plans for our wedding have been made. The twentieth of the month. Lolo said you would need a little time to get acclimated. There will be callers, you know. I think Lolo plans to invite friends to meet you. And, of course, your aunt."

The twentieth. She calculated the days. That was the coming Friday.

Richard seemed drowsy but was still far too perceptive. He said, troubled. "I know that is Friday. Next Friday. But you aren't superstitious about Friday, are you? You see, that proved to be the best day for all the arrangements Lolo has made."

"Oh, no. No, I'm not superstitious. Friday—yes—" And this was Sunday. So soon. She said, feebly, "We didn't have time—at least we didn't take time to see to all my trousseau. It's to be sent out here."

"Darling, who cares about your trousseau?"

She rallied a little; she managed to smile. "I care!"

He laughed again, his kind, charming laugh. Oh, a very desirable husband, she thought; but her startled, whirling, foolishly confused mind added, But I don't desire him.

It was too late for such treacherous thoughts. She said, firmly, "Flo Bel—my aunt—will see to everything about our wedding." She got it out without choking.

Richard's arched eyebrows rose a little. "But, dearest, I told you. Lolo has already made the arrangements. She'll tell you all about the plans."

Yes, very soon she was going to have enough of Dolores'— Lolo's decisions. She looked at the great white cast on the leg that lay upon the mass of cushions. "I was so very sorry to hear of your accident. How did it happen?"

His face became still, but slightly puzzled rather than evasive. She hadn't meant to bring up the subject of the accident; it had only offered a conversational topic. There was another gas log in the fireplace between deep curtained windows. The steady heat of the red and blue gas flames was almost suffocating. Just for a second the likeness between the cousins seemed to her to be accentuated. Richard's chin was rather pointed; his jaws rather wide, his cheekbones rather prominent, his forehead was high above those deep-set eyes. What was strikingly handsome in Richard, however, was different in Dolores. A man's good looks are never a woman's good looks, Mallory told herself, but absently, wishing she hadn't brought up the subject of the accident, for there was a shadow of something uneasy in Richard's eyes. He replied, looking at the gas log in the fireplace rather than directly into Mallory's eyes, "I really don't know how it happened. I was just at the top of the stairs, starting down and— I must have tripped. It's a very long flight. I fell all the way to the hall. The doctor said it was surprising I didn't kill myself."

"Richard, how dreadful!" She was genuinely shocked, thinking of that long, that deadly long, flight of stairs.

"Ah, well..." He turned to her again, smiling. "I wasn't killed. But I'll have to go to the church and altar in a wheelchair, they tell me. I hope you don't mind too much."

"Oh, Richard!" A genuine pity caught Mallory. "How could anybody mind! I'm only so sorry—"

"It's all right now," he assured her, happily, his eyes brightening. "The doctor says I may have a slight limp, but that's all. You're not marrying a cripple, darling."

"No—" But I am marrying you, she thought; it was inexorable, it was going to come true and there was nothing she could do about it.

Dolores said softly from the doorway, "I don't like to take her away from you, Richard. But dinner—they are waiting and—dear Richard, I'm sure you are happy but perhaps a bit tired."

Mallory wanted to say, decisively, that he was not tired, that she had not tired him. Better not; she checked words almost on her lips.

Dolores turned brilliant eyes to Mallory. "He insisted on being out of bed and sitting up to see you. The doctor permitted it. But he said that I must see to it that he didn't get overtired. Come, Richard dear. I'll call Cheng to help you."

"But surely—" Mallory began, and stopped. A broken leg was of course very painful, but still—how long had it been? Surely it was not necessary for Richard to be treated like an invalid.

She wasn't sure of that; his thin face did look pale and tired.

Dolores put a white hand—sparkling also with diamonds and the strange blue-green stones which Mallory later learned were aquamarines—on Richard's hand. "Come, Richard. Say goodnight to Mallory—"

"No. Lolo, I haven't given Mallory her present. I got him for you, Mallory," he said happily. "Just wait. Where is he, Lolo?"

Lolo nodded. "Murphy has him. I'll get him. But you really must not excite yourself, Richard. You know what the doctor said."

She went quietly away. Richard smiled. "Wait till you see. I got him just before I fell on the stairs. Murphy—he's our coachman—has been taking care of him. I meant to give him to you when we arrived back here, after our honeymoon. You said you'd never had one."

She stared at him. *"A dog!"*

One of her epic battles with Flo Bel had been when she found a stray, hungry and scared, on the street and brought him home. Her aunt had told her to go to her room and stay there. She rang for Gorham to take the dog away. Unluckily for Mallory, Uncle Peter was not at home; she had felt sure that he would have permitted her to keep the dog.

Gorham, later, tried to comfort her, bringing cocoa and little cakes to her room and telling her not to cry about the dog; he would see that it was taken care of. "And fed?" she demanded tearfully. Gorham said yes. She believed him, for Gorham liked dogs.

But this and all her other childish differences with Flo Bel had been forgotten when she saw how her aunt, courageously, adamantly, never yielding, had conducted herself

76

after the doubly crushing blows of Uncle Peter's death and the subsequent knowledge of the almost complete lack of money.

But now—a dog! Mallory hadn't told Richard of that faraway episode; she remembered, however, that she had once told him she had always wanted a dog.

Richard was nodding, so pleased and happy that Mallory's heart reproached her. Then she noticed how exhausted he looked.

"I haven't tired you, have I?"

"No, certainly not! It's just that—oh, the doctor and Lolo and Henry and all of them seem to—that is, they take such good care of me, you know."

They are making an invalid of you, she thought rebelliously, and yet, again, with pity.

Dolores came back into the room, holding at arm's length something brown and furry and wriggly. It struggled against Dolores' hands and gave a tiny but angry growl.

Richard laughed. "A little dog with the heart of a lion. Take him, Mallory."

She reached out both hands and got the wriggling brown body into her hands and into her arms; he had an oddly squashed-in face, long fluffy ears and wide dark eyes. His pink tongue went out, he gave her hand a tentative lick and then stretched up to nose her cheek tentatively, too, as if finding his way.

"Oh, Richard!" Mallory held the little body closer. "I've never had one—oh, you know that! But now—oh, Richard!"

Richard's face lit up as he saw how pleased she was. "He's yours. You'll have to name him."

"What kind of dog? I mean—I've seen one, but—"

"Pekingese. They came originally from China. I got the smallest one I could find. The very small ones were stunted and called sleeve dogs because the court ladies could carry them in their sleeves. But some call them lion dogs, too. Despite their size, they are fighters!"

She snuggled the dog under her chin, and Richard looked so happy that she again felt a throb of something like pity. Dolores, still standing in the doorway, said, "Here is Cheng to help you back to bed, Richard. Your dinner will be sent up in a few minutes. Shall I take the dog, Mallory, until you—want him?"

Mallory clutched the warm bundle. "Oh, no. May I—" She checked herself. She didn't intend to start the marriage that was before her and the years of living in that house by deferring to Dolores. "I'll put him in my room. Su Lin will see to him."

"As you wish." Dolores moved aside to permit an elderly Chinese, plump, polite and bowing, to enter. "Now, Richard, let Cheng carry you—"

Richard glanced almost apologetically, timidly, at Mallory. "I can help myself."

"It's better to take no chances," said Dolores. "Help him, Cheng. I've explained."

"Yes, Missy." The Chinese advanced, still bowing, to Richard's chair.

Mallory couldn't stop that wave of pity for Richard that kept coming over her, striking at her heart—and her conscience? Conscience had nothing to do with it. Anyone with human feelings would sense something sad and helpless in Richard. She was tired; she had been emotionally stirred— a moment or two on a chugging ferry, seeing the outline of a city against the twilight sky and a man beside her. She must not keep thinking of that.

But that recent scene flashed through her mind even as she stopped, holding the little dog close, and kissed Richard's clammy forehead. "I'll come in after dinner to say goodnight," she promised.

"Darling," said Richard and smiled at her. "You do like the little dog."

"Yes! Oh, yes!"

"Ready, Mallory dearest," said Dolores.

Cheng, plump and strong-looking in his black trousers and black blouse, was bending over Richard. Dolores put a hand on Mallory's arm. "Su Lin," she said at Mallory's door. "Take care of the little dog. He might like a walk..."

Su Lin, smiling, took the small dog, who rolled big, perplexed eyes toward Mallory as if he wanted to say, Where are you going? Why are you leaving me? We've only met. Don't you like me?

Mallory patted the silky head, and at Dolores' rather peremptory "They're waiting for us," went with her down the long flight of stairs. What a hideous place to fall!

"They" proved to be Flo Bel, in her black moiré, the plump and bearded Henry Beaton and the tidy Ernest Grenay, who, colorless and quiet, gave her a keen look from very keen eyes.

Henry Beaton was hospitable. There were vast armchairs and tables in the hall. He poured sherry and urged it upon her. He talked of their journey. "And you found young Suydam a pleasant escort," said Henry.

"Yes." Mallory sipped at her sherry.

"Very smart young fellow. His *Madrone*—well, I don't remember which one—left this evening. He owns a shipping line. Calls all of his boats the *Madrone* something. After a house of his—I think it must have been his grandfather or grandmother who built it."

"Grandfathers," said Ernest Grenay remotely, "are a little scarce in San Francisco."

Henry wasn't pleased with the remark. "Call me a newcomer if you like. So are you. Most of us are first- or, at most, second-generation San Franciscans. But all the same, it's our city." He was obviously proud of the fact.

Ernest Grenay nodded approvingly. "Did the *Madrone Concita*" (He would know the exact name of the vessel, Mallory thought) "bring in a shipment for you, Henry?"

"A very good one." He spoke to Mallory again. "I have a store here—"

"Gallery," said Dolores, "the Beaton Art Gallery."

"Now, now, Dolores. Everyone knows my place simply as Beaton's. Good enough for me. Yes, Scott's ship brought in a very nice supply for me last week—hard to get now, you know. I haven't had time for an inventory, but one of the finds was—I think, at least—haven't had time to make sure—but I think it could be a T'ang horse. Most unusual if I'm right." He chuckled. "Man who got it for me last year disguised himself as a peasant woman, smuggled out the little horse. But it has taken many months, and many palms to grease, to get it. White nephrite."

"Jade," said Ernest Grenay to Mallory, who probably looked as she felt, puzzled. "But not likely a T'ang."

"Now, I can't go too fast. May be a later period. Likely to be, but I'm hoping. Have to be very careful about making claims, you know," Henry said fussily. "You must come to my store." He smiled at Mallory. "Full of beautiful things—quite beautiful. Some of them very hard to get since the Boxer Rebellion. I have only a few pieces which were smuggled out during or after the looting of the Forbidden City. You know, the old Empress' palace—"

"I don't think Mallory is interested in Chinese art," Dolores said.

"No, well—now then." Henry poured more sherry for himself. "Speaking of young Scott Suydam. It was like him to think of going to New York himself to bring you here, my dear—may I say Mallory? You are to be my sister-in-law. All in the family..."

Mallory said something; it must have been agreeable, for Henry nodded and went on talking. So Scott himself had suggested that trip to bring her to San Francisco. Why?

Flo Bel was remarkably silent, yet Mallory, knowing her so well, knew that her aunt's wits were by no means still. Dinner was served in a huge, rather gloomy dining room—a room which all but demanded at least thirty people around the long table. It, too, was vaulted, a high ceiling with frescos painted above a heavily plastered and ornamented dado. Huge, ornate silver candlesticks stood on the table and their light was strong enough to give Mallory a dim view of the frescos themselves, a rather surprising glimpse, for they seemed to concern mining operations—men with curious hats, what she guessed must be ore cars on short railway sidings, pickaxes, shovels, but mainly the strong figures of workingmen. So Richard—or his father, whoever had built the house—respected and wished thus to remember the men who had helped him to found his enormous fortune. She had heard that that fortune had been based on gold, but the business enterprises, coming later, she knew, had traveled far. On two teakwood stands across the room stood big Chinese vases, which Mallory recognized as Famille Rose and almost priceless. Yes, it was an impressive room. It was also cold and cheerless.

Only one end of the vast table was laid, but that was laid

in state. There was a silver bowl of red and white flowers on a lace tablecloth. Real lace, Mallory could almost hear Flo Bel thinking. Waterford glasses for wines, tall goblets for water. China of the most exquisite fragility. Heavy, too heavy, silver. Her napkin of damask, with lacy inserts, was so big that it might have served as an outsized tray cloth.

Ernest Grenay saw to the pouring of the wine, although Kai Sing, neat and silent as usual, served the dinner—and that consisted of course after course: soup, fish—very delicate, pheasant with bread sauce, then slices of a roast, done precisely to a tender pink, with asparagus.

Sunday supper at the Bookever house—in the old days before Uncle Peter's death—had been just that, a light, sometimes cold supper in order to allow the servants, numerous then, an evening off; the theory was that they had the opportunity thus to attend church. Later, of course, if they were alone, Flo Bel and Mallory had scrambled eggs or cold meat and salad Gorham had prepared and left for them. It was obviously different here, but the elaborate dinner might have been arranged because she and Flo Bel were newly arrived guests: it also might be because it was Easter Sunday.

She did wonder who had cooked it, but then Dolores volunteered that information. She tasted the incoming custard ice, nodded and said softly that really the cook she had employed for the time being had been quite efficient. "I may keep her on until after the wedding."

"She lives in Chinatown," Henry said. "She may not want to travel up and down the hill."

Dolores dismissed that. "Murphy can take her."

Flo Bel ate lightly and said nothing, so markedly that Mallory began to feel a little uneasy about her; her utter stillness, and a kind of chill in her manner, boded no good. Flo Bel said nothing even when the talk turned to grand opera and the opera house of which San Franciscans were so proud. Caruso was due to sing; the rumor was that an entire train of Pullmans had been engaged to carry him and the Metropolitan Opera Company from New York to the city.

Henry stroked his beard and said it wasn't likely that they needed an entire train. Ernest Grenay commented dryly that he understood that some local singers had been engaged as

81

part of the chorus for the production of *Carmen*, scheduled for the night of the seventeenth. Mallory thought: Seventeenth, eighteenth, nineteenth, twentieth.

Now and then something was asked about their journey westward. And Mallory tried to make polite replies, but Flo Bel gave only a few occasional nods.

After dinner the ladies withdrew, at Dolores' gesture, to a small and charming room. Dolores continued to ask rather bored questions about their trip. Mallory answered as best she could, but Flo Bel remained coldly silent. Eventually Dolores led them into a library. This was another vast room, but it had a friendlier air than the dining room, for it was lined with books and there were deep leather easy chairs and settees and Oriental rugs of crimson hues. A gas log hummed here, too.

There were huge paintings in wide gilded frames. They were rather somber, conventional products of the Victorian period, unlike Uncle Peter's collection. He had been adventurous in accruing art and had even bought a few paintings of the new school, called the Impressionists. To her own surprise, if not Flo Bel's, these paintings had fetched far more money than the older pictures.

Flo Bel's dignified silence seemed to chill the entire room in spite of the heated glow from the enormous fireplace. She sat erect in an armchair. Mallory had settled herself in a brown leather-covered sofa; a frigid glance from Flo Bel reminded her that she must not lounge. She couldn't help lounging, she thought crossly; not with so much food inside her, to say nothing of wines, and not in that soft sofa. The men had joined them by now. Henry stood before the fire. Ernest Grenay sat almost as erect and cool as Flo Bel. Dolores had curled up in the other end of the sofa, beside Mallory; she was slight and graceful as a smug and pleased cat with a gray silk tail curled around her. They were all to go to the opera on the seventeenth, she said.

"There is the Welbeck box, of course. People will expect to see you, dear Mallory. I'm sure you and your aunt have brought suitable gowns and your jewels."

This last was a dart. Surely Dolores knew that there were no more Bookever jewels. Richard had known of the circumstances of Uncle Peter's death; he must have seen and noted the barren appearance of the one-time elegantly decorated Bookever house. Besides that, acquaintances would certainly have informed him of Uncle Peter's collapse and death. And if acquaintances had not, as Mallory was perfectly sure they had, especially, she felt meanly, those mothers who had marriageable daughters, then Flo Bel would have tackled their financial situation frankly and head-on.

Flo Bel's eyelids barely flickered; if she felt the jab, no one could have detected it. Now she broke her long silence and said, unbelievably, "Certainly, my dear Dolores."

What did she mean by that? There was nothing left but some fake pearls, which Flo Bel had had made, copying her fine pearls for wear when traveling. She might possibly have had some other of her finest jewels copied. If so, Mallory had never seen these imitations.

After that, Flo Bel, subtly, yet definitely, indicated that they had had a long trip and were tired and she must say goodnight. Instantly the men were on their feet. Mallory glanced up, rising just in time to see Ernest Grenay bending over Flo Bel's hand and a look in Flo Bel's eyes which astounded her. It couldn't be as cold, as grim, as completely inimical as it looked!

She was certain that Flo Bel had never seen Ernest Grenay before.

Mallory's imagination was running away with her; no question of that. She was tired, really tired. She still had not had time to sort out, arrange her feelings about those few moments on the ferry, at the railing with Scott. She was thankful that he had not come to dinner.

She said goodnight to Mr. Grenay, who bowed slightly over her hand. Dolores led the way. Then Flo Bel went up the stairs ahead of Mallory, her back as erect as a steel rod under the rustling black moiré dress. She left Mallory with a murmur, nothing more. Dolores hoped that her room was comfortable and told her she must tell Su Lin to call for anything she wanted.

"But I promised Richard to come in and say goodnight."

"Oh, no, Mallory dearest. The doctor was here, you know, while we were at dinner. I heard him—" (Mallory had not heard that arrival, but then, she had not been listening for it as clearly Dolores must have.) "So," Dolores continued gently, "Richard should be asleep by now. The doctor gives him sleeping medicine. It is very important for Richard to get his strength back." She gave a soft little laugh. "All of us, the whole household, have made his complete and quick recovery our sole aim. Why, Henry stays at the gallery only as long as he must! Oh, by the way, I forgot to explain why you came by carriage. Richard's new motor, he ordered it from England, it's called a Daimler—it is not just now available." She shrugged lightly, her thin gray silk barely moving. "Murphy, our coachman, says there is something wrong with something. I couldn't possibly say what. So we still use a carriage and horses. Goodnight, Mallory."

"But I don't think Richard will be asleep yet. I did promise."

Dolores did not even reply to that. She leaned over, delicate and softly perfumed, planted a brief kiss on Mallory's cheek and walked gracefully down the hall.

So what should she do? It was very likely that Dolores spoke the truth and Richard was asleep. It was also important that his rest not be disturbed. Yet a broken leg wasn't like some long-drawn-out, potentially dangerous illness.

The gas fire was still flickering cheerfully in her room. The little dog lay happily on a blue silk eiderdown, on the great bed. Su Lin had turned down the bed and put out night things.

The dog gave a kind of low gurgle, meant for a warning growl. Someone knocked on the door, and when Mallory opened it Gorham stood there, looking very dignified, his black coat, white collar, darkly striped trousers immaculate, and he was, incredibly, smiling. "I took the little dog for a walk, Miss Mallory. A nice little dog, I might say. I fed him, too, none of that Chinese stuff in the kitchen but good pieces of roast beef. I'll see to him for you, Miss Mallory."

"Thank you, Gorham." He went away. Probably his pocket was gorged with poker money—she had never seen him quite so openly cheerful. But then, he was British and the British had the reputation for liking dogs. She must choose a name

84

for this one, who now stood on feathered legs and yawned, showing a pink tongue under his snub nose.

She decided to risk going to Richard's room; after all, she had promised to see him.

She opened the door to the hall, and Dolores, in a floating pink negligee, was walking gracefully past. "Oh, Mallory, I just peeked in! He's asleep. Better not disturb him. By the way. Everything has been so hurried and upset, I didn't have time to have proper wedding invitations made and sent out. Besides, Richard insists upon a quiet wedding. Just a few of us, in the church. I'm sending little notes around to invite the close friends here for a reception after the ceremony. I've ordered announcements of the wedding, however. I expect them to be delivered tomorrow or next day and we can address them ourselves. Or get a young man from Grenay's office to help. I'm sure you'll have your own list—"

"Yes," Mallory said on a breath that sounded like a sigh.

"I thought you would agree. I couldn't think of any more suitable plan. Goodnight, dear Mallory."

"Goodnight," Mallory said and closed the door again. It was settled; nothing could change it now.

Eight

She was alone. She must think about Scott and her feelings for him, even though she knew there could be no change—no different course for her to take. The wedding day, the church, the announcements were arranged.

But her thoughts persisted in going over and over recent events. Finally she fell into a troubled sleep—her feelings still unresolved.

Mallory didn't see Scott the next day at all. She knew Richard expected him, and would probably grow a little fretful when he did not arrive, so she ventured to Richard's room again. But she was stopped at the door by a bowing, respectful and adamant Cheng, who told her, smiling, that Mr. Richard was about to have his massage and exercises, and that the doctor, who had made another call that morning, early, felt him to be overtired.

Dolores was mysteriously busy at the telephone and at writing notes, and later, in the afternoon, receiving callers.

For callers came, rustling decorously in silks and leaving beautifully engraved cards in a great silver dish on a hall table.

Flo Bel did unbend when she noted some of the names and when it developed that most of the callers had traveled not only to New York but to Paris, London and Rome.

The conversation was precisely what suited Flo Bel; her native social grace blossomed, full of charm and dignity. Mallory told herself that she must develop a keener ear for names and a wider knowledge of the people of San Francisco. She hoped that would come if she worked at it, as she resolved to do.

The silver tea service was impressive, and had been rubbed to a soft patina, so it shone pleasantly in the firelight. Kai Sing was on duty, padding around silently, anticipating Dolores' brief nods. The talk was mainly of the coming opera and the coming wedding. Mallory thought, but wasn't sure, that the callers approved of her.

Later that afternoon, boxes containing her bridal gown and the rest of her trousseau began to arrive. Flo Bel came to her room to examine each item, advise Su Lin as to folding or hanging, and for the first time in many days seemed fully content as her face relaxed into smiles. "They've done well," she said, examining the white wedding dress with its short ruffled train, its sleeves widely puffed to the elbow, the long white gloves that went with it, the white satin slippers. In a separate box the veil was packed carefully in layers of tissue paper. Only then did Flo Bel's face grow a little sad. "I wish I could have kept your mother's veil. And mine. Both really priceless laces. Dear Mallory, I am so sorry."

Mallory was looking with dismay at the wedding dress, the white gloves, everything. To avoid her aunt's keen eyes, she rose and helped Su Lin.

However, when Su Lin had gone to take the little dog to Gorham, she tackled Flo Bel, knowing her aunt was probably anticipating her question. "Darling Flo Bel, you told Dolores we had brought jewels, but how—"

"Good heavens, Mallory, we couldn't come here with no jewels!"

"But—"

"Oh, I rented them, of course. My credit is still good, especially since it is so well known that you are marrying the Welbeck—I mean Richard. But I think it likely that Richard may give you something to wear to the opera that night. Almost like your debut party over again, although," Flo Bel added, eyeing the ruffled dressing table, "it will not cost us anything this time."

This entire trip may cost more than you know, more than you can possibly guess, Mallory thought so strongly that she suddenly was afraid she had said it aloud. But no; Flo Bel said, absently, "Remember to slit the left-hand glove—you know, the third finger for your wedding ring. When Ella Garry was married, nobody had remembered that and somebody had to fetch out a penknife. It was absurd."

Wedding ring, Mallory thought. So very soon.

After a moment she ventured another question. "Flo Bel, you don't like this...this Ernest Grenay?"

Instantly Flo Bel's face took on its careful, restrained look. "What on earth makes you say that?"

"I could see it."

Flo Bel merely looked at her for a second or two.

"And I don't think you like Henry—I mean Dolores' husband."

"I know he's Dolores' husband. *Lolo's*," said Flo Bel, an edge to her voice.

"She has been good to Richard."

Flo Bel gave her a sharp and very perceptive glance. "She is making an invalid of him," she said tartly. "I never heard of a broken leg's lingering on and requiring unremitting care. Good heavens! Your uncle would have been up and at his desk, propped up, perhaps, but able to eat. And swear," she added with the tender little smile that accompanied any reference to her husband.

Suddenly Mallory thought, Suppose I snatch this moment, when she is like this, and tell her I can't marry Richard: tell her I'm fond of him but I'm in love with Scott, and I won't marry Richard, nothing can make me.

Too many things weighed against it. Even the empty boxes, the drifts of tissue paper, the lovely dresses, carefully put away now on sacheted and padded hangers in the big dressing room adjoining her bedroom, added their small yet inexorable weight to the scales.

Everything in the house was what one would expect of a great mansion; there was central heating and open gas fires. And it was a balmy spring night, certainly. But the evening fog—Scott had called it the tule fog—creeping in seemed to bring a deadly chill with it.

Flo Bel rose, adjusting her flowing black moiré skirt. "My dear, I'm sure you will be very happy with Richard. I have been so pleased about your marriage."

"It's not marriage yet," Mallory said before she could stop herself.

Flo Bel gave her a calm smile. "The same thing, really—only the formality of the ceremony. Of course, that is essential, but the important thing is that you and Richard are so happy together," she said firmly. A spark came into her sharp eyes. "You will laugh, but on the train west, once or twice it occurred to me that you were a good deal too friendly with Scott Suydam. He is an estimable young man, certainly. Most polite and attentive. But I'm sure you would not forget for a moment that you are Richard's financée. And Friday you'll be his wife. My dear child—"

Gorham knocked respectfully, and at Flo Bel's word came in. "The little dog, madam."

The dog wriggled out of Gorham's clasp and sped across the room to Mallory. Flo Bel again gave her an affectionate, really loving smile. "The dog will be a comfort to you," she said and rustled away. Gorham followed, closing the door gently, as was his long-trained habit.

Something in Flo Bel's parting words struck Mallory with dismay. Surely Flo Bel did not mean that—that married to Richard, she might be in need of comfort, even the comfort of a little brown dog with a smashed-in face and wrinkled nose.

She had been perceptive, though, about Scott, too perceptive, but her attitude said, Now they were in San Francisco, all was well.

For a moment the warm coziness of the private car seemed like a retreat, a quiet yet wonderful kind of nest. That was wrong; Mallory could never return to it.

"I've got to give you a name," she said. The dog lifted his face intelligently. "Heaven knows what!"

Su Lin came in after her own special soft knock. "Mr. Richard asked me to tell Missy he'd like to see her."

"Yes. Thank you, Su Lin." But she held the dog as if for comfort already, and went to Richard's room. He was propped up as before, his cast-enclosed leg straight out before him on the mass of cushions. His red dressing gown was cheerful, but his face was again too pale. "I've missed you all day. Lolo tells me a number of callers arrived. Did you like them?"

"Yes."

He gestured toward a chair near him and she sat down. "I know they liked you. Have you talked to Lolo about the wedding arrangements yet?"

"Yes. Some. There hasn't been much time."

"I know. Your trousseau came today. I'm sure you'll be so beautiful. Darling, are you sure you'll not mind a wheelchair at the altar?"

"How could I mind?" Again, weakening any lingering notion she might have had to refuse marriage, run away, do something, anything, she felt a surge of pity.

He said, happily, "You like your dog. Have you named him?"

"No, I can't think of a proper Chinese name."

"Forget the Chinese. Call him Caruso. Everybody is talking about the great tenor's coming here. Caruso—or— No, just Cho. That suits him." He lifted a white hand toward the dog, who hesitated, then wagged a plumy tail cautiously. It delighted Richard. "You see! He knows already that he belongs to you. Now then, about the wedding. I do hope a small wedding will be all right. I know that you had planned to have bridesmaids. Lolo thought she ought to select some of

89

the girls here. But I said no. They would be strangers to you. And besides, well, honestly, a string of bridesmaids and grooms down the aisle, and me waiting in a wheelchair—it seems a little—a little—"

"Unusual?" she asked, smiling. Here was the old Richard, the dear, kind young man she had promised to marry and intended to marry.

His face sobered. "Will you look in the upper drawer of that little desk over there?"

The desk he indicated was a delicate French piece, Empire, she thought, quite near his bed. She went to it and opened the drawer. "Take out the box you see there," Richard said.

She took out a long purple velvet jeweler's case.

"Open it." He was smiling as happily as a child.

She opened it and gasped. Pearls! She knew enough about jewels to know at once that they were magnificent gems.

"You like them?"

"They are beautiful. Oh, beautiful!"

"Come here. I want to put them on you."

She turned, absently, to close the drawer from which she had taken the pearls, and saw a bottle. She stared at it for a moment and then turned to Richard. "You aren't taking laudanum?"

"Oh, that! Only a little to sleep. Only what Lolo or Cheng gives me."

She returned slowly to him, thinking hard. She leaned over so he could fasten the jeweled clasp of the pearls around her neck and said, her face turned away from him, "How often do you take it?"

"Whenever she or the doctor thinks I need it," he replied casually. "There! Now let me see you."

She had to persist. "How often is that?"

"Oh, now and then. Ah—my darling, they suit you. I knew they would. You can always trust Shreve's."

Shreve's? Oh, yes, surely someone sometime in her hearing had mentioned the famous San Francisco jeweler.

A bottle of laudanum and Richard's languid air of sickness!

She wished suddenly that she could talk to Scott about that.

90

Richard said, beaming, "My lovely bride! The pearls aren't good enough for you. But there are all the Welbeck jewels. We'll have them reset."

"Oh, Richard, the pearls—"

"You'll wear them with your wedding gown."

"Yes," she said after a second or two. "Yes. Richard, this laudanum—"

"Oh, it's only to help me grow stronger."

Or to help him grow weaker? It was an irresistible question. Since the bottle of chloral hydrate had disappeared, and the disappearance was still not clearly explained, a tinge of uneasiness concerning any drug remained with Mallory. Surely Richard couldn't need much medicine, not now.

He said, dreamily, "I knew I was right about you. I knew I couldn't have been mistaken."

"Mistaken?"

"About you, of course. Naturally, several people had told me of your uncle's death and...and the reasons for it. I knew— Forgive me, Mallory, but I couldn't help knowing that you had no prospects. Financial prospects," he said hesitantly. "We'll not talk about that. It didn't matter. I fell in love with you. It didn't matter to you, either. I am sure of that. You didn't care at all about the Welbeck money. But Scott—" He checked himself.

Scott! "He suggested coming to escort me here."

Richard's pale face was tinged with pink. "Well, you must understand. Scott— You see, he has known me all my life— and I went to New York and met you and fell in love and we decided to marry, and Scott only wanted to make sure that—"

"That some poverty-stricken adventuress was not trying to snare you into marriage? Was that it?"

"No, no!" He leaned forward and grasped her hands. "Believe me, darling, it wasn't that. Scott did have business in New York. And, well, he is cautious and—"

"And thought he'd better get acquainted with me before you married me. Your accident gave him the chance to come to bring me west. I see."

At the moment she could cheerfully have strangled Scott. His offer to escort her across the continent to oblige Richard was perfectly comprehensible, even laudable. His offer to act as a judge of her and her motives was infuriating. Richard was embarrassed, confused, regretful. "Darling, forget it. Scott had only my best interests at heart."

Your best interests, she thought in a sweep of anger. So he talked to your fiancée, he walked with her; he made her fall in love with him.

The moment on the ferryboat in the dusky twilight, surrounded by the cries of the gulls, the faraway wails of ships and foghorns—had Scott intended that to happen? A cruel kind of test?

She straightened her shoulders. "That was very sensible of Scott," she said without choking. "I wanted to see you last night, Richard, but Dolores said you were asleep."

"Yes, I took the medicine, doctor's orders, you know. I'm sorry, Mallory. You'll stop in to say goodnight tonight. Scott is coming to dinner, and Ernest Grenay."

The door into the hall was open; someone was preserving the proprieties; perhaps she had left it open herself. Scott Suydam said from the doorway, "May I come in?"

Richard smiled happily. "Scott! I've been hoping to see you!"

Scott spoke to Mallory, avoiding her eyes. "Good evening," he said pleasantly but formally. "Richard, don't move. Dolores tells me you must not be permitted to move around too much."

Scott came closer as Richard held out eager, welcoming hands. "I understand you accomplished the journey across the continent with the greatest of comfort."

"Indeed we did." As Richard motioned to a chair near him, he hesitated, shot a glance at Mallory, who said, "I'm just leaving," and Richard said, "No, no, don't leave yet, Mallory. See the pearls, Scott. Like them?"

Scott looked at her again, briefly. "Beautiful," he said. And unexpectedly added, "Your bride is everything you said she was, Richard."

So, that was fine! He gave her a reference, did he? A testimonial! Mallory felt the angry color in her face. It didn't matter. Neither man was observing her. Richard was beaming at Scott. She gave a quick glance at Scott, who was looking extraordinarily grave, almost shocked. He was leaning toward Richard, "See here, old fellow, you really are getting along, aren't you?"

"Heavens, yes. Such care I have! And now Mallory is here, all is well. I'll be quite fit and able to get to the altar Friday."

After a second or two, Scott said, "Friday? Dolores has made all the arrangements?"

"Oh, yes. Everything is arranged. Mallory's trousseau arrived in time. The fates were with me. Even the wedding dress, veil—everything arrived today." He glanced happily at Mallory. "Su Lin told me. Everything in this house does come to my ears, I think."

"That's all right," Mallory said in a stifled way. Scott did not, would not, look at her again. She added, "I'll leave you two. I must dress for dinner."

"Remember to stop and say goodnight to me this time," Richard reminded her. She said yes, murmured something polite in Scott's direction and went to her room.

So Scott had decided to investigate this girl Richard had fallen in love with and proposed to marry.

She was still angry, yet...Scott *couldn't* have intended that moment or two on the ferry. He couldn't have done such a clever job of acting. Perhaps he could.

Su Lin helped her dress; she clasped the pearls around her neck. They glowed against the white skin of her throat and as much bosom as the gown Flo Bel had chosen for her allowed to show. The dress was from her trousseau; she was wearing it ahead of time because she had little else sufficiently new and elegant. Dolores' big eyes, with those rings of white showing below the pale iris, would have instantly detected a shabbier dress. This one had lace at the shoulders, lace in a cascade down the pale-yellow crepe de Chine skirt. It was a new fabric; it draped gracefully.

She gave herself a long look in the mirror before she left the room and was warmed by the frank admiration in Su Lin's dark eyes.

But when she opened the door, Scott was waiting for her in the hall. "There's a room over here. I think we must talk. Come with me."

He didn't explain; he led her quickly along the balconied hall, past Richard's door, now closed, around a corner and into a small room, comfortable, lined with books; there was a desk there and chairs. "Richard's special study," he said. He leaned his arms on the back of the chair at the desk. "Mallory, what is going on?"

"What—"

"I mean Richard. What are they doing to him?"

"Oh, Scott, I don't know! Surely a broken leg would have improved by now. He takes laudanum. I discovered that."

"Who gives it to him?"

"His doctor. Or Dolores at the doctor's orders. He says. Dolores says."

He eyed her for a moment and then unexpectedly said, "You are very beautiful. That dress, your eyes and hair— and Richard's pearls." His voice had changed subtly. For a moment he had been natural and at ease. He became abruptly formal again.

She said, as abruptly, "You suggested the plan to bring me here so you could see what kind of woman Richard had chosen."

"But I…" He faltered, then looked squarely into her eyes. "Yes, I did."

"I understand you gave me a good reference."

"Mallory—don't! Let me explain."

"I don't want to listen to anything!"

Scott's face tightened. "You've got to understand that Richard, that I—"

"Have been friends since you were children."

"Yes, certainly. And he's not been really happy, you see. For some time it had seemed to me that it would be a good thing for Richard to get away, go somewhere, go to New York, say, and meet other people. He and Dolores made one or two short trips in the private car. But that was all. He was becoming almost a recluse."

"I see—"

"No, you don't see, not yet. I insisted, and Richard went to New York by himself. I even made him use a Pullman, not his lonely private car. I wanted him to see people. I got letters of introduction for him. In New York, I was sure that he began to enjoy life, and then he met you. His letters were of nothing but you. And all at once, very suddenly, you were engaged to be married."

"Is that so remarkable? Richard is a very—"

"I know. A very handsome, charming young man. He is also very rich."

"I *didn't*—" She sat down and clutched the arms of her chair.

"Oh, don't bother about that! I knew almost at once—well, I think now the moment I met you I knew that Richard was also a very lucky fellow. So I—" He came around the big chair and sat down also. "Mallory, I don't know when I began to feel that I mustn't see much of you. I tried to stay away. But then—then I couldn't. Neither of us—"

This was fact. She had to believe him. She said, not angrily but steadily, "That is in the past."

She didn't say what was in the past, the very recent past, as a matter of fact, but there was no need to put it into words. Scott said, "Tonight, when I saw Richard—he's much worse. Actually, he wasn't too bad when I left. But now he's a different man. The same kind and friendly Richard but—different. Think, in spite of all these massages and special foods and this new man, Cheng, to see to him, and I gather the doctor is here constantly, two or three times a day. For a broken leg! But the main difference is something I can't explain—a kind of languor. It's as if somebody is trying to keep him an invalid. Or as if somebody—Mallory, you remember that ugly business, just before we got to Chicago?"

"Of course." Even now her skin crawled.

"And then the bottle of sleeping stuff that disappeared. I almost convinced myself that it had simply rolled off a table or shelf and one of the servants had thrown it out. I was never really sure. And if— All right, I'm going to say it. Suppose somebody wants to prevent your marriage—"

"Flo Bel thought it possible, but everyone has been so kind, welcomed us, all that."

He shrugged impatiently. "What else could anyone do, openly? There'd have to be a strong expression of the greatest friendliness and welcome. But there we are, you see. Richard is really a very rich young man. If—I mean," he said, looking rather white, "when you marry him, the money aspect will
95

be different. His wife could control Richard. I don't mean that he's weak-willed. But he can be persuaded. And now that he is in such a . . . an odd state of health." He kneaded his hands together. "Richard was always just as you know him—that is, knew him in New York. He expects the best of everybody. He'd never question what anyone close to him would do."

"Dolores." It was not a question.

"Dolores has been a great influence in Richard's life, ever since they were children. You must have known that."

"I guessed it. Yes."

"But still—his generosity, his affection for her are valuable to Dolores. Surely she wouldn't risk losing that." He seemed to be arguing with himself.

She thought for a moment. "But does Dolores need money? That's what you're talking about, isn't it?"

"Yes. As a matter of fact, I suppose she could use Richard's fortune. It came from his father and the Welbeck Bonanza Mine—in the beginning, that is. Later Richard's father branched out into all the other Welbeck enterprises. But in the beginning it was the mine. Oh, it's still operative. But you see, Dolores was his father's brother's daughter. The brother seems to have been kind of a misfit, couldn't get anywhere in spite of the terrific opportunities offered here. Tried all sorts of things, I believe—everywhere. Died years ago."

"You mean Dolores—" she paused, then said, "Lolo—" She said the name in a biting tone of voice.

He glanced at her. "You don't like her, either."

"You think that she—and her husband, of course—need money?"

"I don't know. Henry has a reasonably good business, rather profitable, I think, although he must gamble on some of his imports. Really, that's all I know. But, Mallory, if she is trying to, say, keep Richard an invalid" (Or murder him, Mallory thought wildly) "you've got to help him."

"Yes." It was almost a whisper; her throat felt numb.

Scott linked his hands hard together; his eyes were dark and deeply troubled. "We can't let it go on like this. He's so much feebler, so much worse than when I went away. I don't

96

know what it is—too much laudanum, perhaps." He swallowed hard and said, "I feel so sorry for him."

Nine

"Yes, I know. He is helpless— Oh, Scott, I don't know what I can do!"

"You'll have to do something. You are the only person with the...the authority to save him. He'll die if this goes on. That accident on the stairs—I was never sure it was really an accident. You guessed that I was holding something back?"

"I wasn't sure. You didn't want to talk about it. I could see that."

"Your aunt could see it, too. I must be very transparent. She kept asking me about it. But I couldn't accuse anybody. I just felt that Richard wouldn't have fallen. When we were kids, we often chased up and down those stairs. They're slippery. But Richard was always agile, quick, never had to clutch the railing as I did sometimes. And he rarely drinks, you see. Besides—oh, I can't explain it, but I wasn't sure."

"You said you arrived just after the doctor."

"I was stopping in to see Richard, often did. He was so pleased about...about you and his coming marriage. I was to be his best man. I saw the doctor's rig outside and ran in, and there they all were, gathered around Richard. He was lying at the foot of the stairs, unconscious. Oh, I told you and your aunt all this! Dolores had sent Murphy for the doctor. Henry, Dolores, even Ernest Grenay were huddled around Richard, Dolores crying. The doctor made them shut up and give him space and he put splints on Richard's leg then and there. Then he gave him something in his arm and Murphy and I carried Richard up to his own room."

"But you thought—"

"I didn't think anything just then. The doctor said Richard was all right except for the broken leg. A bad break, yes, but Richard could have been killed by that fall. So I began to wonder. I couldn't help thinking that a light push could get him off balance. But there were Dolores, Henry, Grenay—all in the hall. They said they had been in the library and heard the crash and Richard screamed and— You see, there is no evidence of any violence."

"Who could have ... have made him fall?"

"Nobody! If they are telling the truth. Kai Sing was there, too. I did get him aside one day and questioned him. All he could tell me was that he was cleaning silver in the pantry, he heard the commotion and ran out, and they were gathered around Richard and Dolores told him to call Murphy and send him for the doctor."

"I think Kai Sing would tell the truth."

"I believe him. Besides, he had nothing to gain—"

"You can't mean—"

"Wait. I'm not sure I mean anything. But Richard is so very rich. Dolores, Henry, either of them just might want to stop his marriage to you. I can't think either of them would try to murder him. And yet— Oh, I don't know, Mallory. But I was uneasy. I wanted first to see you in New York. I wanted to be perfectly sure that you hadn't—forgive me, Mallory— hadn't entrapped Richard because he has so much money. If you were in love with him, I wanted to get you here, quickly, get the wedding over with, give you a position of real authority in this house. And ... and so I did," he said. "Like a fool. So I did. And Richard is not to suffer for it."

"But, Scott—"

He said quickly, "No, Richard will never know."

"We'll know," she said in a whisper which, although low, was almost like a shout.

"Yes," said Scott. He looked steadily at the handsome red and blue figured rug. "We'll know. I ought never to have spoken to you. I was very wrong." He lifted his eyes to her own and said miserably, "I couldn't help it."

"I couldn't help it, either," she said again in a whisper.

"And, Mallory, there's that other thing. It could be the answer. I mean—well, the Gary affair. The threat to you."

"Nobody—"

"Somebody tried to. I wish I could be here every minute, every second. Promise me—" He stood up abruptly. Something flashed in his eyes like a blaze of fire. He reached for her hands. "My God, Mallory, do you realize what I'm asking you to do?"

She didn't trust herself to speak; she put her hands in his but he didn't seem to be aware of it. He cried, "I'm a blasted damn fool! I'm asking you—"

"To marry him," she said. "I'm going to."

"Then we are both fools. I was thinking only of Richard. I was so shocked at his appearance, his languor, his— But my God, you *can't* marry him! I won't let you."

"I've got to." But she only whispered it—that, or he did not hear. Unexpectedly she thought of all those boxes of beautiful clothes—not paid for. All Flo Bel's debts, debts made for her, Mallory—unpaid. But she also thought of Richard's thin face, smiling and happy because she was to be his wife. She had to marry him; there was no way of avoiding it.

Scott said, explosively, "Sidney Carton! I always thought he was a great fool. Losing his head to promote— But that at least was quick. I've lost my head and my heart, too, and— What am I talking about! No, you are not to marry Richard. I know the date is set, everything is ready and planned. But I'll not let you marry him." He drew her close against him and for a fleeting moment she thought, Perhaps he can stop this marriage. Perhaps— The door opened quietly.

It mustn't be Dolores, she thought, and turned and—it was Dolores. She stood there, simply looking at them with those white-framed eyes. For a second she seemed almost like an animal, sending out waves of sensitivity. Surely, though, there was a flicker of something like satisfaction in her expression.

Then her arched eyebrows lifted; she said, sweetly, "I didn't mean to interrupt you."

Satisfaction? Mallory thought again, incredulously. Could Dolores actually have hoped that during the long trip across the continent, propinquity might have its influence—so the thing that had happened between Scott and Mallory had an opportunity to happen? Oh, no, Mallory told herself, she couldn't have been hoping for, say, a broken engagement, at the last minute!

On the other hand, Dolores did not seem to be really angry about what she must have overheard. There had been that swift flash of almost delight in her catlike face.

Scott said, shortly, "You didn't interrupt." His hands had dropped to his side. "Mallory and I have been talking about Richard—"

"I'm sure," said Dolores gently.

Scott ignored that. "We aren't satisfied with his progress. What does the doctor say?"

"The doctor! Why, dear me, Scott, he is perfectly satisfied. You have known Richard so long and so well that you must realize he never has been strong. So, naturally, it may take him some time to recover fully."

"From a broken leg?"

Dolores' wide eyes became still wider, her smile still sweeter. "The shock. You must realize that such a terrible fall was a great shock. So the doctor says."

"I'm sure it was." Scott had recovered what self-possession he had momentarily lost. "That is still Dr. Fairing, isn't it? He came when Richard fell."

Dolores nodded. "He is so very thorough. So dependable. We are very lucky to have him as a family doctor. Now, my dear"—she turned to Mallory—"dinner— Oh!" Her wide eyes showed an almost alarming flash of white. "I see that Richard gave you the pearls. Lovely on you. Very becoming. Don't you think so, Scott?"

"Yes," said Scott. "But really, Dolores—"

"Can't you say Lolo?" she asked, still eyeing the pearls at Mallory's throat. "Everyone does. It's been Richard's name for me since we were little children and—after my father died. That was very tragic, Mallory," she said in parentheses. "Perhaps Richard told you. I was so young. First my mother and then my father—but Richard's father took me in and treated me like a daughter. After my marriage, of course, Richard expected us to live here. Naturally, I feel great gratitude toward Richard. There is really nothing I wouldn't do for him!" She gave a soft little laugh. Mallory thought, like a dart, Or do *to* him? There was the money. There was the fall on the stairs. There had been two hands gripping her ankles, trying to force her downward! But that had been a man; the strong grip of those hands had almost certainly been a man's.

In spite of herself she looked at Dolores' hands and was shocked to see that they looked so strong—big, ridged, the hands of a laboring woman, or even a man. Dolores quite evidently tried to divert attention from those hands, manicured and creamed though they were. She wore such heavy bracelets, so many jewels, that it was not easy to avoid their glitter and see the hands alone. Yet Dolores herself could not—*could* not—have been on the platform at Gary, or on the train itself. Scott, in his many trips through the railway cars, seeking a possible assailant, would certainly have discovered her. Anyway, she had been in San Francisco at the time. But she could have hired someone to...to try to kill me, Mallory thought—but couldn't believe it. Murder? A broken engagement due to Scott? Could anyone plot so devious a scheme? If one attempt to stop her marriage to Richard failed, might another succeed?

She felt half ashamed as these thoughts raced through her mind even as Scott spoke. "Well, then, Lolo. It does seem to me that Richard doesn't need such constant care—"

"Oh, but he does!" Dolores cried reproachfully. "You don't understand Richard."

Scott didn't quite grit his teeth; but Mallory felt that he was barely restraining himself. Dolores went on, "I was about to say that we must go down to dinner, but, Scott, I see you aren't dressed for—"

"I meant to explain. Something has come up. I can't stay." He turned into the hall and held the door wide for the two women. He wouldn't, or at least didn't, look at Mallory as she passed him. In the hall he paused for a second at Richard's door. It was closed. Dolores said, "The doctor is with Richard now. I'm so sorry you can't stay. However, we'll see you tomorrow night at the dinner before the opera. As Richard's best man, Scott surely must be included in our party," she said to Mallory.

Scott showed nothing at all in his expression. They had

reached the top of the stairs when he said, "By the way—Lolo—show Mallory just where Richard fell."

Dolores gave a delicate little shudder, rippling the diamonds at her throat. "What a dreadful thing to ask. Dreadful! Just don't think about it any longer, Mallory dear."

But she did think of it. She herself grasped the railing harder than she had intended and stepped down very carefully, measuring each step in her gold cloth slippers. No one spoke until they reached the enormous hall, where Scott said a brief goodnight. Kai Sing, bowing and smiling, opened the outside door for him, and Lolo—I might as well get accustomed to it, Mallory thought—led her into the drawing room. This, too, was almost overpowering in its splendor. The Bookever house in New York had been beautiful, but this was baronial, full of treasures, Mallory guessed at her first glimpse. Two ladies, swishing in silks and glittering with jewels, came forward; there were also four gentlemen, bewhiskered and glossy as to shirt front; two of them were Ernest Grenay and Henry Beaton, touching his whiskers as if he'd been drinking something. Flo Bel was already there, looking her elegant best.

Dinner was almost a repeat of the previous night's, possibly even a little more elaborate.

Halfway through it, Mallory turned from the whiskered gentleman on her right, who was telling her of the Welbeck Bonanza Mine and its enormous and continued productivity, when she felt eyes fixed too steadily on her. She looked up uneasily and met Dolores' pale gaze. Dolores sat at the head of the table, her triangular face set and determined. Mallory thought, Why, she hates me! She'll stop my marriage to Richard by any means she can employ!

It was like a mute warning, so violent a wave of telepathy that no one could have avoided it. But then, at once, Dolores smiled and turned to the man at her right, and Henry Beaton, on Mallory's other side, began to talk of the opera.

It was midnight, this time, before the guests departed and Flo Bel, still reserved and yet at her usual social ease with the four guests, barely permitted Ernest Grenay to bow over her hand before withdrawing it as if she had touched a snake.

Lolo hates me, Mallory thought again, and I know why.

But I don't know why Flo Bel seems to hate this Ernest Grenay.

That was Monday night. The four guests—the women furred and veiled and talking pleasantly and eagerly of the next night's opera and their dinner and their pleasure at meeting dear Richard's bride-to-be—at last were gone. There was the muffled thud of trotting horses on the long driveway.

Mallory didn't quite run up the stairs, although she wanted to. When Dolores called to her she made the dog her excuse, and said goodnight.

The dog was waiting, scrambling up when he heard her open the door to her room, his plumy tail wagging, his black nose making snuffling welcome noises.

Su Lin was waiting, too, in the luxurious dressing room. She helped Mallory out of the yellow dress, with all its tiny unreachable hooks and eyes; she turned the gas log lower. She said that Gorham had had the little dog out and had fed him. She said, "Goodnight, Missy."

Mallory at last settled down in a chaise longue near the cozy blue and red gas log; the dog pawed and scrambled his way onto her lap. She stroked his ears, drawing them through her fingers. The sapphire ring with the diamonds around it glittered in the light from the fire. So—now—she must concentrate on the day's happenings.

Scott had said he wouldn't let her marry Richard.

But he couldn't stop it. She couldn't stop it. Dolores *would* try to stop it; she was instinctively yet rationally sure of that. Was it possible that Dolores was jealous? Cousins had been known to fall in love with each other. But—no. She rejected that vagrant reflection at once. There was nothing at all in either Richard's or Dolores' attitude to suggest the remotest semblance of a romance. It was simply, completely out of the question. She didn't need to ask herself how she knew that; she simply knew it. But there might exist another kind of jealousy, that of possession—of the use of Richard's house, his money, even his private car, and the position and luxury his name gave her. Who but Richard could have given Dolores all her jewels? And it would be like him, trying to repay her for the attention she had apparently given him for most of his life.

Dolores might certainly feel that Richard's marriage would threaten all those things, and she was a strong and ingenious woman, devious and certain of getting her way. Her way, just then, was to prevent Richard's marriage—if she could.

On that subject, in a peculiar way, Mallory and she were in agreement, but Dolores did not know that. It was possible, of course, that Dolores had encouraged the idea of sending Scott to New York to escort Mallory to San Francisco. There had been that fleeting but identifiable gleam of satisfaction in Dolores' face when she had found Mallory and Scott together, and she had almost certainly heard something of what had been said.

That did not matter, however. The marriage was a settled thing. When the time came, she would have to deal with Dolores as best she could. It was not a happy prospect.

The dog twitched his ears, seemed to listen to something, gave a little tremor and settled more closely against her. Somewhere, not far away, a horse was restless, kicking at his stall in the distant stable. She was suddenly too tired to even try to think any longer. She went to bed, and the dog, after trying and trying, finally scrambled up onto the silk eiderdown and contentedly wriggled against her, snuffling happily.

Otherwise, it was a silent night, warm and still. Actually, a light breeze came from the ocean but Mallory knew nothing of that. That was Monday, April sixteenth. By the time she drifted into weary sleep, it was Tuesday, April seventeenth. Three days until her wedding.

The next day went swiftly; more boxes of clothes came and were unpacked under Flo Bel's sharp eyes. Wedding announcements, beautifully engraved, came and were sent to Ernest Grenay's office and an obliging clerk. Also that day, wedding presents began to arrive, sent on from New York. Dolores helped unpack them, then took Mallory to a room already filled with gifts from the friends in San Francisco who knew of the altered plans for the wedding. A smiling Dolores and a serious Flo Bel made lists. "No use trying to do your thank-you cards now," Flo Bel said.

Mallory looked at the mounds of tissue paper, the glints

of silver and crystal, swallowed hard and said she would write the cards later.

Richard sent for Mallory twice; once he told her to bring the dog and she did, and watched with a pang as Richard's face lightened while he stroked the silky ears and laughed at the little dog's blunt face and his rasping pink tongue. Su Lin came to tell her that her aunt wished her to try on a dress. Later in the afternoon she had a quiet tea with Richard, the gas fire alight again, although it was a warm night. "Always like this when the wind is from the sea. You'll like it."

He talked of plans for changing the house. It was so large, he couldn't do much about that; but he could change some of the heavy grandeur which had been a part of its Victorian conception. His father had been a self-made man, pleased at his success. "No reason he shouldn't display his wealth if he wanted to," Richard said simply. "It was the fashion then, but you and I needn't live with all this—" His hands made a sweeping and comprehensive gesture. They were not like Lolo's hands. Richard's hands were thin, the fingers long and gentle. Lolo's hands looked quite as if she could grasp anything in the world and keep it, too.

Mallory did ask a question. Were Dolores and her husband to continue to live in the house? She toyed with one of the dog's paws as she spoke and didn't look at Richard. She heard the surprise in his reply.

"Why, of course. Lolo has always lived here, since she was a child and orphaned. And surely there is room for them in this great house. But now—" Anxiety came into his quiet voice. "If you don't want them, you have only to say so. I'll see to it that they have the money to buy a house of their own—and keep it up, too. Henry, well, Henry has a little money, but he doesn't have enough for a house like this. And...and Lolo— But if you want me to, I'll tell them they must have their own home. Of course, Ernest Grenay doesn't actually live here, but he stays here often. Convenient for me and convenient for him so he doesn't have to get across the Bay at night. He has a charming little house near Sausalito. But if you mind Ernest or Lolo and Henry being here, I'll tell them as soon as we get back from our honeymoon."

105

The honeymoon was to be in Mexico somewhere; there would be mountains and magnificent views of the sea and a splendid climate—and Cheng would go with them, Cheng and Su Lin, to be their valet and maid.

Cheng came in before she could make any kind of reply. He gave her a sleepy glance from his slanted dark eyes; his oval yellow face was bland as usual. He said, almost too respectfully, that it was time for Mr. Richard's massage.

Dinner again; another trousseau gown. Flo Bel came in as Mallory was dressing. She was wearing black, of course, a handsomely cut dress which revealed still-beautiful white shoulders. She was carrying white gloves in one hand and a cluster of sparkling jewels in the other, and was actually wearing a diamond-set tiara in her reddish-silver hair.

Mallory stared and Flo Bel laughed softly. "I really intended the tiara for you. But in New York you wouldn't be wearing a tiara, not an unmarried girl. So I decided to wear it myself. Now you have the pearls—and here are bracelets and a brooch."

More diamonds. Mallory looked at them with alarm. Surely her aunt hadn't carried such a fortune in jewels across the country in her dressing case. She guessed at Mallory's dismay and smiled. "They were quite safe."

All rented, Mallory thought dazedly. When Su Lin went out of the room for something, Mallory whispered. "Are they insured?"

Flo Bel lifted her eyebrows. "My dear!"

Su Lin came back with a wrap, white velvet touched with ermine, silky and soft. Her dark eyes glowed as she said, "Mr. Richard sent it to you, Missy."

Pearls, and now a long, lovely cloak to cover her finery— and rented jewels. Flo Bel said, "You'll do very well, my dear. That white is becoming and suitable."

An extremely elaborate dinner; guests; more silks, more feathers, more jewels. More talk of the opera to come and of the opera of the previous night, *The Queen of Sheba*, which, it developed, no one at dinner had heard but the *Call* had given bad notices; the rumor was that Caruso had been furiously angry at the various newspapers' unbridled and adverse remarks.

Scott did not turn up at all, but no one mentioned his absence. The vacant place at the table was filled by a short young man, with small, almost pretty features, thick yellow hair and a long, drooping yellow mustache. Mallory did not, then, discover his name, and if he said anything at all, she didn't hear it, but from something someone said, she had the impression that he worked for Henry. Probably Dolores invited him when she needed an extra man. He was very polite to everybody, but once he seemed to get his big mustache entangled with soup and spluttered and dabbed until Gorham, on self-imposed duty, came swiftly forward, brought a fresh napkin and contrived to fleck away drops of soup on the young man's formal coat. Dolores shot him a glance that could have killed, Mallory thought with rather wry humor, if the young man had not pulled out a pince-nez and adjusted its fine gold chain in his lapel quite as if he were making an excuse for clumsiness. Gorham, face long and expressionless, retired, holding the soupy napkin as if it were a plate.

Kai Sing imperturbably continued serving. Coffee was brought to the table to save time. The ladies rustled away into a sumptuous cloakroom; jewels, coiffures and laces were adjusted. Then closed carriages arrived and coachmen hastened to open the doors. The carriage Flo Bel, Mallory, Dolores and Henry rode in was well sprung and well built, but even so, it jounced and joggled as it went over cobblestones and down steep hills.

Then the opera. The Welbeck box. Opera glasses turned steadily toward the box and toward her, Mallory.

She tried to ignore the glasses and their remorseless observation. Flo Bel held herself like a queen. Dolores was beautiful that night, too; Mallory had to admit it, grudgingly. Her black hair, so black it was almost blue, was done up in a full kind of roll all around her pointed face; she wore a small tiara and, Mallory thought, gave a rather searching glance at Flo Bel's. Dolores' pale face was always very white, but that night it appeared to have an extra coating of whatever she used, some kind of liquid powder, Mallory unkindly suspected. Her dress was pale-blue satin, glittering with sequins. She wore bracelets outside her long white gloves.

After some preliminary fiddling and tuning on the part

107

of the orchestra, and a number of hushes aimed at the still-conversing audience, the overture to *Carmen* began.

It was to be a historic opera. Of course, Mallory did not know that then. She did not know, either, that Caruso had had a historic battle backstage, still angered at the reception given *The Queen of Sheba* and now angry at that night's audience, who, he felt, would not appreciate *Carmen*. Mainly, he was angry because he had consented to make this tour at all, and particularly angry at Madame Fremstad, who was to sing in *Carmen* with him and with whom he had had a running argument during the entire tour. The quarrel was patched up sufficiently to send the singers to their dressing rooms. Here, too, Caruso became difficult, for newspapermen were in wait to ask him questions. How many trunks, really, had he brought with him? Forty? What did he think of the eruption of Vesuvius? He said furiously that he was thankful he was not in Naples and pushed them out of his dressing room.

Naturally, no one in the audience knew all that. As the curtain rose, there was only respectful quiet—the rustling silks seeming to settle against the stark black and white of the men's evening clothes.

Mallory knew *Carmen*. She had heard Caruso before. Probably he had never sung better, but she scarcely heard a single glorious note of it.

She was aware when gentlemen came to the box between the acts, as was the custom. They were introduced to her and Flo Bel. Mallory was reminded, briefly, of the opera house in New York and the members of the Opera Club there, a group of men, many of them young, who had seats in a special box which was well situated for observing the ladies in the audience, although it was not so well planned for observing the singers on the stage. She was aware, too, that Scott did not come to join them at the opera, just as he had not appeared at dinner.

At last, incredibly, it was over. Incredibly, she and Flo Bel and Lolo were crushing their skirts together in the carriage. Incredibly, the lights streaming from the opera house were left behind as the horses began to climb—and climb and climb, Mallory thought, jolting over cobblestones.

She knew only that an interview, which she realized, now, had to come, and which she dreaded, was inexorably approaching. She must tell Flo Bel about the decision she had made—her ears deaf to the music of the opera—the decision that could change the course of their lives.

The horses seemed possessed with a nervous kind of energy and the carriage rocked from side to side. Henry Beaton, the ubiquitous Ernest Grenay and the blond young man had taken another carriage. It drew up behind them as they reached the porte-cochere; the young man hurried, his opera hat dangerously over one ear, to hold neatly gloved hands up to assist the ladies. Henry and Ernest Grenay came also, and the coachman, still clutching reins and trying to hold in the horses, said, "They're mean tonight, Mr. Beaton."

"You tried to drive too fast uphill. Don't do it again," Henry said sharply.

The coachman was stubborn. "Couldn't keep them at a steady pace. Kept getting ahead of me. I don't know what's got into them."

"Probably something has got into you," Grenay said. "Surely you had a drink, or two or more, during the opera."

"No, sir. No, sir, I didn't. Stayed with the horses. They were acting up—funny, it is."

The coachman in the rear carriage added quietly, "He's right, Mr. Beaton. My team seemed kind of restless, too. Nervous somehow."

"Bah!" said Henry, but under his breath, as Cheng opened the massive hall door for them. Lights streamed out.

No one seemed disposed to linger. Flo Bel swept majestically up the stairs, but not until she had thanked Lolo, most politely, for the pleasure of the evening. Henry muttered something about nightcaps, and the three men, shrugging off their black opera capes, disappeared toward the library.

When Su Lin had unhooked Mallory's white chiffon dress and taken her gloves and evening bag, Mallory sent her away and crawled into her shabby red flannel dressing gown. She looked around for the dog, but apparently Gorham had taken little Cho for an airing, late as it was.

The velvet and ermine cloak had been carefully put in the dressing room. The pearls had been returned to their purple velvet case. The rented jewels were placed carefully in a drawer.

Scott had not come to dinner, had not arrived at the opera. Why not?

Simply because he didn't want to? But she felt, deeply, that perhaps, just perhaps, there was a more urgent reason for his absence.

He had said, hadn't he, that he wouldn't let her marry Richard? But there was nothing he could do. There was only something she must do herself.

The flannel dressing gown was meant for cold New York Aprils, not for balmy San Francisco, yet she was cold, her hands were icy, and the dressing gown felt oddly reassuring.

Gorham came to the door. She knew his knock and told him to come in.

He did so, quietly as usual, but he did not have Cho with him. Instead he carried a small rolled-up leather case. "Madam sent me for the jewels, miss."

"The—oh—in this drawer." She got them out and watched as Gorham seemed to know precisely each of the small stitched-in pockets for their care. "The tiara Madam wore and the other jewels go here—" He indicated the spaces.

An amazing surmise struck her. "Gorham! Did you carry those things all the way across the continent?"

"Why, yes, Miss Mallory. Certainly."

"But—"

"No danger of losing them. No one could have guessed that I carried them. Madam had to rent them. She said she had told you." He rolled up the leather case expertly.

"Oh," said Mallory inadequately.

"By the way—Mr. Scott—I should say Mr. Suydam—left this for you. He spent some time with Mr. Richard while all of you were at the opera. When he left he gave me this. His instructions were for you to keep it safely."

He handed her a long, thick white envelope. It was inscribed merely with her name.

"What— It looks so...so official!" Could Scott have discovered some legal reason to prevent her marriage! But that was nonsense.

It was indeed nonsense. Gorham said, "Mr. Richard's will,
110

I should guess, Miss Mallory. At least, I was called in to witness his signature. As I did. Also Kai Sing."

"His—will! But he's going to get well."

Gorham's pale-blue eyes were rather sharp. "You are going to be married, too, miss. Goodnight, miss."

She didn't want him to leave; every second he stayed postponed the thing she had to do. "Where is Cho? I thought you had him."

"Oh, no, I had him out sometime ago. Dear me! Where is the little fellow?"

The little fellow was discovered, after a swift search on Gorham's part and a swifter one on Mallory's. He was huddled, a bundle of drooping brown fluff, under the bed. He gave a small whimper when Mallory reached in to get him, and he was shivering. She could feel the tremors in his small body.

"What's the matter with him?"

"I can't say, miss. But—" Gorham touched Cho's nose; he looked into his eyes. He felt the small body carefully, and said, "I don't understand it. He seems frightened. There's nothing to be frightened about. Just hold him. Keep him warm. He's perfectly well."

"Gorham," she said on a tangent, yet in her heart she knew that she was trying to keep him there, talking, putting off the task ahead of her. "You remember that dog? The one I found on the street and brought home. Oh, long ago—"

"You were about nine," said Gorham.

"Yes, I suppose— Gorham, I've been wondering. What did you do with him?"

"Dear me, miss. Why didn't you ask me at the time? Why, I kept him for a few days in my care, then I gave him to Mrs. Helmerson's coachman. The Helmersons had decided to get along without a footman, times were getting difficult, so the coachman let the dog ride on the box with him. The little dog turned out to be part black and white terrier. It was quite a sight." Gorham permitted himself a smile. "Seeing the little dog sitting up on the box, like a king."

"I see. Yes. Well—thank you, Gorham. Cho will be all right, then?"

"Nothing to worry about, I assure you. I understand the

opera was a great success. But I hear that Mr. Caruso was not at all satisfied with his first rooms in the Palace Hotel. They were obliged to give him a suite once used by a former President of the United States, Mr. Grant. Dear me!" Gorham allowed himself a slight but chilly headshake and added, surprisingly, "A wop."

"Gorham! He's a very great tenor!"

"Yes, Miss Mallory. I'm sure. But still—" He took the leather case, put it under his black jacket and nodded gravely as he started away.

"Wait, Gorham, exactly which room is my aunt's?"

His eyebrows lifted slightly. "The second door to the left, miss. Goodnight."

Cho gave a snuffled kind of murmur and nestled closer. She slid the envelope in her pocket, where it rattled crisply. Richard's will; so that was how Scott had been occupied, inducing him to make a will and get his signature witnessed properly, while the others were at the opera.

She wouldn't look at it. Anyway, it was probably sealed. She had no doubt that the will concerned her: his bride on Friday. Yes, Richard would have thought of her in that way. Scott would have told him firmly that Mallory must be protected.

So now she could no longer postpone the interview she dreaded. Grasp the nettle, she told herself; but this was a very painful nettle to grasp.

She wrapped the dressing gown closer around her, took a long breath, leaned over to put Cho down, went out of the room. The second door to the left.

She knocked a little more sharply than she had intended. Flo Bel replied in a startled way, "Gorham? Is that you?"

"Me," said Mallory and went into the room. She closed the door behind her.

Flo Bel was sitting at a dressing table, wrapped in her own rather shabby blue damask dressing gown, brushing her still-luxuriant hair. She met Mallory's eyes in the mirror and whirled around on the bench. "What on earth, Mallory! You're white as a sheet."

Mallory stood against the closed door; it gave her some support.

112

"I'm not going to marry Richard."

Flo Bel gave her a brief look, turned back toward the mirror and calmly started brushing again. "All girls feel like that just before marriage. Go back to bed."

"Aunt..." Only in very serious moments did Mallory address Flo Bel as "Aunt." Flo Bel's brush paused.

"Aunt," Mallory began again. "Please listen to me. I mean it. I am not going to marry Richard."

Flo Bel waited a moment, then put down her brush and again turned around to face Mallory.

"But you are going to marry him."

"No. Please, Aunt—"

"You can't stop the marriage now. It's impossible."

"It is not impossible. I'm not yet married to him—"

"Almost as good as married. You accepted him. You came all the way across the continent to marry him. You— Good heavens, Mallory, you don't mean this!"

"I do mean it."

"Do you have any sleeping pills?" Flo Bel said gently.

"You must believe me. I'm not in a state of premarriage twitters. I am simply not going to—"

"Stop saying that!"

"All right. I've told you." Mallory made a move toward the door.

Flo Bel said, "Stay here! I want to talk to you. You say you have decided not to marry him. Well, then, have you considered the alternatives?"

Mallory paused. "I've considered enough."

"Enough? Are you sure? Do you plan to return to New York—no marriage, no—" Flo Bel bit her lip and did not say *no money.* "Nothing to do but remain an old maid, and a poor old maid."

"But—"

"If you think that anybody will want to marry you with such a scandal hanging over your head—well, nobody will. At least, nobody who could give you anything worth having— name, position—oh, well, yes, money."

"Flo Bel! I do remember everything you've done for me. I am grateful."

"Grateful! Telling me something like this?"

113

"I can do something, get some kind of job or— oh, that doesn't matter—"

"It matters a great deal. In fact, it's your whole future."

"I can—stay here—" Mallory wished she hadn't said that as soon as the words were out.

Flo Bel stood. *"Stay here?* After backing out of a marriage at the last moment! You are out of your head. In fact—that is the answer, I suppose. Bridal nerves—"

"Bridal nerves, nothing!" Mallory almost shouted.

"Well, then what? Leaving a man like Richard Welbeck! After your much-publicized engagement! Your trip out here—your—" Flo Bel cast about for arguments, and cried, "Even your trousseau. And all those wedding presents to send back!"

"I've thought of all that. I'm sorry it will hurt you. But please believe me, I cannot go on with it."

Flo Bel thought rapidly; Mallory could almost feel her authoritative, agile mind racing around. "But you like Richard."

"Yes, of course I do. How could anyone not like him?"

"Have you thought of the pain this silly—this childish notion would give him?"

"Yes, yes, and I'm sorry, but—"

"Now listen to me, Mallory. You were a comfort to your uncle and to me. You were also inclined to be a rather spirited, indeed sometimes a rather rebellious, child. It took considerable patience and—yes, and love on our part. You can't remember yourself growing up—"

"I didn't grow up!" Mallory said suddenly, as if seeing herself clearly. "I didn't grow up at all. I just did what was expected of me."

"Not always," Flo Bel said tartly.

"I did what you told me to do because it was easier. Besides, I always thought you were right. And after Uncle Peter died you had so much courage—"

"Then, you see—"

But Mallory swept on. "I just now grew up—at least I feel a new kind of confidence in myself, I think—I think only in the last few days. Sometime. I don't know. I don't understand—"

114

Flo Bel cut in sharply. "Scott Suydam! I did wonder about that. But you can put him out of your stupid, childish head. He is Richard's best friend."

"Aunt, you must believe me. If I have to ... to do anything, find some sort of job, anything, I'm not going to marry—"

"What kind of job? We've talked of that. There's nothing you're qualified to do."

"I can work in a store. I can—"

"You can go straight back to bed. I've had enough of this childish nonsense! If you insist," said Flo Bel as if granting a great yet reasonable favor, "we can talk of this notion of yours in the morning. Not now. I'm too tired. You are in a— in a very confused state. Tomorrow morning, yes. Now then, goodnight, my dear." She swept over to Mallory and kissed her cheek lightly.

"All right," Mallory said gracelessly. "But if you think you can change my mind, you can't."

Flo Bel had one last remark to make; as usual, a practical one. "How do you think we can get back to New York? I have no money."

"I can—I can sell or pawn Richard's pearls!" Mallory cried in a reckless and utterly futile effort to convince Flo Bel, who merely smiled, almost indulgently, and said, "Goodnight, my dear."

She opened the door; she didn't push Mallory out, but she stood there as if politely waiting for her departure.

But she hadn't won.

Mallory went wearily, drained, loving Flo Bel and deeply resentful at the same time. Flo Bel might be reasonable, sensible. But nothing would shake Mallory's decision.

At the beginning of this evening, she had thought she had everything straight in her mind. She knew she must marry Richard. Then, oddly enough, it was during the opera that it had become clear and imperative that she could not. How could she marry Richard when she was in love, truly in love, with another man?

Her decision encompassed more than that, Mallory thought; it meant that she had begun to mature, at least, had learned something of reality, during the eventful journey across the continent.

115

She was tired to her very heart. She crept into bed, still with her dressing gown tucked closely around her. She left the rose-shaded bedside lamp burning; that, too, was vaguely comforting; she would turn it off later. Cho settled himself against her ear, so she had to move him. He kept returning, however, his little body trembling.

It was a restless night. Again, but this time more insistently, she seemed to hear horses kicking, rattling against wooden stalls. One of them, quite nearby, neighed and neighed and another snorted. A restless night.

She did not reach out to turn off the lamp beside her. But she did eventually fall into sleep, for she was asleep when the bed shook itself, the room shook itself, a pillow shot from her head to the floor. The whole room was shaking. Cho gave a sobbing yelp. Something crashed heavily upon the ceiling—no, down the chimney; bricks clattered wildly on the rug. The room heaved; the bed trembled. Somewhere across the room a vase fell and shattered like a small scream. Then thunderous crashes came from somewhere, everywhere, and Cho scrambled up on short legs and barked defiance at the something he could not see but must attack.

The little bedside lamp wavered and fell over, crashing on the rug. Mallory was flung to the floor as the bed tilted to an impossible angle. She managed to get to her feet as the door into the hall was flung open. Gorham, a startling figure in long white nightshirt and heavy black overcoat, clutched the leather case of jewels in one arm and Flo Bel in the other. Flo Bel had her dressing gown tight around her; she said in distinct, and certainly disapproving, accents, "It seems to be an earthquake. Come here, Mallory—"

Gorham said, "Here under the doorbeams. It's said to be safer. Things," said Gorham with true British understatement, "are coming down a bit."

The second shock then came.

Ten

It was a devastating, unearthly strong shake that almost nothing could withstand. The sounds alone were deafening. It was as if the whole world had given itself up to an uncontrollable universe. Chimneys crashed, windows shattered everywhere. The house shuddered violently. The long marble stairway humped itself upward, a block of steps fell, crashing on the floor below. The wrought-iron railing twisted. The terror, the thunder, the unearthly power unleashed seemed to last an eternity.

Mallory sneezed and sneezed and found herself lying sprawled across an undulating floor, choking with fright and with dust from falling plaster. She felt her head vaguely; something seemed to have struck her. Gorham was crawling across the floor, calling her name. Flo Bel—where was Flo Bel?

Gorham got to her and tugged at her sleeve. "She's all right," he yelled. "She's all right."

Mallory must have cried out, screamed probably for her aunt. Flo Bel was on the floor, too, but now she lifted her head and said, with cold disapproval, "Dear me!" She, too, began to crawl.

There was no electric light. Everything had been shaken away. But somewhere a pale light shone. Dawn?

Mallory tried three times and finally sat up, on a perilous slant above the marble stairway, now with a gaping hole, like an enormous mouth with some gigantic teeth wrenched away.

Gorham tugged again at her sleeve. His face was bloody from a cut on his forehead. He still clutched the case of jewels. Flo Bell crawled across a shambles of fallen plaster and a chair, broken so splinters stuck out jaggedly and blocked her for a moment; then she crawled carefully around it. "Mallory! Mallory!"

"I'm all right; I'm here—" Mallory didn't know where her voice came from. She could see Gorham, turning to hold one arm toward Flo Bel; she could see Flo Bel.

Gorham yelled, "If there's not another—try to get over here, madam. Safer—"

Nothing was safe. The world had swung out of its orbit. There was a continuing hideous crescendo of sounds, crashing, thundering, everywhere. Above it, through it, there were church bells coming from somewhere. Church bells! Well, they needed a church, Mallory thought, and said to herself, "I'm hysterical. I must keep my head. Richard!"

Richard, unable to walk, unable to find a safe place! Anything might have happened. The hall floor leading to his room was broken, cut in irregular pieces.

Flo Bel reached her and clutched at her. "Mallory, you're hurt. Your head—"

"No, no, it's all right. Richard—"

Gorham seemed to be listening to something, his long face pale except for the streaks of blood on his cheek. He lifted the hand that still clasped the leather bag. "I think it's over, madam. I think it's over—"

But there were still deafening crashes from inside the house, from outside, from everywhere—and the church bells kept ringing. They waited as if paralyzed, uncertain, grasping at anything at all that seemed firm and steady. A long, long moment, another— Yes, perhaps it was over. In the quiet pause a horse screamed; it was an agonizing, terrifying and terrified sound, long and high and indescribably horrible. Another crash followed it.

Gorham said, "The stables, I think," almost calmly, but sweat was mingling with the blood on his cheek. Something stirred beside Mallory and whimpered, and unbelievably, Cho lifted his head and barked and growled. He had known something was coming, hadn't he? He'd tried to tell them something was coming, and now that it was here he was determined to defy it. How the little dog had managed to stay with her, Mallory didn't know, didn't pause to think about. She must see to Richard.

118

There was a jagged gap in the floor of the hall between where she sat huddled, and Richard's room. His door hung open and a faint light streaked out of a split in the heavy wood. She called out, "Richard—Richard!"

Dolores answered. She came sweeping past the sagging door to Richard's room, her black hair wild around her shoulders, her pointed face white as wax. She glanced at them, light eyes blazing. "It was a bad one," she gasped. She added, as Gorham had said, "I think it's over."

"Richard!" Mallory cried.

"He's all right. Nothing fell—at least nothing to hurt him. I've got him up and in a chair. If he'll only stay there—Henry!"

Henry was scrambling awkwardly, on a slant, from an open door along the opposite side of the encircling balcony, clinging to the twisted wrought-iron railing as he came. He looked grotesque, his bearded face ashen above a long white nightshirt and a violently purple silk dressing gown, embroidered—later Mallory remembered the design and wondered that she had noticed it—in great golden dragons.

He shouted, "Get downstairs before the roof falls in."

Dolores looked at him. "How?" She gestured with one of those thick strong hands toward the broken stairway.

"Back stairs, of course." He crawled to them. "Here—you can get across. Give me your hand."

"I'd better stay with Richard."

"Is he all right?"

"Oh, yes. Yes." Dolores put both hands up and shoved back her thick hair. Her triangular, pale face seemed to glisten. "Take Mallory and her aunt—take them down the back stairs. Hurry, you, Gorham—"

Gorham looked at Flo Bel. Flo Bel brushed dust from her face and said, "Do you think it really is over?"

"Oh, yes." Dolores seemed certain. "It was a bad one. I don't think we have ever had such a bad one. But they never last long—"

"Too long," said Gorham sourly.

Henry adjusted his dressing gown. "Dolores, come with me. I'll help you."

"No, I'll stay with Richard. He can't walk, and if—"

119

"There won't be another." Henry spoke confidently, as if he'd received assurance from the powers that had let loose such havoc. "All right, then. But the roof might go—"

"We'll stay here, I think," Flo Bel said. "Your room, Mallory. It looks fairly safe from here."

Flo Bel scrambled over the slanting floor of the hall, looking, in spite of her unusual position, still dignified, still self-possessed. Gorham sighed, and crawled after her. They vanished through the dimly lighted doorway of Mallory's room. The frame was still in place.

Dolores said across that chasm of ruined flooring, "The house is well built. Probably perfectly safe now."

But the world outside was not safe, for Flo Bel called from somewhere inside the room. "Gorham! It looks as if there's a fire! See! Over there!"

As Mallory started across that buckled-up flooring, she called out something to Dolores, but she didn't know what and Dolores paid no attention, for she had lifted her silky dressing gown, displaying extraordinarily thick and muscular legs, and was cautiously negotiating fallen chunks of floor. Henry told her to go back, go back, be careful; he chattered distractedly. Cho crept after Mallory. They reached what seemed the haven of her room, although it was also a shambles.

Bricks lay scattered from the fireplace. The gas log was still in place, but tables were overturned, windows were shattered. From outside, audible through the gaps in the broken glass, there were screams, confusion, shouts from everywhere.

Gorham cried, "My God, look! Look over there."

Dolores had joined them, peered over Mallory's shoulder—and screamed.

Henry Beaton managed to reach them, too, and began to swear, heavily.

A ruddy leaping flame surged up in the distance. Far away from it, in a remote part of the city, another flame shot a scarlet finger into the air.

And Richard! Mallory thought dazedly that Dolores had not stayed with him—as she had said she would. She turned to go back to his room.

"Look! Look—it's all over there, too! Where are the fire engines?" Dolores' voice rose, shrill with terror, above the uproar.

Henry's deep voice answered. He was at another window, the shards of broken glass framing his bearded head. "The water mains must have been broken. If there's no water—no electricity—"

Gorham said, "This is not good, not good at all."

"Not good!" Henry whirled on him. "Do you realize what you're talking about, man! The whole city could go up in flames. Those houses down there, most of them are wooden. They'll go like matchsticks. There's more— Look—*look!*"

No need to tell anyone to look. The scene had a dreadful fascination.

"They'll have to dynamite," Henry shouted about the tumult that came up the hill from the city. "Only way to stop it if the fire gets hold."

Cho gave another threatening growl. He didn't think it was good either, Mallory thought with a touch of hysteria. But who wouldn't have hysterics, that night!

"Richard!" Dolores cried shrilly, and whirled around toward the doorway. Richard stood there, clinging to the door casing, white and strange, his eyes glassy. Dolores caught him as he made an effort to come into the room. "Oh, Richard, you shouldn't have moved! Henry, help me get him back to his room."

The dawn light in the room was pallid, ashen as their faces. The confusion in the city below was like a bad dream— screams, shouts, the pounding hoofs of horses. Richard struggled away from Dolores and sank down on the floor, his cast-wrapped leg straight out. His eyes sought Mallory, who stumbled on a brick and fell against him. A man loomed in the doorway, sobbing and waving his hands. She recognized his face; surely it was the coachman. He cried out, sobbing, "I got them out. But they would go back into the stable. They *would* go back. They were terrified. I couldn't stop them. And then the stables went, crashed down. My beauties! My beauties! Oh, Holy Mother of God!" He put big hands over his face. His bald head glistened.

Dolores said, sharply, "All right, Murphy! All right, come
121

along. We've got to get Mr. Richard back to his room. His bed is still standing."

"No," Richard cried. "No. Mallory—"

"I'm all right, Richard. I'm not hurt."

Henry Beaton was glued to the window, staring out and down. "My God, look at the fires. They're everywhere! Look!"

"We'll be all right," Flo Bel said. In spite of the confusion her voice was still cool and reasonable. "The house has stood, so far."

Richard said in a gasp, "It will stand. It's solid. The quake is over."

Another figure ran into the room. Mallory had no sense of surprise when she saw Scott, wrapped in a coat, blood dripping from his hand. He caught her glance. "It's all right! I only cut my hand. Thank God, this house is built to stand. The shock is over, I think."

Henry at the window said, "I believe—yes, I believe—the Ferry Building is still standing. I can't see—the smoke is too heavy. Oh, my God, there's my store—"

There was such nightmare implausibility everywhere that, later, when Mallory tried to recall just where everyone was at what time, it was impossible. She did know when Ernest Grenay appeared, and apparently with him or else at the same time, the young man with the doll-like face and drooping blond mustache. He huddled down on the carpet, in a corner, his hands over his small face. Mallory thought wildly, He's crying; well, why not? She'd like to cry herself, but there wasn't time.

There wasn't time for anything—only an instinctive grasp at anything at all that seemed to promise solidity and safety. Dolores had boosted Richard to his feet. "Help me, Henry. Help me, Murphy," she gasped.

Mallory started after them, stumbling again on the bricks that lay on the floor. Scott caught her arm. "Stay here. I'll see to him—" He was gone, holding Richard himself, an arm around his body. Dolores clung to Richard's arm. Murphy apparently didn't hear, or didn't want to hear, Dolores' cry for help, for he stood in frozen fascination at the window.

Flo Bel said, "The whole city is on fire—everywhere—" as coolly as if she were witnessing some theatrical effect.

122

Gorham still hugged the bag of jewels as he craned to look over Flo Bel's shoulder. Henry's hands were frozen to the windowsill. Every time anyone moved there was the snap and crunch of broken glass. Yet, later too, Mallory realized that there was in fact little movement. There was only a stunned paralysis and the shocking commotion from the city, which seemed to deaden feeling as the quake, in a sense, had done. Murphy must have finally moved, for she saw him, in the gray light, leaning at another window. "The church bells—" he said. "It's St. Mary's, in Chinatown."

Sometime later Scott came back, gave Mallory a swift look, went to the washbasin and washed his hands. Gorham's trained sense was instantly aware of this; he moved, he found a towel, he bound up one of Scott's hands. Scott said something to Mallory. She heard only "Richard—he's all right." He went out again.

Small things happened and were clear, but much happened which was not clear. The shock, the fright, the confusion, the continued crashes and storming tumult from the city, even the church bells which kept ringing, seemed to combine to shake everything and everyone, so the whole was like a giant kaleidoscope. The complete picture could not be comprehended. Even time seemed to have taken on some wry dimension, altogether out of kilter with normal time. But certain pieces of the kaleidoscope did stand out clearly. Mallory knew that at some time Ernest Grenay must have slid out of the room as unobtrusively as a slim gray shadow. The young man with the drooping mustache was gone, too—that, or he was lingering somewhere in the room, behind the enormous cupboard perhaps, somewhere, it didn't matter. She knew it when Henry suddenly shouted, "The servants! They've gone, have they, Murphy?"

Murphy grunted without turning from the window. "Aye, yes, sir. That new cook, too. Ran like the rats they are to Chinatown—"

"They'll not last long there," Henry said grimly. "All those wooden shacks and—"

"Aye, sure, sir. It'll go. The whole city."

"Not yet," Henry said. "If they can get some water. The Palace Hotel has whole vats of water in case of fire."

"There goes— Isn't it the Singer Building?" Murphy said hoarsely. "I can't see through the smoke."

Mallory knew that full morning had come, for the light was strong now, yet it was a curiously foggy light, smoky and acrid, burning her throat.

Henry said loudly, as if astonished, "Why, it must be six-thirty," and disappeared into the hall.

Murphy's elbow moved as he dragged a watch from some pocket; his head moved in silhouette as he looked at the watch. "Seven," he said, added "sir" and staggered, as if drunk or as if he could not bear what he was witnessing, out of the room.

Flo Bel was transfixed; Mallory felt almost under a spell as she stood there, stunned by the spectacle below and the noise from the raging city. The fire was spreading.

Muffled shrieks, continued crashes. Oh, it is a nightmare, Mallory thought, clinging to Cho.

Flo Bel said, so firmly that Mallory knew she was restraining tense nerves, "Whatever happens, I'm going to dress." She went out, and Gorham, huddling in his overcoat and long white nightshirt, gave a murmur of excuse and went out, too.

So Mallory was alone in the room when she heard the first loud crack of a gun above the sounds of the terrified, raging city. It sounds close, she thought. Peering through the smoke and flaring reds of fires, here, there, everywhere, she thought dully, I suppose the policemen are trying to prevent looting. The gunshot had seemed very near, almost in the house. Gorham, who had dressed with magic swiftness, came back into the room. "I heard a gunshot—"

"Yes. Out there somewhere. The police, I suppose."

"Possibly. There's a fort nearby. Called the Presidio. I daresay the military must prevent looting. All those buildings, all those houses—"

Mallory thought, I should get to Richard, even if Scott is with him. If Dolores—and even Richard, with one leg in a cast—could manage to get around that widening gap in the hall floor, she could. She started to leave the room. In the growing light of morning the wild flames from the city still cast dancing, reddish hues obscured only by clouds of smoke.

Scott met her at the door. "Go back. *Go back—*"

There was now a distant fusillade of gunfire from the streets. "It's no use," he said close to Mallory's ear. "You've got to go back. Don't go near Richard's room. Mallory, you must understand—"

"Understand?"

"You can't go in there. You've got to stay here, with other people. They'll say you did it. You've got to be able to prove—"

"Did what?" Was that her own voice? It was like a whisper and like a scream.

He leaned very close; she could feel his breath on her ear. "Richard is dead. He was alone in the room, at the window. A bullet struck him. He's dead."

"It—can't—be—"

"I found him, like that. Almost as if he'd been leaning out the window and was hit by a stray shot. There's shooting below now. General Funston's men from the Presidio. Trying to keep order. Richard lay on the floor below a window. I put him on his bed."

"I can't believe—"

Suddenly, as if he had a sixth sense, Gorham turned from the window where he'd been looking out and started across toward them. Flo Bel, sedate in a black dress, came quietly into the room and stopped to listen.

Scott beckoned urgently. "Gorham, see to Miss Mallory. A terrible thing has happened."

"I heard a shot," Gorham said. "It seemed very near. Did you say that something has happened to Mr. Richard?"

"Yes," said Scott. "Now keep Miss Mallory here. I'll do what is necessary."

It was difficult to comprehend the look that went between the two men, yet instinctively Mallory did understand it. She whispered, "You mean that someone shot him. Someone *meant* to shoot him—"

"And did. It was murder," Scott said bluntly. "But they can't think it was you. So stay here. See to her, Gorham."

Flo Bel did not move.

"Yes, sir," said Gorham. "Come back here, Miss Mallory."

She hadn't known that she was clasping Cho, who growled

125

as if in warning. Gorham thrust her back beside Flo Bel. A bright reflection of flames leaped up in the room for a moment and then died down.

Eleven

It had to be some stray shot from one of the soldiers now in the city.

But it was not. She had heard one gunshot, close at hand, moments before the distant shots from the soldiers in the streets below.

The havoc in the city, the havoc in the room, the nightmarish havoc all about her seemed to drop away, revealing one fact too clearly. In the midst of the shocking confusion and terror, someone had killed Richard.

It had to have been a swift decision. An opportunity that had been seized.

For an instant or two it seemed to Mallory that she was thinking with inordinate clarity. Someone had shot Richard. That someone had to be in the house.

Gorham, his long face very grave, went out, probably to Richard's room, in spite of Scott's request. Flo Bel found a chair, righted it and sat down as if she had collapsed.

The room was in wild disorder, broken china and glass on the floor; bricks spilled out over the carpet.

Gorham returned.

"Gorham..." Flo Bel began, and he said, "Yes, madam. Mr. Richard *is* dead."

A long, thin scream came from somewhere. Gorham said, "It's Miss Dolores. We had to let her see him. It seems..." Gorham paused, his long face bleak. "Mr. Scott believes it best to say publicly that Mr. Richard was looking out a window in his room and a stray shot from one of the patrolling soldiers struck Mr. Richard. And killed him," he added un-

126

necessarily and precisely. "Mr. Scott does not himself believe this."

In the distance Dolores began to sob, so loudly, so frantically that they could hear it clearly and hear Henry's deep voice speaking to her.

Flo Bel moistened her lips, looked at Gorham and said, "A soldier?"

"Yes, madam," said Gorham steadily.

Flo Bel seemed to withdraw into herself. Something faraway crashed down. Buildings and houses were still falling, some probably as fire ate into their walls, some from weakened timbers or brick giving way, but as yet there were no fires near Nob Hill. At last she said, "Yes. No matter what anybody thinks, we'll say that."

There was a movement at the door. Su Lin crept in.

"Su Lin!" Flo Bel saw her first. "We thought you'd gone..."

"Oh, no, madam. Not to Chinatown. I was afraid—" She stopped, caught her breath, glanced around at the wild disorder of the room.

"The back stairs are all right," said Su Lin and looked piteously toward the window. "Chinatown?"

Gorham shook his head soberly. "We don't know, Su Lin, but let us hope the fire hasn't reached there yet."

"All my people!" Su Lin went to the window.

Scott returned. "Oh, Su Lin, I thought you had gone with the others. It's an inferno out there. Perhaps your father will not try to get to Chinatown—will come back here."

"Perhaps," said Su Lin.

Gorham shook his head gravely, as though he had no hope of that.

Scott turned to Gorham. "I don't suppose you have access to anything in the way of—"

"Certainly, sir," said Gorham, "I understand," and left the room.

Flo Bel cried, thinly, "Scott, I still can't believe Richard—"

"It's true. I wish it weren't." Gorham came back with a bottle and glasses on a tray. He handed one of the glasses to Scott, who gulped down the whiskey before he continued. "I'll try to see to...to everything. It will be difficult. But all those people—nobody knows how many were killed in the quake. Falling chimneys, falling buildings. There's no water, no electricity." He turned to Gorham. "I think the ladies could use a drink, too."

"You got here," Flo Bel said, automatically accepting a glass.

"I live quite near. My house is still intact. Of course, this house will never go. Built to last."

"How did you get in?"

"A broken window, downstairs. The front door was locked and, I'm afraid, jammed."

"Mr. Grenay was here a few moments ago."

"Yes. I believe he stayed here last night after the opera. He usually stays here, especially when it's late. Also, young Gerald."

"Gerald?" Flo Bel might have been at a formal reception.

"Gerald Flower. You know—young, small face, big mustache. Works for Henry. Has rooms over in Marin County, near Grenay's place."

Su Lin's eyes were dark slits, her face waxy. "Please, sir, what did you say about Mr. Richard?"

Scott bit his lip, but then said firmly, "Mr. Richard was accidentally killed by a stray shot from one of the soldiers. You can hear them now—down in the streets—"

"I hear them." Su Lin stood very still for a second, then she put her hands over her face and ran out of the room. There was another faraway, scattered crackle of gunshots and the roar of leaping fires, tumbling house walls throwing debris everywhere.

Mallory sipped the whiskey, which now seemed to stir her to activity, if not to clear thinking. "Scott I must go to Richard."

"No," Scott said. "There's nothing you can do—" He broke off as a tremendous crash shook the house and sent more plaster dust everywhere. It was so loud and so close that even Gorham was appalled. *"What was that?"*

"The ballroom, I think," Scott replied. When the sound of falling masonry had died away, he added, coolly, "A good thing they built it out at one side of the house. Not on the third floor, as was first suggested."

Well, at least the ballroom was gone, Mallory thought

wildly; I needn't worry about presiding at formal balls. Then she thought, wildly too, But of course I needn't think of presiding at formal balls or anything at all here in this house. Richard is dead. I'll not have to take my place as Mrs. Richard Welbeck.

She felt a sense of release, which appalled her. She hadn't wanted to marry Richard, but she had never wished him dead.

Murdered.

Oh, no. Scott had to be mistaken.

She started unsteadily for the door, still under a compulsion to do something, she didn't know what, for Richard. Scott reached her with one stride and pushed her back. "No! No need, Mallory. Stay here!"

The drink had revived Flo Bel. "You actually said murder."

"Obvious. The soldiers patrolling the streets are too far away. It had to be a shot nearby."

"You *can't* really mean—"

"I don't know what I mean," Scott said. "Just keep quiet until we can—see our way."

"You told Su Lin a stray bullet." Flo Bel considered for a moment; then nodded. "But you don't believe that."

"I don't know what I believe. All I know is he's dead."

"And it was you who found him." She seemed compelled to want to hear all the details.

"Yes. I had been around the house, crawling over heaps of broken chairs, tables, chandeliers splattered on the floors, a Famille Rose vase in shards—I was trying to see how safe the house is. I made almost a tour of the place downstairs. There's damage, plenty of damage. But I honestly don't think we need be afraid of fire even if it gets this far. I came up the back stairs and went to Richard's room and—there he was. On the floor. Below the window. But— Mrs. Bookever, Richard was shot before Funston's men began to patrol the streets."

"Police, then." Flo Bel said firmly. "Firing at looters!"

"Not this far up the hill. In the streets below, perhaps. But a bullet wouldn't carry this far."

Gorham said, "No. I heard the sound of the shot that must

have killed him. I thought it was very near. I was in the Boer War, sir. I remember. But then—I didn't think of this," Gorham said flatly.

"No! No," said Scott and went out again.

Dolores' screams had died away. Henry's deep voice had stopped. Gorham stood like a black pillar beside Flo Bel.

Full daylight revealed the ghastly havoc in the room. The crash of falling walls, somewhere, continued.

Mallory gathered her dressing gown around her and crept out of the room; she hesitated at the broken floor of the hall, but only for a moment.

A smoky light hung over Richard's room and Richard himself lay on the bed. A cover had been placed over him. But she could see his face, which was strangely tranquil—strangely, Mallory thought, until in the back of her mind she remembered that Uncle Peter had looked at ease and peaceful when she had been permitted to see him, too.

Someone had closed his eyes. Someone had arranged his hands at ease along his sides. Oh, dear, harmless, confiding Richard.

Scott said behind her, "So you came. Of course, you had to. Dear Fellow. You know, Mallory, he never had a happy time. He was always the poor little rich kid. He was so kind—so—" Scott's voice faltered.

"I know." Mallory tried to swallow the hard lump in her throat.

She put her hand out toward Scott and he took it. Richard had stood in their way, yes; but they had both, in different ways, loved him.

A loud fusillade of gunshots echoed from the city below. Smoke swirled in through one of the broken windows. Scott said, "There would be no use even trying to get the police—anybody. We'll be lucky to get a doctor's certificate or a burial permit."

Richard seemed quietly, calmly asleep. "He couldn't have suffered," Mallory whispered.

"No, there wasn't time. He must have died instantly. I'm going to find out who killed him," Scott said as if he were making a vow.

Dolores came to the door; her eyes were red-rimmed. She

shouted in a hysterically high voice, "So now there is nothing to prevent *your* marriage, you two! How could you bring yourself to shoot him, Scott? How cruel! How senseless! He always thought of you as his brother."

"I didn't kill him."

"Remember, I saw you and Mallory!" she screamed hoarsely. "I heard what you said. You both wanted to get rid of Richard. Mallory only wanted his money. Everybody knows that. Well, now she'll not have it. I know who shot him and why!" Dolores swirled around and dashed out of the room.

Scott said, quickly, "Richard made a new will last night. Have you got it, Mallory! I told Gorham—"

"That! I never thought—" Amazingly, she still had it wedged down in her pocket. She drew it out, and held the long white envelope toward him. "Take it."

"No. You must keep it safely. I know what's in it. I know Richard's wishes. Almost everything he had will go to you."

"But I wasn't his wife! I couldn't take—"

"You'll have to— Oh, there's no time now for talk. Keep that will so it's safe. Give it to that man of yours, Gorham. He'll see to it. It means a great deal to your aunt, you know."

Flo Bel, yes. Mallory shoved the envelope back into her pocket. Scott led her out of the room. She gave one pitying glance back at Richard, looking as peaceful and kind as he had been in life. Tears came all at once; Scott saw them and took her hand to help her over the rubble.

"Now dress and go down the back stairs. They're still standing. Better get some suitable clothes on."

He went out. She fumbled at the envelope. Su Lin had returned to the room and was moving around like a yellow wax doll. Mallory asked her to find the beige suit she had worn across the continent.

What did one wear at an earthquake, a raging fire eating remorselessly at a beautiful city? After a murder? I'm hysterical, Mallory thought.

Yet, somehow, the house began to take on a peculiar kind of order.

Although there was no electricity, there were lamps and candles, which Gorham had lit to dispel the gloom caused by the smoke-darkened atmosphere.

131

There was no water from the faucets. But Murphy reappeared at Mallory's bedroom door and said that he had managed to drag up pails of water from a separate cistern near the demolished stables. It was obvious that he had been crying again. His beauties—all gone, with the stable. He put down two pails of water and went away.

Mallory caught a glimpse of herself in a mirror and could scarcely believe what she saw. Hair disheveled, hanging down her back. Face streaked and smudged. Her lower lip had been cut slightly and her hands were scratched and sore. There was a purple-red lump on her forehead.

Flo Bel returned and said that the dining room had apparently escaped severe damage, except for broken windows. "And there are pieces of glass all over the house, Gorham tells me. Wear your street shoes." As Mallory flung off her dressing gown, the paper in its pocket rattled; she drew out the envelope and looked at it for a moment, soberly. Richard's will. Scott was right: give it to Gorham to care for. She shoved it inside the tight belt of her suit skirt. Flo Bel said, "What's that?"

"Richard's will," she replied briefly. Flo Bel said nothing. The back stairs were solid; there was no difficulty in making their way down. Gorham was waiting, dressed now in a neat black coat and striped trousers, as carefully as if he had been receiving callers in the New York house. "Mrs. Beaton is in the dining room, madam. Murphy thinks he can find wood for the kitchen range. I feel sure we can manage a meal of some kind. Just go that way, through the pantry."

Mallory wondered briefly what he had done with the bag of jewels. She drew out the will. "Take this, please, Gorham. Take good care of it for me."

His eyes flickered swiftly over the official-looking envelope. "I'll see to it, Miss Mallory," he said as he put the will carefully into an inside coat pocket. Mallory followed Flo Bel through the pantry, littered with broken glass and china, to the enormous, now shadowy and chill dining room.

Dolores was there, bending over the huge table, covering it with some kind of cloth; the snowy linen looked eeerily normal. Shards of glass from a tilted buffet crackled under Mallory's feet. Dolores' jewels—necklace, bracelets, rings—

sparkled in lights from a drunken-looking candelabrum, twisted out of shape but still holding candles. The flames were not dimmed by the smoky daylight, but the upper part of the room looked all wrong, and Mallory was puzzled by it until she looked straight up and realized that there were great cracks in the plastered frescos, and the painted figures, lamed and cut in pieces, were hanging down.

As Flo Bel noticed the way Dolores' arms and neck glittered, she said dryly, "You're wearing your jewels."

"I was afraid of looting. I was afraid we'd have to leave the house. I was putting these on when ... when Richard was shot."

Henry came lumbering in; he, too, was dressed but, oddly, in dress trousers, a tweed jacket and no visible shirt. He had heard Dolores speak of the jewels and said angrily, "Take them off. If we have to go out into the street, some thug will snatch them—kill you if necessary. The streets must be full of looters."

Cheng appeared—somehow returned from Chinatown—bowing but not smiling, and asked Dolores for orders. Dolores pushed back her hair distractedly. "Food, I suppose. We must have something—anything. Oh, your ... your Gorham, Mallory, said he would see to that. Help him, Cheng."

Cheng nodded, both hands tucked into his flowing black sleeves. Mallory pulled a chair upright. After looking at it for a moment, only half aware of it, she sat down. It seemed the thing to do. Mechanical dolls, all of them—stunned and unable to comprehend the magnitude of what had happened. Henry righted a chair, too, and sat down heavily, elbows on the table. "Ernest has gone down into the city. God knows if he'll get back. Said he had to try. His office building—I think my whole place has burned. That new shipment from China—" Abruptly, Henry, as Murphy had done earlier, simply put his bearded face in his hands.

Finally they were sitting around the table. Flo Bel absently straightened the satiny cloth. No one had anything to say.

The silence was broken by Dolores, who said, steadily now, less hysterical, "Henry, I'm telling you again—Scott murdered Richard!"

Henry lifted his face, gave her a look, then lowered his head.

Flo Bel said, "You cannot accuse Scott! He was Richard's best friend."

"He intended to stop the marriage. He told your niece, I heard him! He said he would stop the marriage. And he did."

Again Henry merely lifted his head, stared at Dolores for a second but said nothing, and dropped it again.

Scott came in from the hall and paused a second to look at them; he seemed out of breath, as if he had been running. His face was begrimed; the towel that was wound around his hand was splotched with red. A deep cut, Mallory thought; he ought to see a doctor, have it sewn up. Scott said, "Well, so here we are. Where's Grenay?"

Henry mumbled from behind his hands. "Office...trying to save papers. He can't do it."

"Perhaps he can," Flo Bel said, and added, enigmatically, "If he really wants to save them."

Nobody asked what she meant. Nobody really cared what anybody said. They were like figures in a painting.

Richard had been killed. But his house stood, when so many had been shaken off their balance, crashed down, fallen into rubble. Mallory found her voice. "Scott, were you outside? Is...are there..."

"I couldn't tell." Scott miraculously understood her. "The streets are crowded. Hospitals already full, a man told me. He was running past me. Had a top hat in one hand and a baby in the other. He was wearing a nightshirt," Scott added as if details were important. All of them were obviously suffering from shock.

Flo Bel was probably the most alert. She said, quite coolly, "Dolores has just accused you of shooting Richard."

Scott's smoke-smeared face did not change. He came forward, pulled a chair from the wall where it had slid, brought it to the table, sat down in a leisurely way and said, "Yes, I know. She's already said as much to me. But she's mistaken."

Henry said heavily, "Richard was shot accidentally. He wasn't murdered. Dolores, you shouldn't say that Scott—or anybody—killed Richard. It was a stray shot."

134

Just then Cheng came softly in, accompanied by the clink of silver, and there was complete silence while he padded around the table putting down forks, knives and spoons. It was incredibly normal and domestic.

Scott looked thoughtfully at Henry, and after Cheng padded out of the room, said, "No, Henry. You'd best have the truth. It was not a stray shot. It occurred before General Funston's men arrived from the Presidio. And it was not from a policeman's gun, either. All the police were down in the city trying to control what...what they could control." He sighed. "I didn't see much, but enough. It's a shambles. Everybody making for the ferry. Trying to escape the fires. I couldn't reach my office. I'm sure it has been burned. Streets are a bedlam. Just the same, no stray shot killed Richard."

Dolores fingered her bracelets. "No! You killed him yourself! I heard you tell Mallory that you intended to stop the wedding. So you stopped it!"

Scott said, "Why are you wearing so many jewels, Dolores? And where did you get Mallory's pearls?"

Dolores' big hands flew to her throat. Mallory saw them, then; the pearls looked like those Richard had given her. They had been hidden by the diamond and blue-green flash of two other necklaces.

"Give them to Mallory," Scott said.

"No. These are mine." Dolores' hands clasped the pearls as if Scott might tear them off her. The way he looked just then, Mallory thought it possible that that was precisely what he might do.

Henry said, heavily, "You never wore pearls. Come on now, Lolo. If you did take the pearls, who has a better right? But don't bother to deny it."

"She doesn't have the right to take anything of Mallory's." Scott still spoke in that reasonable, matter-of-fact voice. "Richard made a new will last night. I was here. He left almost all he possessed to Mallory."

Dolores' pale eyes widened. She leaped to her feet. Henry stared at Scott.

"All he had! That's impossible!" Dolores cried shrilly.

"But a fact," Scott said, still equably. "Richard left something for you, Dolores. For Henry. Enough, I think. But

135

everything else—the entire bulk of the Welbeck money—goes to Mallory."

"*So*"—Dolores planted both jeweled hands on the table and leaned over, her eyes blazing fire—"so you had more than one reason for killing Richard! The girl and the Welbeck money. I knew it! You'll get neither. I'll see to that—*Ernest, where have you been?*"

Twelve

Ernest Grenay staggered into the room, stumbled across to the table and leaned against it. "My God, my God! It's terrible. I can't tell you..."

Henry stirred from his heavy lethargy, rose, supporting himself on the table, shoved Ernest Grenay into the chair he'd left vacant and went awkwardly, as if blind, around the room to find another chair. Grenay sank down into Henry's chair and stared around as if he saw monstrous things instead of a big mahogany table, so solid that it had withstood an earthquake. "The streets," he gasped. "The people. Everything. Houses down, buildings, Market Street on fire. Fires everywhere."

Cheng came in carrying a tray, and the fragrance of coffee was another strangely homely and normal facet of the lives that had been thrown so suddenly, so chaotically into total disorder.

Cheng must have noted Ernest Grenay's stricken, horrified attitude, for he set down the tray, cups clinking slightly, then poured a cup full of coffee, black and strong, and took it to Ernest.

Just what we all need, Mallory thought blankly and rose. She went to the tray and helped Cheng pour coffee for the others. When she gave Flo Bel a cup, steaming and fragrant, her aunt nodded, pleased at Mallory's self-control, Mallory knew. But she hadn't any real self-control. She was numb, acting out of sheer habit.

Henry had bumbled around until he found a chair, and was now dragging it, screeching across the floor, glass crackling in his path. He set the chair squarely at the table and sat down, leaned on his elbows and stared at Ernest Grenay. "Did you see my store?"

Grenay shook his head. "I couldn't get near. The flames, the people—I'm afraid it's gone, Henry. Did you have things insured?"

"Some of them. But not any of the shipment that came in last week. A prize shipment." Henry groaned, wiped his face with his sleeve and said to Grenay, "Did you reach your office?"

"It's all gone. Everything. I had put last week's receipts in the bank, as usual. But with the heat, they'll not be able to open their vault for some time, I think. Of course, the old records are safe in my house in Marin County. Unless the fire reaches that— But no, it can't leap the Bay. Although I'm not sure. You haven't seen what I saw—"

Scott said, "I saw some. It's bad. In the worst areas some gas mains are broken, hissing. Water mains broken. The big reservoirs must have been damaged by the quake—Crystal Springs Lake and San Andreas Lake. Electricity gone. Rails for the cable cars twisted like spaghetti."

Grenay passed grimy hands over his face. "I saw people— the hospitals aren't big enough. The graveyards won't be big enough. The fireman—the chief—was hurt, fell. Concussion, someone said. In the hospital—one of the first I saw—Oh, I can't talk about it!"

Flo Bel was stirring her coffee. Mallory wondered vaguely where she had got the sugar, and then saw the silver bowl on the table. Flo Bel said, "You keep records in your own house, Mr. Grenay? Not in your office? How very prudent."

Ernest Grenay mopped at his sooty face, absently. "I keep only old records at my house. I didn't think of such a thing as an earthquake—fires. No, I've done that merely because my office was too crowded with old records. The later records— I may have to replace some, get duplicates. A tiresome business. But," he said in a reassuring way, "I'm sure I can
137

get duplicates, if necessary. All the firms we deal with are good and reliable." He looked at Dolores. "Nothing to alarm us about that."

Flo Bel folded her hands, one above the other, and looked at them. Now that she knew that Richard had left the Welbeck fortune to her, Mallory thought fleetingly, it would be like her aunt to want to nail down anything that might affect her.

Cheng had vanished quietly, and as quietly returned, but this time Gorham came in too; stately and calmly he deposited covered silver dishes on the table. Cheng assisted him. Cho clawed at Mallory's skirt. Mallory hadn't realized until then that the dog had followed her step by step down the back stairway. She took him in her lap and lifted a piece of bacon from a dish before her and fed it to the dog, who audibly munched and crunched, but no one said anything about it. Even Flo Bel seemed to think it quite proper to feed the dog at the table that morning.

Unexpectedly, Flo Bel said, "I think, in view of Dolores' statement, we ought to say—one at a time—just where we were and what we were doing when...when dear Richard was shot. I was dressing. I heard the shot, I thought it very near, too near to come from the street. Gorham felt the same. Gorham is a man with battle experience."

Henry's thick eyebrows lifted. Gorham said politely, "The Boer War, sir. I was at Mafeking, as a matter of fact. Toast, sir?"

Henry's hand went out for the toast as he stared at Gorham. His hand was shaking. Gorham went on to Dolores, who reached out too, her hands sparkling with jewels. Candle flames on the table wavered slightly and everyone jerked to alert attention. The chandelier above the table shivered and its crystal prisms trembled, but even as they stared up in almost breathless silence, it settled into quiet.

"Dangerous," Henry said. "Let's shift the table."

Somehow they did move the heavy table, all of them pushing, the women trying to steady the china and coffee service, until it was out from under the trembling chandelier. After a second or two of waiting silence Henry said, "It's all right, I think," and they sat down again.

"Can't be another quake," Scott said dryly. "Well—there could be, I suppose. But I really do think we've had all the shocks we're likely to have."

"But not the fires," Henry said. "Suppose the fires reach us, here. I'll get water going— No, there's no water."

This, Mallory thought wildly, is delirium, but the dreadful fact is that it *is* happening.

Dolores suddenly scrambled to her feet, clutched at her throat, pulled the pearls off and flung them across the table almost in Mallory's face. "Be thankful I saved them for you," she said shrilly.

Flo Bel caught them as expertly as an athlete. She looked over the pearls, so obviously trying to satisfy herself as to their authenticity that Dolores leaned angrily over the table. "They are the right pearls! They were in Mallory's room. She shouldn't have left them there when she went to look at Richard. I tell you I saved them for her!"

"So I see," Flo Bel replied calmly. "I'll take care of them for you, Mallory." She was wearing a white net collar, boned in an upright position around her neck; it was probably intended to prop up a sagging chin, but Flo Bel had no sagging chin or wrinkled neck; she wore the collar above her black dress merely because it was fashionable. Now she fastened the pearls carefully around her neck and dropped the long string of the necklace beneath her black blouse. Clearly she did not intend to give Mallory a chance to carry out the childish threat to sell or pawn the pearls. Even then Mallory felt a wry twist of amusement. But, tragically, now there would be no such need.

Flo Bel said, "As I said, I was in my room when I heard the shot. Mallory was in her room, watching the fires. Gorham was, I suppose, dressing, too. I'm not sure about Murphy or Mr. Grenay or that young man who sat in the corner and cried. I don't remember if or when he left. Or when Mr. Grenay left the room."

"It must have been before any shot. I'd have heard it from there," Grenay said promptly. "I was worried about my office. The fires were getting near the building, I could see that. So I hurried out of the house thinking perhaps I could save something. I was confused, I think everyone was confused."

139

"Certainly," Flo Bel said smoothly. And looked at Dolores, who was still standing.

"You needn't look at me," she cried. "My cousin, my only relative! I've cared for Richard for years. He was always frail and withdrawn and he needed me. I wouldn't have hurt him. I wouldn't—"

"All right, Lolo!" Henry was crumbling toast nervously. "You're hysterical. Nobody in the world would ever accuse you of hurting Richard. Much less—for God's sake—killing him!"

"Such foolishness!" said Ernest Grenay around a mouthful of eggs, which sputtered out a little with the vehemence of his words. "Everybody knows that Lolo has devoted her life, practically, to caring for Richard. As for me"—he swallowed the eggs and spoke more clearly—"I cannot believe that Richard was deliberately murdered. I tell you a stray shot—"

"But we know better," Flo Bel said. "Oh, I agree it's wiser to call it a stray shot. But we knew better. Don't we?" She looked at Henry.

"No—no—I mean, yes. That is, it had to be an accident," Henry said defiantly, but he seemed flustered. "I had been at the window in your room"—he nodded at Mallory—"then I thought I might get a better view from the room Richard called his study. I remember hearing the shot and thinking it was very near. But that's all. And—Lolo, we've got to do something about Richard's . . . Richard's . . ."

Scott said, "It's been done, Henry. Murphy and I got him on a stretcher. The Daimler always worked all right. Murphy just preferred his horses. We took—" Scott's voice grew husky, but he went on, "Richard is now at St. Mary's Hospital. In the . . . the room with others. The Sisters will care for him."

Something odd, frightening in its way, an atavistic recognition of need, seemed to flow over the room, almost a sigh of relief, thankfulness—Mallory didn't know what it was. She only knew that everyone felt an instinctive release because Richard, harmless, kind Richard, had been removed, taken out of the house in which he had lived all his far-too-short life. Yes, it was comforting to know that the Sisters would care for him.

Flo Bel broke the moment of quiet. "I'll have more coffee, please, Gorham."

He emerged from the corner of the room, his long face unhappy. He said, "Beg your pardon, madam, but perhaps you ought to...to continue. I mean—where we all were at the time of the shot. I believe the Chinese had gone sometime before. Su Lin was still here, but—"

"I was not here," Cheng said softly, appearing at Gorham's elbow. "I had started for my home. Then I saw conditions. I came back." To the question in Gorham's eyes, Cheng replied, simply, "I thought it safer. This house is strongly built."

Dolores was sitting again, nervously toying with her jewels, eyes shining like the stones in the bracelets. "I had gone to my room to get my jewels. These. I heard the shot, but thought nothing of it." She looked at Scott. "You have not admitted anything, have you? You needn't! We know where you were—"

"What's that?" Flo Bel's bright head jerked toward the kitchen area.

There was a confusion of sounds, first low, excited, then growing louder, then low again, like the mingling of many voices.

"Chinese refugees," Gorham said, listening. He waited a moment; they all waited, then Cheng said, low, "And many others. The fires—they know this house is safe—"

"They can't stay here!" Dolores leaped to her feet. "Filth, trash, heaven knows what riffraff! People from the Barbary Coast perhaps—in my own beautiful house. Get rid of them, Cheng!"

My own house! But Richard would have permitted them to stay. Mallory stood up. She glanced at Scott, who, understanding, gave her one slight but approving nod. Mallory said, "They stay here. You can't turn them out. There's plenty of room."

Dolores' eyes were like pale-blue fire. "I said they were to be sent away. I'll not have them—"

"They can stay. There's the big drawing room. And see that they have food—coffee—whatever they need, Gorham."

Gorham, too, gave her an approving nod: this was the way a lady ought to act. "We'll see to it, miss," he said and walked out just as a thundering blast rocked the house, sending down drifts of plaster dust. The chandelier danced, but still held. They all jumped up. Someone—Dolores?—screamed.

Scott shouted, "It's dynamite. Only dynamite."

Only dynamite, Mallory thought irrationally—what kind of world are we in—so early this morning! Cho crept up to paw at her hand, and gave an indignant whine.

Scott seemed to shake himself. "The Daimler will make a good ambulance. Murphy can go with me. Henry, you and Grenay might be able to patch up that break in the stairs. Crowbars and planks might help."

Gorham cleared his throat respectfully. "I'll go with you, if you'll allow me, Mr. Suydam. I've had some experience—"

"Leaving us!" Dolores cried. "Mobs—looters—"

Flo Bel eyed her coldly. "We do not require protection. Your husband and Mr. Grenay and Cheng can help here. But outside..."

Gorham, pausing at the door, said, "Thank you, madam. People are injured and need help. I'll just get on different clothes, Mr. Suydam."

"Right. Thanks. I'll meet you at the back door."

Mallory put Cho in Flo Bel's lap. "I'll go, too, Scott. I'm strong. I can help."

"No, you can't," he said sternly. "There's not room enough in the car. We'll need every inch of space. But if there's anything at all you can do later, I'll tell you." He ran out the door to the pantry.

Afterward it occurred to Mallory that the first, futile attempts at trying to discover anything—anyone—responsible for Richard's murder had to give way to immediate needs.

It was a day of desperate and exhausting labor. Flo Bel, Mallory and Su Lin straightened out what they could: chairs, small tables, objects hurled from their places. They got dustcloths; they got brooms and swept up shattered glass. They worked savagely, afraid all the time that another quake might come. Cheng, rather unwillingly, went to help Mr. Grenay and Henry shore up the broken slabs of the stairway.

Yes, Mallory thought vaguely, it was like a nightmare come true: Richard's death and the earthquake merged into unbelievable reality.

The dynamiting kept on at intervals and rocked the house, blasted their ears, terrified everyone. The refugees set up an eerie wailing, until Flo Bel assured them with her air of authority that it was only dynamite, intended to block the fires by creating a space across which, it was hoped, the flames could not jump.

Cho pattered after Mallory until his short legs tired. Then he crawled up on an immense footstool in the library and lay with his chin on his paws, watching—and listening.

Everyone that day seemed to be listening at every moment.

A scanty sandwich lunch was eventually put on a platter in the library. They ate wherever they found themselves. The men working on the stairway pounded and swore in low voices, but continued to pound and heave.

The sky was still almost obscured by drifting black smoke.

Tales from the outside began to arrive—who brought them, no one knew, probably other refugees. Bars and saloons had been closed; there had been problems with drunkards, which added to the mad confusion the soldiers and police were desperately trying to control. Mayor Schmitz had issued the closing order. From Henry's face, when he reported this to Mallory and Flo Bel, they took it that Mayor Schmitz had not been universally admired. "Some good, anyway." Henry wiped his red face and went back to work.

Later he came back, flopped down in a chair and told them that Caruso had been heard singing out the window of the Palace Hotel. Some said it was in the hope of cheering the people who were running helter-skelter in the streets, trying to escape, trying to get to the ferry, trying to rescue others caught in the falling bricks and stone and timber. Others said that he was afraid the shock had injured his voice, that someone had encouraged him to put his head out the window and sing—and the sound of that liquid voice was probably the only note of hope on that dreadful day. After that, someone reported, he had escaped from the hotel.

Some of the stories that drifted in from the refugees were, in a way, encouraging: buildings with steel girders and concrete were gutted by fire, but many of the structures themselves were still standing. The eighteen-story Call, or Spreckels, Building could be seen from the Welbeck windows. Fire had leaped through it, but the framework remained. The same with the Flood Building.

Henry ceased in his labors now and then and went to the windows overlooking the city to observe and to report. The St. Francis Hotel and the Shreve buildings seemed intact. Henry squinted through drifting smoke and murmured, like a litany, what buildings were gone, what buildings still stood. "And my own—that is," he explained drearily, "the building wasn't mine. I rented it. But my whole business was there. Most of the things were insured. Thank God for that. But that new shipment..." At intervals during the day he had mourned the T'ang horse—if, that is, he could have proved it to be of the T'ang period. He had not actually seen it, only a quick glimpse in its wrappings. And certainly, while there existed other works of art from the T'ang period, a jade horse would be unusual. Now, wherever it was, probably it was lost forever.

Some refugees drifted away; but by nightfall, most were still milling around in the kitchen. These were mainly from Chinatown; some, Henry said, probably came from the Barbary Coast, that nest of gambling, brothels, stabbings, drunkenness, probably the entire lexicon of vices, which lay along the Bay, two hundred feet below Telegraph Hill.

Mallory told Su Lin and Cheng to get blankets for the refugees and to let them sleep on the floor of the big drawing room. Dolores had emerged, and hearing that, ostentatiously removed the jewels she was still wearing, retreated again to her room and, Mallory was thankful to note, remained there. Eventually the men succeeded in shoring up the broken slabs of stairway. There was nothing to be done about the twisted wrought-iron railings.

Always in Mallory's mind, during the awful confusion and urgent needs of that day, was the tragic fact of Richard's death. Certainly it must be imperatively at all times in the consciousness of the others—Flo Bel, Henry and Dolores, Ernest Grenay, even the blond young man who had turned up again, and stayed huddled below the portrait of Richard's father which hung askew but still clung to the wall above the library fireplace. His face was not pretty now, but

144

smeared with smoke; his mustache was awry, his pince-nez gone entirely, and his eyes were red-rimmed.

The fires continued. Su Lin told Mallory that a few of the refugees had decided to return to their homes to try to salvage property. Others, she had heard, had gone to St. Mary's to pray at the high altar. "We could all do some praying," Mallory said wearily. "It wouldn't hurt us."

Evening came, and the fires lighted the sky and the devastation below. The dynamiting stopped. Someone said that the supply had been exhausted. The crackle of gunfire continued as the troops and police still did what they could to patrol the city.

It was dusk, but eerily alight with an ever-deepening red glare, when Scott and Gorham and Murphy at last returned, their faces smoke-grimed and lines with memories of the tragedies, the fears, the helplessness and hopelessness they had witnessed and tried to aid that day. "So many people with no homes. They have set up temporary hospitals wherever they can. Food for the people in Golden Gate Park— everywhere they can gather. They're trying to save the waterfront. The Navy is sending in ships bringing water—the fires are spreading. A committee of fifty has been named to do whatever can be done to bring order out of chaos. You can't really lick San Francisco," Scott said; a gleam of love and pride came to his face. He had searched out several of the men who worked for him in his office. All of them and their families were safe—safe but frightened. "I'm thankful all my ships are at sea. Not one was in the Bay." He then rubbed at a cinder in one eye, and Flo Bel neatly removed it with a corner of a spotless handkerchief, probably the only clean thing in the city, Mallory thought absurdly.

Chinatown was burning: the wild flames could be seen racing through the warren of wooden buildings and the tunnels, Henry said, which lay below them.

Nobody entered Richard's room. But everyone except Dolores returned at intervals to stand at the windows of Mallory's room—gazing almost hypnotically at the writhing, struggling city below.

Mallory said once, horrified, "All those people in Chinatown."

145

Flo Bel, always realistic, said, shortly, "And rats, too, I daresay."

Henry heard that and would probably have looked white if the smoke stains on his face had permitted it. "We've never had plague here! You did mean plague? It's not possible!"

"I'm sure I hope not," Flo Bel replied, without turning a hair. She had procured from somewhere a very large white apron, which was tied tightly around her. She, amazingly, contrived to look perfectly dignified, a lady.

But at the same time, oddly, Mallory had the feeling that Flo Bel was always conscious of Ernest Grenay, who certainly was only trying to help, trying to keep them informed, trying to keep them calm. The blond young man, Gerald somebody, appeared again from nowhere and sat down, his hands over his face. Nobody paid any attention to his spasmodic sobs until Ernest Grenay told him rather sharply to get up and make himself useful. He gave Grenay a haunted glare from his round doll-like eyes, waved his hands feebly and disappeared again.

Supper, at last, was somehow assembled and served from a table in the big library, which had regained some slight semblance of order. Tables and chairs were returned to their usual places, fallen paintings stood with their faces against the wall; books had been gathered up and stacked in corners; even the rug had been almost straightened. Gorham, face and hands clean now, saw to it that generous drinks were poured. Flo Bel downed what looked like a hefty slug of whiskey, which would have astonished Mallory if she had been capable of astonishment any more.

Dolores emerged for supper and ate with gusto. She had put away her jewels and combed up her heavy hair; her triangular face was set in lines which boded no good for anybody. Henry looked nervous, kept glancing at her. Mallory was so tired, she felt that it would be a long time before she cared what Dolores said or did.

But after Dolores had finished her coffee and set her tray aside, she said, "Now then, how soon can we get the police here? I want them to arrest Scott and charge him with Richard's murder. Scott and his accomplice."

"Lolo—" her husband began.

146

"Nothing else to do," Dolores said. "Motive—he and Mallory planned to marry. He said he would stop her wedding to Richard. And so he'd get the girl and Richard's money. I tell you that's what he did! That's why he induced Richard to make a new will!"

"But that was reasonable," Ernest Grenay said hurriedly. "Richard and Mallory were about to marry—"

"As a matter of fact," Dolores persisted, "I'd like to see this famous will, leaving almost everything he had to Mallory. Where is it?"

Scott did not so much as flicker an eyelash. "It's in a safe place. No use looking for it. It's legal. I brought a copy of my father's will in order to copy the correct phrases."

"All the same—"

Scott was digging in a rumpled, sagging pocket. He brought out a small bottle, rose and took it to Flo Bel, who glanced at it, then looked at it hard and uttered a slight sound. It wasn't a scream but it had the effect of one.

"Your bottle of chloral hydrate?" Scott asked her wearily.

"Yes! You can see. It has my name on it. But—"

Scott nodded. "So I really do wonder how it got in the drawer where Richard kept his medicines. There it was—and also a remarkably large supply of laudanum. You gave him the laudanum, Dolores. But this bottle of chloral hydrate—what about that?"

Dolores just stared at him. Henry rose, than sat down again. Ernest Grenay put his hands together, neatly linking the fingers. Gorham, in the background, stood like a very tired statue. Dolores finally said, "You must have put it there yourself, Scott! Intending to give it to Richard. You were on the train. You had a chance to take it."

Thirteen

"How did you know the bottle was presumably lost on the train?" Scott spoke softly, yet his voice seemed to echo through the big room.

Dolores kept staring at him, as if she hoped her brilliant gaze might shrivel him up. Then she moistened her lips slightly, letting them curve upward in her own thin, oddly feral kind of smile, and said, softly, "Why, you told me, didn't you? Or—no, I'm mistaken! It must have been Su Lin. Or—why, yes, I remember! It was Kai Sing. He told me it had been lost and all of you had searched for it. So why did you give it to Richard, Scott? I know why. You hoped he would take that instead of the laudanum, which he knew how to measure. I say we must get the police at once—"

Flo Bel said, clearly, "You can't. Not now. As a matter of fact, Dolores, I think you will make a great mistake if you insist upon arresting anybody, and forcing a trial. San Francisco will never forget it. You may not come out of it very well yourself, you know. Having to admit how much you enjoyed Richard's money. Much better to acknowledge that it was a stray bullet that—sadly, tragically—killed Richard."

Dolores was suddenly so white that she looked ghostly. "So *you* say," she cried. "*I* say Scott killed him. This...this Mallory was his accomplice. Scott was with Richard when we heard the shot."

"No." Scott returned the ugly little bottle to a pocket. "As I recall, we got Richard back to his room and left him on the bed. But it seems he didn't stay there. He must have gotten up—wanted to look out the window. When I found him, he had fallen just below it."

"When you found him!" Dolores said scornfully.

"When I found him. He was dead then. Now, you were,

you say, in your room selecting jewels to take with you just in case we were obliged to leave the house. Henry—"

Henry shouted, "I told you! I was in Richard's study. I was looking out the window the whole time after you and Dolores helped Richard back to his own room!"

Scott said, "Murphy helped me carry Richard. Dolores rushed off—to get her jewels, she says."

Dolores leaped out of her chair, her strong hands clenched. "What do you mean 'she says'? Are you implying that I...I shot Richard?"

"I'm not sure," Scott said gravely. "There was the chloral hydrate. And when Richard came to Mallory's room he was already full of laudanum. I could tell. You must have given it to him."

"Listen, Scott," Ernest Grenay said patiently, dusting off a smeary coat sleeve. "I really think you're mistaken. Zealous about your long-time friend, but mistaken. I assure you that nobody in the house would be at all likely to kill Richard. The idea is simply preposterous."

"It happened," Scott said obstinately. "Oh, I agree. It seems best to keep it among ourselves—for now. But later, when law and order have fully returned to the city, then I think—I know we've got to report Richard's death as murder."

Henry tugged at his ear. "But, Scott—even if you should be right— Oh, my God, nobody can ever prove anything! Perhaps one of the servants—"

"Why?" Scott asked.

Henry lifted heavy shoulders. "Oh, for any reason. Upset about something. Blamed Richard. Took advantage of the confusion. It could never be proved—"

"It *can* be proved!" Dolores flashed. "I told you! Scott came here last night. He persuaded Richard to make a new will, in favor of Mallory. He had told her he wouldn't let her marry Richard. I heard him. I tell you! The wedding was planned for Friday. What time was there for Scott to intervene and stop the wedding except as he did? There's plenty of proof, if only you will admit it—"

Ernest Grenay rose. "Dolores, you know that I would protect Richard's interests and your own. I believe Scott is wrong. The manner of Richard's death must be attributed to one of those dreadful, regrettable accidents which do sometimes happen. This is by far the most reasonable conclusion. Last night—this morning, I mean—anything could have happened."

Flo Bel said unexpectedly, but with a weary air of forced interest, "Did you say you kept the Welbeck records in your home, Mr. Grenay?"

Ernest Grenay turned to her, surprised. "Why, yes, Mrs. Bookever. All the old records. Only recent records were in my office."

Henry gave Flo Bel a puzzled look. "All of Richard's affairs are in Ernest's care. Have been since Richard's father died. Mr. Grenay—Ernest's father, I mean—was trustee for Richard until he reached twenty-one. Then Richard took over for himself but retained Ernest, who had succeeded to his father's office and duties so admirably that Richard wished to continue—"

"All right, Henry!" Dolores snapped. "No need to go on about that. We all know. Just remember this. No matter what anybody says, I'm not going to let Scott Suydam get away with murder—and Richard's money." She went out of the room, her muscular legs pounding hard on the still gritty dust on the floor.

It was like a signal. They all got up to leave. Scott and Gorham were white with fatigue. They were all inexpressibly tired. There was a feeling of emptiness all over the house.

Yet when Mallory went by the drawing room, she saw several blanketed shapes move, and a few faces turned and stared at her. Refugees. Well, they were taken care of for the night. Tomorrow there would be more camps, more fully equipped, food kitchens, everything done that could be done. She followed Flo Bel up the mended stairway; it was no longer a beautiful, curving sweep, but it had been shored up, blocks of marble and planks had been placed with sufficient care so it was no longer dangerous. Not dangerous, that is, if one moved close to the wall, for the railings were still twisted and drunken-looking.

Cho hopped along after her. Flo Bel untied her white apron, said goodnight and went on to her room. Gorham stalked after her and opened the door as the dignified figure in black, with its shining hair, moved into the room. Mallory waited until Flo Bel had lighted a candle. Then Gorham murmured something, closed the door and disappeared into the dim hall, which still smelled of smoke. Everything smelled of smoke.

Flo Bel, Mallory thought suddenly, almost staggering out of the clothes she had snatched that morning—only that morning, she thought with disbelief—Flo Bel was interested in the Welbeck records. Now, of course, in view of Scott's information about Richard's will, her aunt had a right to make sure that all the Welbeck records were intact. And she hadn't liked Grenay; that had been clear from their first dinner in the Welbeck house. My house! Mallory thought with a quick shock. She couldn't live there! She'd have to do something about it, sell it—if anything now in the city was salable.

Dolores had asked to see the will; yet she undoubtedly knew Scott well enough to know that he had given her the correct details. Mallory could not reasonably refuse to accept so generous and loving an act on Richard's part. That money was desperately needed by Flo Bel; Flo Bel had gambled on this marriage. No, she wouldn't refuse Richard's money, but she couldn't possibly take the whole amount.

She was so tired, every muscle in her body ached; she was too shocked, still, and too tired to reason. Su Lin had left night things out, and a lighted candle stood, carefully placed for safety, on a table in the middle of the room, far from any blowing curtain. Someone—Gorham, Su Lin, somebody—had placed cardboard over some of the gaping holes in the windows. The bed had been propped up. She blew out the candle and lay down, aching for sleep—but it did not come.

After a long time she rose and went to one of the windows. She pushed aside a piece of cardboard and was appalled to see how much nearer the fires were. Even as she watched, the whole interior of a house not far away became clearly visible, all its door and window frames starkly black against leaping red flames. A balcony crashed down. Small figures of men were running around near the house; she thought they were trying to lug out paintings, furniture, anything.

151

Suddenly there was a tremendous crash inside the house, and the black, silhouetted figures leaped back, away from it.

It seemed to her, now, that the flames were creeping closer and closer—but she told herself, wanting reassurance, that all of them had said the Welbeck house was safe.

The Welbeck house and all the Welbeck interests might have to become, at least for a while, her own concerns. The Welbeck interests! She shivered as the night grew chill, which seemed improbable with fires raging everywhere. But the house *was* safe, she kept telling herself, and crawled back into bed. The reddish glow from the fires lighted the room eerily.

Richard had told her something of the widespread Welbeck interests. She tried wearily to remember just what. She knew there were steel interests, mining interests, naturally, sugar interests, she thought, something or other that necessitated trips to that, to her, completely unknown world, Hawaii. Now that Richard had written a will making her his legatee, that could be considered a motive, throw suspicion on her, or would in the face of public outcry. Scott's explanation of Richard's death to outsiders would probably shield her, Mallory, from ugly inquiry, and delay the revelation that no one was with her when the shot that killed Richard was fired.

But she knew, also, that Scott rejected that explanation; he hadn't hesitated to make his real feelings clear. For the moment, he would stick to his own suggestion, but only outwardly. It wouldn't matter how sensibly Ernest Grenay spoke or how firmly Flo Bel decided that it was best to say it was an accident.

Suddenly Mallory went to sleep, as if she had been drugged. It seemed to her that through her unconsciousness there still went on the shouts and commotion from the streets; certainly the smell of smoke persisted. Cho was restless, growling softly to himself whenever a crash came too near to suit him. Once or twice he even barked, but by that time Mallory was so drugged with sleep that she was barely aware of the sound.

But then, all at once, Cho crept up to her face, pawed furiously at her and sneezed. "No, no," she mumbled. "It's too early to go out."

He gave a sharp bark in her ear, so sharp that it thoroughly awakened her. "Really, Cho!"

Then she smelled it—another odor, not smoke. Something gagging, something reminiscent of the big kitchen in New York when the gas heater had gone wrong, something that seemed to turn her body to stone. She leaped out of bed and heard the light hiss of gas escaping somewhere in the room.

The smell was nauseating. It was also deadly. She stumbled for the door, automatically scooping up Cho. She flung the door open and screamed for help.

Gorham came dashing along the corridor. "Good God! It's gas—" He ran into her room, shouted and came running out. "My God! The gas is strong!" He had a fold of his overcoat over his face.

Mallory clung to a chair, which someone had returned to its place against the wall.

"Gas?"

"The gas log. In the fireplace. It must have broken. I'll shut the door until it seeps out into the air. Good God, Miss Mallory, it could have killed you!"

There was a light downstairs, in the hall, a candle in Scott's hand as he leaped up the stairs, *"Mallory! I smell gas. Gorham—"*

"The gas log was turned on in her room," Gorham shouted. "I turned it off."

"How did it get turned on?" Scott put the candle on a table near Mallory.

"I don't know—Cho sneezed."

"Sneezed!" said Scott, and Gorham said promptly, "Very sensitive nose. Saved your life, Miss Mallory. I daresay you were sound asleep after all that shocking day."

Scott put his arm around Mallory.

Flo Bel said from behind him, "Another accident, was it?"

A second glimmer of light from the stairway wavered nearer. Everyone turned to watch the candle flame approach; it was held in a woman's hand, emerging from a green blanket. It shone on a woman's face, a rather oddly painted face, grotesque because only spots of color were left. But it was a young face; glowing yellow hair peeked out from the blanket, also a vehemently pink, short skirt spangled with sequins.

153

"You got her out! I smelled gas. I was coming to tell you," said the girl.

"It's all right now," Gorham told her. "It's quite all right." He echoed Flo Bel, but rather uneasily, "An accident."

"An accident?" said the girl. The candlelight sent up sharp shadows on her face and accented her darkened eyelashes. "Gas. I know the smell. Florence used it when she— It was a gas oven that time. It was awful." She stared at them above the candle flame and added, huskily. "I found her, you see."

Henry shouted from somewhere in the space of darkness, "What's the matter? What's wrong?"

Dolores said something, high-pitched, not clear. The girl gave an apprehensive look in the direction of the voice. "I'd better get back downstairs. I don't think she wants us here. That is—I—I'm glad everything is all right."

Flo Bel said, suddenly, gently, "Thank you, my dear." Flo Bel had almost certainly never before encountered a dance-hall girl or a girl of a profession which all but advertised itself—but she was thankful to her for trying to come to Mallory's rescue.

Scott went to the door of Mallory's room. Gorham followed him. Both men stopped, waited a moment, and then, as Gorham said, "It's better. Most of it is gone," both men went inside.

There was still, though, a lingering and nauseating odor of gas. Nothing could have induced Mallory to return to that room.

The girl on the stairs shot another apprehensive glance in the direction of Dolores' voice, mumbled, absurdly, "Thank you," and fled down the stairs, but cautiously, too, staying close to the wall.

"Our thanks to you," Flo Bel called after her warmly and took Mallory's arm. "Come. There's a sofa in my room. You can't go back there."

The sofa in Flo Bel's room was not very comfortable, being a firm product of its Victorian era, but it felt like bliss to Mallory.

Flo Bel carefully examined the gas log in the fireplace, groping with her fingers, sniffing at the air, before she lighted a candle. "You must have put out your candle," she said absently to Mallory, who remembered her own casual, seemingly unimportant, gesture of leaning over to blow out the candle. Flo Bel sat down on the bed; she was again wearing her faded wrapper. After a moment she said, "Put that blanket around you. Now then, we'll wait until Gorham has looked things over."

Mallory turned to look at her aunt. She felt weak with fright. "Flo Bel, there was the man at Gary. There was the bottle of chloral hydrate. And now—"

Flo Bel did not reply. She rose and started to walk toward the door.

There was only the faintest whiff of gas, not dangerous now, coming from the hall. Dolores appeared in the doorway, glanced in and said, "How could you have been so stupid, Mallory? You could have blown up the whole house."

Flo Bel gave a short, dry laugh. "Now really, you are too silly. Did you open the gas jet yourself?"

"Me! Good heavens! I'm getting tired of your accusations!" Dolores flashed out of sight. Henry's voice rumbled distantly.

Mallory said stiffly, as if the words were frozen in her throat, "I think someone did turn on the gas. I was confused, all the noise in the city, the fire coming nearer and nearer—Cho barked and growled, but I thought nothing of it and—yes, Flo Bel, somebody must have turned on the gas log. There was no smell at all when I went to sleep. I don't know—I don't see how I could have slept—"

"We were all sleeping," Flo Bel said after a moment. "Now we are going to do the safe thing. As soon as we can get to the ferry, you are to get back to New York. Scott Suydam is a businessman; he can help me straighten out affairs here later. But you must get back to New York. At once."

Back to New York, Scott remaining here to settle everything. Yes, her aunt was right. Get away, reach the ferry, find a train, any way to escape. She was badly frightened and only now beginning to feel the full shock of her near-approach to—well, to being murdered, she thought with incredulity.

The third attempt—yes, now she fully believed there were two other attempts. Dolores? Only Dolores could profit by

Mallory's death. Only Dolores, now, could reasonably expect to be Richard's legatee.

Flo Bel said, thoughtfully, "That's settled. Now—later—I must do something for that girl. The one who came upstairs to warn you—to try to rescue you, really. A girl of courage."

"But...she..." Yet nothing her aunt said or did ever ought to astonish Mallory.

Flo Bel said, "A girl of courage. Wants to do what is right. Let me tell you this, Mallory and remember it. Courage and kindness rate in the very highest bracket of human qualities. I'd choose them over almost anything. Honesty automatically accompanies both. Well, that's my moral lesson. Yes, I know the kind of girl she is. But she's young. I'll do something about her—"

Scott came to the open door. His face looked white and strained in the wavering light from the one candle. He shook his head slowly as he put out his hand toward Mallory—but couldn't seem to find words to express his feelings. Gorham loomed up beside him and said, firmly, "The gas *was* turned on, madam. It's hard to believe that it was an accident. Of course, in the quake something might have jarred loose. But if you'll permit the suggestion, we should leave San Francisco at once. That is—as soon as we can get to the ferry. We'll leave everything here to Mr. Suydam."

Scott's eyes were dark and troubled. But he said, "Yes, I agree. It's too dangerous for you, Mallory. You mustn't stay here. I don't know what—or rather, who is so—"

"So determined," Flo Bel said in an icy voice.

Scott nodded. "Yes. I'm afraid so. The gas had been turned on and not lighted. It's hard to see how it could have happened this morning, during the quake, without our noticing it earlier. In the morning Gorham and I will see to it that you get to the ferry, and will stay with you until you are safely on board with other people. There was a long line today. But we'll wait. I don't know how soon you can get a train from Oakland, but you must leave—"

Mallory said, "No."

The candle flame flickered in some current of air. Flo Bel, Gorham, Scott simply stared at her. Scott then came across the room and took her hands in his, leaning urgently over

156

her. "You must leave, Mallory. It's the only safe thing. Unless we're wrong, this was an attempt to kill you. Think—"

"I'm not going to leave."

There was another pause. Then Scott said, "Why not?"

Why not? "Because I won't."

"But, Mallory—"

"My dear child—"

"Really, miss—"

Mallory rose. "I'm not going to leave. I'm not going to run away—"

"There's no sense in being stubborn. You've got to get out of this." Scott caught her by the shoulders and shook her. Cho, who had been at Mallory's feet, apparently not fancying Scott's manner of expressing himself, growled, showing his teeth and shooting out between Mallory and Scott.

Scott, diverted, cried, "Shut up, you damn little mop," which Cho took as a personal insult and launched himself at Scott's ankle. Scott jumped adroitly to one side, but scooped up the dog, who still growled, then unexpectedly stopped and gave his tail a wag. There was a slight but indulgent smile on Gorham's lips. "He's upset. He's a good dog, really."

"God's sake!" Scott said indignantly. "I'm only trying to help Mallory. She's *got* to leave."

"I won't," Mallory said flatly again.

Flo Bel turned suddenly, as alert and elegant as a greyhound. "There's another smell. It's not gas..."

It wasn't gas. It was the nearby smell of smoke. Gorham whirled out into the hall. Scott dumped Cho into Mallory's arms and leaped after him. Somewhere, somebody screamed. There were more screams, shouts, an indefinable and frightening hubbub of voices, feet running, thuds, crashes as if windows were again being broken.

Then a woman nearby, Dolores, screamed clearly, "It's here—it's here—"

It was there, surging into the house, sending out the acrid smells of rapidly charring wood and burning wool carpets. Sending swirling black smoke all over the house. Sending leaping tongues of scarlet flame everywhere, seeking out anything and everything to be devoured.

Fourteen

The magnificent Welbeck house, with all its elegance, all its lavish absurdities, all its treasures, went down into the roaring tide of fire.

Again kaleidoscopic memories were to remain with Mallory—Scott not there, then dashing back again, his arms full of clothes. Gorham shouting something like "Stay here—I'll be back," and running out and presently back again; the screaming of the refugees, scattering for the front door, Flo Bel said, like so many ants. Flo Bel had swiftly gathered up an armful of clothing, too, wrapped her coat around her and gone out into the hall. Mallory followed after her. She heard the screams, she saw the fleeing black figures of the refugees, she knew when Scott thrust her coat around her, knelt down and shoved her feet into street shoes, the shoes from which a buckle had been torn. Then he pulled her and Flo Bel to the back stairway. It would be the last part of the house to go, someone—Gorham—shouted. He then shoved at Flo Bel, who didn't need shoving but ran down the steps as swiftly as a girl. Dolores was somewhere near, too, and Henry panting and red. Someone shouted, "Casa Madrone—Casa Madrone—" Scott?

The streets were bedlam. People—shouting, screaming, dimly seen, bumped into, running. The flames behind them soared as if in triumph.

Cinders fell like black snow; sparks made flashing red streaks. Mallory coughed, half strangled in the billows of smoke. Only Scott's arm seemed a solid reality in an increasingly delirious nightmare. He boosted, hurried, harried, made her run until she was not only coughing but gasping for breath, stumbling over bricks, paving stones, vaguely seen debris.

She had no idea of how long that terrible flight continued. Then, suddenly, she felt Scott's arm thrust her against a wall of.something that felt like concrete; later she found out it was time-aged adobe. Grenay was there all at once, panting and shouting; Dolores, too, was shrieking above the tumult. A wide door, a wooden door near Mallory, was pushed open; she was herded by Scott into a courtyard paved with cobblestones. She stumbled across it at the pressure of Scott's arm, and another wide door opened.

Grateful silence and darkness fell upon them. They must be inside a house. Someone was lighting a lamp; there was the sputter of a match, Gorham's long face eerily hanging above its flame. Cho was miraculously in Mallory's arms, clinging to her and furiously muttering, probably Chinese curses, she thought wildly.

A long room, low-ceilinged, came into being. The walls were white, the rugs mainly red; there were deep chairs. Flo Bel pushed up her hair, wiped at a grimy face, took a long breath and calmly sat down.

The room was not cold, but had the damp chill of an old house. Scott snatched paper from a table, went over to an enormous fireplace, gingerly touched a match to the paper and held it up toward the chimney, watching carefully until the flame of paper shot smoothly upward, catching the draft. "The chimney's all right. It has stood for many years." He took logs from a basket nearby and stacked them up on iron firedogs. He continued to watch carefully, until he seemed satisfied that the chimney had not been damaged. A portrait hung above the mantel.

Dolores, wrapped in her white satin opera cloak, her black hair in disarray, was squatting on the hearth rug, clasping a towel, bunched up to hold something to her throat. Ernest Grenay stepped out of the shadows, looking absurdly disheveled in tweed trousers and a black tail coat. Behind him came the young blond man, Gerald, absurd, too, his mustache drooping, his opera cape over gray trousers, a pink ruffled shirt in one hand and a hat box in the other.

The house door swung open and Su Lin came in from the outside, Murphy propelling her. He was panting. "It's all going, Mrs. Beaton. All going. Nothing can be done." He closed the door and leaned against it.

Dolores only nodded. "I've got my jewels," she said numbly. So that was what she had bunched together in a towel. Gorham said to Scott, "I think perhaps..."

Scott nodded. "In the next room. The cabinet isn't locked."

Su Lin sank down beside Mallory. "My father—" she whispered, barely audible. "He thought he could help. He went to Chinatown and—he didn't come back." She started to sob.

Mallory wanted to say something, but could not think of any words to console her. She could think only that her breath was becoming more regular, that the air here was pure and fresh.

Then Gorham was in the room again; a tray was in his hands and glasses were on it. Scott followed with a bottle and poured recklessly into each glass.

Brandy. The fruity fragrance, like raisins, Mallory had always thought, was incredibly welcome. Flo Bel drank quickly, didn't even gasp, and held out her glass for more. A good idea, Mallory thought, and drank her own brandy as if it were coffee. The logs in the fireplace began to give out warmth.

Casa Madrone: Scott's home. He had said that he lived near the Welbeck house. How far had they come, struggling through the smoke and burning cinders that fell around them? It seemed miles; probably it was not more than a half mile, if that.

The house was definitely of Spanish design. The thick adobe walls—walls that had kept the house safe from the fiery city—were visible at the window seats. Heavy red curtains hung open over them, until Gorham drew them together, making the room feel even more protected, shut away from the horrors of the night.

The portrait over the mantel was Spanish, too; a woman— no, one would have to say a lady—erect and stately, in a green dress, with jewels in her high-piled black hair and an enormous comb like a fan. A black lace mantilla was draped across one white arm. She seemed to be looking disdainfully at the disheveled huddle that had gathered together in her drawing room.

Scott's mother? No, she had to be someone married to a long-ago Suydam. Whoever she was, it was evident that she had had a strong personality—and beauty. Gorham was saying something to Scott, who replied; Mallory heard only a few words. "—plenty of bedrooms. The house sprawls all over. There's a long bedroom wing. Added on to—but it's safe, I think. The roof can't catch fire. It's tiled. We're just out of the fire zone, the way it seems to be traveling, I mean."

It was reassuring, yes.

The brandy had affected all of them. Suddenly Dolores gave a high-pitched laugh, just short of a giggle. She called to the mustached young man, "Here—here, Gerald, take my jewels, see to them."

He moved reluctantly, it seemed to Mallory, from a corner. His doll-like face was smudged with soot. Dolores shoved the bundled towel into his grimy hands. Oddly, again it struck Mallory that Dolores' hands were big and strong for a woman, almost like the young man's hands. He took the bunched-up towel and looked around him worriedly. Gorham, who anticipated every need, said to Scott, "I believe I saw a safe in the pantry, Mr. Suydam."

"Safe?" Scott shot him a puzzled look over one shoulder. He was kneeling at the fireplace, adjusting the logs with great iron tongs almost as tall as Mallory. "What— Oh, a safe. Yes, in the pantry. I'll open it." A flicker of a grin crossed his dirt-streaked face. "Dolores, huh? Her jewels. Dear me! We must keep them safe."

"Well, they belong to me," Dolores snapped. "I'm glad I saved something."

"Certainly," Scott rose and went with the young man out toward what Mallory assumed was the pantry and kitchen.

Flo Bel had managed to carry the small dressing case she held on her lap. She said, "I think I'll take some more brandy."

More brandy; she had taught Mallory that one must never say I'll take *more* of anything at all. Silly to think of that just now! Henry said, "Me, too," and went for the bottle, which stood on a handsome, solid-looking table of some polished dark wood. The house had, to Mallory, a beautiful fragrance, an aromatic scent from the logs and, of course, a hint of the Orient, of sandalwood; floors, chairs and tables were

161

all of polished dark woods; there was a certain air of elegance and dignity which spoke of many years of gracious living.

Ernest Grenay came in quietly as an eel through the wide front door; she had not known that he had gone out. He went to the fire, rubbing his hands. By then, even though still smeared and streaked with soot, he had recovered sufficiently to look unshaken and neatly if oddly dressed. "The Welbeck house is almost gone," he said dryly. "The inside of it, at least. The outer walls and the porte-cochere seem to be standing. The frames of windows can be seen. One of the turrets has collapsed."

"Like the other houses." Henry downed more brandy.

Scott came back into the living room and walked over to Flo Bel. "I've lighted a fire in a room for you. There's a dressing room adjoining it for Mallory. I think you'll be comfortable." He glanced around the room. "There are bedrooms enough, I think, if you want to stay."

"Scott," Henry said thickly. "All we want is to stay here! Find rest. Forget this dreadful—forget—" He gave a groan which was like a sob. Dolores said, "You're drunk, Henry."

"Not drunk," Henry said ponderously. "Just—just—tired."

Scott nodded. "I'll be back. Come, Mallory. Mrs. Book-ever."

He led them out of the living room and into a long narrow hall which seemed to run the length of the house. He turned right. "This is the oldest part of the house. The other rooms were added later." He opened the door to an enormous, spacious room, Spanish in its effect, with a great bed, a four-poster, heavy blue curtains, a thick rug, a fireplace with shining andirons and a sparkling fire. "It gets cold in the night. The house walls are so thick. This was my mother's room. Some of the furniture came around the Horn."

Flo Bel's blue eyes suddenly, and for one of the few times in her life to Mallory's knowledge, looked full of tears. She said, "We are so grateful. This is the home you told us about, of course."

"Casa Madrone, yes. There are enormous old eucalyptus trees, too—but Casa Eucalyptus..." He grinned a little. "Wouldn't be really a euphonious name. Casa Madrone—everyone calls it that. Trees and shrubs must have been here

162

since the Spanish owned this land. I've got to go now. I'll have to help people if I can. The dressing room is over there." He indicated another door, half open. "There's a small bed, everything I hope you may want. A bathroom on the other side. Now then, look here. The dressing room can be entered only by this bedroom door. There are only small windows in the dressing room, barred, as a rule. But right here— See this bolt?" It was a big iron bolt that could be moved directly across the door and the wall beside it; it was at least a foot long and looked very solid. "When I've gone, remember to drop this bolt into place. Remember—"

Flo Bel said, "We remember. It's the whole dramatis personae, isn't it?"

Scott gave her a long look and then nodded. "I'm afraid so. Cheng has not turned up yet—or Kai Sing, but they may. Now then"—he looked at Mallory—"Don't worry. Sleep, because tomorrow you're going to get started to New York." He closed the door quickly.

Flo Bel swiftly went to the door after him and dropped the huge iron bolt into place with a thud. "How *can* he help anybody in this...this terrible fire?"

"He's got to try. I tell you I'm not going back to New York."

She might as well have talked to the wind—or to the fires raging over the city.

Flo Bel was examining the room, opening a door, exclaiming, "For heaven's sake! It's an old house, certainly, built long, long ago. But here's a modern bathroom."

"You didn't think Scott wouldn't want to wash."

"Now, Mallory, don't take that tone. And— For heaven's sake," Flo Bel said again, "all these clothes on the bed—some of mine and some of yours. Oh, dear! He gathered up some of your trousseau things. Well, I suppose he just grabbed whatever he could find." She sat down in an armchair. "It feels so safe here. But we must remember about the bolt. Now then—we'll leave the door to the dressing room open. Call me if—that is, call me."

But even after she had crawled in between sheets that smelled deliciously of lavender, Mallory lay awake in the small bed in the dressing room, its walls lined with dark wooden armoires and cupboards.

163

The whole dramatis personae! Yes, it was true. Everyone in the Welbeck household (except for the Chinese, who would in all probability, as Scott had said, turn up sometime) was here who had been in the house when Richard was murdered, and when the gas in Mallory's room had been turned on.

Cho was so accustomed a presence that she hadn't really noticed him until he scrambled up on the bed, snuggled close to her and began to snore.

So the Welbeck house was gone. Richard...dear Richard was gone. Bolt the door, Scott had said. She had seen Flo Bel do it, but Mallory lifted herself up on one elbow to peer into the big bedroom through the now-dimming light from the fireplace. Yes, she could see the massive iron bolt in place across the door and casing. Nobody could possibly get into the room.

Unexpectedly, from the room next door, she heard Flo Bel say in a muffled, weary way, "I can't see any connection. But I'll have to talk to Grenay. There might be..."

Her words drifted off as if she were half asleep. Mallory sat up. *"Grenay!"*

After a long moment Flo Bel said drowsily, "I don't know—might not matter—yet, if there is any possible connection—"

"Flo Bel! What are you talking about?"

Flo Bel seemed to rouse. "What—oh, was I talking?"

"Yes. You said something about Mr. Grenay."

After another long pause Flo Bel's voice drifted from the next room. "Never mind. Young Suydam will see to your interests, act for you. There's Richard's estate—"

"Flo Bel, I cannot take it all. I'll accept enough to pay our debts. But Dolores has got to have some—"

"She's got her jewels." Flo Bel's voice sounded satirical. "And that was odd, too."

"What's odd? Taking her jewels?"

"No, I don't think so. Dolores wanted them. Never mind. Go to sleep. It's been— My heavens, it's been a day!"

Flo Bel must have finally gone to sleep. Mallory let herself sink down into a deep, heavy lassitude. The house felt safe all around her. It must have weathered many a storm, many a crisis, many years of living. She wondered, on the edge of

164

sleep, why Flo Bel had said she ought to talk to Grenay, and then refused to explain.

Gorham knocked on the door and announced himself. Mallory caught up her coat for a wrapper and let him in. He bore the early tea tray, which, in Gorham's belief, nobody in her senses could do without. Flo Bel sat up majestically in the enormous fourposter, said good morning and accepted the tea. The fires seemed to be dying out, Gorham said, although there were still outbursts. He would get breakfast. Mr. Suydam's housekeeper had come early in the morning; she had taken time to wash, change her dress and have breakfast. She had told him, Gorham, that there was plenty of food and where it was; she had then gone back to the hospital, where she was helping the frantically overworked nurses. "A middle-aged Spanish woman," said Gorham approvingly. "Keeps the house and the kitchen clean as a whistle. We do have a slight problem about water. It may have to be rationed. But Murphy has brought some in from a covered well in the back." He reached for a pail of water in the hall. "We'll see that it is boiled before using. I boiled it for your tea. I'll take the little dog."

Cho grunted agreeably and trotted after Gorham.

The tea was heartening. Mallory washed in as little water as possible and managed to remove much of the previous night's grime. Looking quickly through the heap of clothing Scott had grasped before they fled the Welbeck house, she found only trousseau dresses, but luckily, among them there was a heap of lingerie. She settled on the dress she had worn on the train, elegant though it was, and went to help in the kitchen, where she was not needed. Gorham and Su Lin were busy and as efficient as usual. Breakfast was placed in covered dishes, also found by Gorham, who was pleased, it was easy to see, at the cleanliness and order of the kitchen—also, perhaps, by the fine china and silver.

Cheng turned up at the back door, coming in boldly through some back entry and asking if he could be of any help. He was not needed, but he did bring news of the city—and it was not good.

The city was a shambles. People were crowded in the park,

165

temporary kitchens were being set up, places of shelter were being provided. He had not seen Kai Sing. Su Lin said nothing, but turned away.

It developed that Scott had briefly returned and taken Murphy away again with him in the roomy automobile. Henry and Grenay had apparently gone to see if anything could be salvaged from the Welbeck house. Flo Bel emerged as Cho and Mallory were sharing crisply broiled chops, and Flo Bel looked as composed and neat as if she had had a lady's maid dress her. Her dressing case had obviously contained a hairbrush; her hair was shining as always; her black dress—well, whatever either Scott or Gorham had snatched up in those confused and terrified moments when the fire swept into the Welbeck house, it had had to be, for Flo Bel, a black dress. She still clung to the pearls; Mallory felt the barest twinge of amusement when she saw their satiny gleam below her white net collar.

The living room, which had been such a scene of fright and confusion, yet a thankfully accepted refuge the previous night, was now in immaculate order. The lady in the portrait seemed just faintly less haughty as she looked down on them. Dolores was sitting in a window seat, outlined against the daylight, a murky yellow traced with clouds of smoke. She didn't reply when Flo Bel said, "Good morning."

Dolores had taken time, even in the crisis of the previous night, to bring at least one dress, a thin wool, blue-green again, clinging to her small figure but also clinging to those large and robust legs beneath the full skirt. Probably she had snatched her satin opera cloak because it was nearest at hand.

Mallory went back to the rooms she and Flo Bel had shared, but Su Lin was already making up the beds. Mallory ventured a word of hope. "I truly believe your father will come. He'll guess that we are here, surely. Everyone must feel that this house is safe."

Su Lin, a look of doubt in her dark eyes, said, "It was thought that the other house, the big house, was safe."

"I know," Mallory said. Presently Su Lin departed. Flo Bel had been quite normally brisk and efficient that morning, but Mallory had an uneasy notion that she was trying to

166

ward off any inquiries into what she had said during the night—that she ought to talk to Ernest Grenay. Flo Bel had been half asleep when she spoke, but it was not in her nature to make a purposeless statement even in that state.

Why Mr. Grenay? Of course, he had been Richard's trustee. And he was a lawyer. But Flo Bel had clearly detested him for some reason. She would have it out with her aunt.

It was not easily done, for while Flo Bel followed her, as Mallory asked her to do, into the big bedroom, she simply sank down in a big armchair and closed her eyes.

"All right now, Flo Bel, you were mumbling something about Mr. Grenay last night. You said you had to talk to him. What about?"

Flo Bel's eyes were closed. "Oh, Mallory, I don't know—don't ask me."

Mallory waited a moment. Then she said, "You must know something. You disliked him from the moment you saw him—yet you didn't know him. So why?"

"I'm not sure—I don't know. It may not matter now."

"It matters to me. Tell me."

A slit of blue eyes gleamed for a second at Mallory; then Flo Bel put her head back again. "You were always a willful child. Rather like your dear mother."

"Like you," Mallory said irresistibly.

A very faint smile touched her aunt's lips. Mallory said, "Come on now. Tell me. What is this about Mr. Grenay?"

Flo Bel sighed. "I don't know. In a way it doesn't seem to matter now. Not after all this. But"—Flo Bel sat up and opened her eyes—"but I thought it mattered!"

"What mattered?" She didn't shout, but felt like it.

"Somebody," said Flo Bel wearily, "is a thief. Somebody in the Welbeck connection. It's either Mr. Grenay, or he knows who it is."

After a moment Mallory said, "You may as well go on."

Flo Bel sighed again. "Remember, I was entirely without means. Of course, once you were married to Richard, I knew that I would be taken care of but"—she gave a tiny shiver—"I didn't fancy that. No! I preferred to be as independent as a hundred thousand dollars, more or less, could make me."

"A hundred— But Mr. Grenay—"

"All right, if you must hear it. Dear Peter, at the last, was very confused. He desperately tried to retrieve some of his fortune. He—well, he gambled. On anything that sounded promising. So—so he bought into the Welbeck Bonanza Mine. Shortly after his death I had a letter from Mr. Grenay saying the Welbeck Bonanza had ceased to operate. The lode of gold ore had been exhausted." She thought for a moment and then seemed to gather strength. "I was wrong. I ought to have gone into Peter's financial affairs more carefully. I—well, I didn't. I took the Grenay letter as a fact. But then I heard from Richard himself that the Welbeck mines were still in full production. So I thought, indeed I knew, that Richard himself would make good Peter's investment. I didn't have an opportunity to bring it up to him, didn't want to spoil your chances. I thought I'd wait until after the wedding. But— Oh, Mallory, after what we have seen here and all that has happened—no, no, I can't care about the money, only the money, now."

"Richard would have seen to it. And, dear Flo Bel, you can't let Uncle Peter's last investment go—his last attempt to restore his name for integrity and to take care of you. Uncle Peter would want you to act. You can't let that go. I'm going to call Mr. Grenay—"

"Mallory, wait. There may be no connection at all!"

"No connection with what? Flo Bel, you don't mean those attempts to get rid of me?"

"Yes." Suddenly Flo Bel sat up, her blue eyes determined. "Listen. Suppose, just suppose, someone contrived to steal that money, wrote that letter to me, thought himself safe, suddenly discovered that you were to marry Richard. And that I intended to come here with you. Don't you think that that person might do anything—anything in the world, including murder?"

Mallory was again lost in a flood of uncertainty. She had felt that the attack at Gary and the gas line open in her bedroom had been deliberate attempts on her life. Yet that surmise had been in a sense unreal, removed from her even though each time she had been frightened. But she had been frightened in a kind of shocked yet remote way, as if neither

168

had in fact threatened her life. That was, of course, not realistic. Face to face with attempted murder for motives which
Flo Bel so succinctly defined, she felt a chill of immediate
fear that was almost—indeed it was—terror.

She made herself reply, "*Oh, no!*"

"Oh, yes! Anything to protect himself. Or," said Flo Bel
thoughtfully, "herself. I only know that Peter's money vanished. I don't care now about the money— All this—the earthquake, Richard's murder, everything seems to change my
feeling about the money. It's just money—can't be of the
importance I felt it was when...when I met Richard and
decided he was the man for you. Now wait—" She lifted her
slender hand imperatively. "I knew Richard owned the Welbeck interests, the mine too. But I also knew him to be a
suitable husband for you. I was not—truly, Mallory—I was
not entirely influenced by money. But now I can't help thinking—just suppose it's very important to someone to get me
out of the way, because I might make my claim known. With
you dead, there would be no marriage, and I would go back
to New York at once. And," she said thoughtfully, "killing
Richard would of course accomplish the same things: prevent
the marriage and get rid of me."

Mallory caught her breath. There was again a chilling
logic in Flo Bel's reasoning. "We'll talk to Mr. Grenay. I'll
get him—" She dashed out of the room. Mr. Grenay was in
the living room, about to go out. She said, "My aunt wishes
to speak to you, Mr. Grenay."

He gave her a look of surprise. "Your aunt?"

"Yes. Now."

"But—well—oh, certainly."

He followed Mallory back to the bedroom, where Flo Bel
sat with, actually, a handkerchief at her eyes. She was thinking, then, of Peter, whose proud name she hoped to restore.
A bleak future lay ahead of Flo Bel unless Mallory did marry
money, but her deep desire was to bring back at least some
of the luster to Peter's name as a man of judgment and integrity.

Mallory said, swiftly, "Tell him, Flo Bel. Tell him."

Mr. Grenay, puzzled, glanced around for a chair. Flo Bel
waved him toward a high-backed, unyielding armchair. "I'll

put it briefly. My husband invested something over a hundred thousand dollars in the Welbeck Bonanza. You sent him a letter saying that the mine had closed down. I have discovered in fact that the mine is still in production."

Grenay turned red, turned white, gasped. "Why, I . . . I sent no such letter. I knew nothing of your husband's investment. I cannot believe—"

"I have the canceled check, and the letter came from your office," said Flo Bel.

Mr. Grenay got a smudged handkerchief out of a pocket and rubbed his face.

Flo Bel said, quietly, "I knew that—sometime—I could approach Richard about this. I knew that he would have investigated for me. But I . . . waited too long—"

Grenay sprang up. "This money—you can't prove—"

"There must be a record of it. Granted I ought to have inquired sooner. I ought to have done this at the time my husband died. But I . . . I didn't," Flo Bel said. "I made the mistake of believing the lies in your letter. Now you say that all old records of the Welbeck enterprises are in your home. If you wish to investigate my claims, it should be simple to look over those records."

Ernest Grenay mopped his face again.

Flo Bel continued, "You may have had confederates. Henry Beaton, his wife, perhaps others. I suppose I could bring you all to trial. You would never be able to do business in California again or—well, actually," she said flatly, "anywhere. So you can get the records and then—we'll see."

"But—" said Ernest Grenay. "You're accusing an honest man! Richard trusted me!"

"Richard died. So he can't help me now to put things straight—as he would have done. Three times attempts were made to kill my niece. Was that—all that done to protect a theft of money? Only money!"

"No!" Grenay cried sharply. "No! I had nothing to do with that gas log last night. Nothing."

"Then who did? It was no accident, Mr. Grenay."

"Surely you do not mean to imply—"

"More than imply! You sent me the letter about my husband's investment in the Welbeck Bonanza—"

170

"I tell you, I didn't. I never saw such a letter—"

"But I have it—"

"Mrs. Bookever!" Ernest Grenay was white with anger, but his face showed something else, a kind of unwilling belief. "You are telling me the truth?"

"Why would I make such a statement if it were not true? Besides, there is the check."

"Yes. Yes, the check. Do you remember the date?"

"Not the day of the month but the year—"

"How long ago?"

"Before my husband died, of course. He was desperately trying to recoup some of his fortune. He died something over four years ago."

"Almost five," Mallory said softly. Neither paid her any attention.

Mr. Grenay stuck his finger below his collar as if to ease it. "Mrs. Bookever, my father saw to all of the Welbeck interests. When he died—about three years ago, a little more—Richard asked me to take over the entire responsibility for his financial interests. I had assisted my father to a certain extent. I was not completely in his confidence about finances, so it was more or less difficult—" He edged his grimy collar looser again. "However, I did my best. Most of the former records of the Welbeck enterprises were out of date. The office my father used and which I took over from him was choked with old correspondence—receipts, all that kind of thing. We had to open an entire new set of books. I tried to transfer anything pertinent. There were only a few stockholders who had bought stock in the Welbeck concerns. I advised Richard to buy those outstanding shares, and he did. I saw to that. Now then—"

"I have my husband's canceled check," Flo Bel said stubbornly.

"Madam, I believe that you—how shall I say it?—believe you have it—"

"I know it!" Flo Bel flashed.

"Yes, madam. That is, you must understand I am an honest man. I have looked after Richard's interests according to my best judgment. Now you come to me with this claim and...and a dreadful accusation of attempted murder!"

171

"Richard was murdered. My niece—"

"No, no! There can't be any connection, but to satisfy you, I'll go to my home and search the old records for anything at all connected with your name. And, "Ernest Grenay said tautly, "to satisfy myself. If I can get a fishing boat or anything to take me across the Bay—"

Had the door wavered just a little during the very heated conversation? When it opened quietly, Mallory had a fleeting notion that she had felt or seen a kind of quiver, a very quiet movement, before Dolores came in.

She smiled her little cat smile. "Ernest, Henry needs your help."

"But, Dolores—"

"Now," said Dolores. "He thinks he may be able to get some of his porcelains out of the ruins of his gallery. He says the heat might not have damaged his jade pieces. Perhaps he can find and save some."

"Dolores, you haven't seen! The whole place—why, it's a rubble. Still smoking, I expect."

"No. Henry thinks the fires have gone far enough past his place so there is a real chance of saving something. It means so much to him, Ernest."

Ernest Grenay sighed. "Well, all right. If you will excuse me, Mrs. Bookever. But I assure you I'll...investigate."

Mallory thought that Dolores' eyes shifted knowingly toward Flo Bel's face when Ernest Grenay said, "I'll investigate."

Flo Bel said, stiffly but a shade more graciously than was her custom with Grenay, "Yes, certainly."

He bowed jerkily, Dolores smiled, and as both vanished into the hall, Flo Bel closed the door; she didn't slam it but she closed it firmly. "That woman was listening. Do you think she knew about your uncle's check?"

Mallory thought it over, then said, "I think she knows about almost everything she could discover concerning Richard's business affairs. But I think she'd be afraid to undertake downright theft. Besides, how could she steal a hundred thousand dollars from Mr. Grenay—from Richard, really?"

"I don't know." Flo Bel's eyes were like blue steel. "But she would if she could find a way! Grenay, himself!"

Fifteen

"Mr. Grenay sounded honest," Mallory said presently.

"Yes," said Flo Bel reluctantly. "That is—yes and no. I don't know. But there are legal ways to track down that money. Of course, they may say that it was a loss—that the mines had ceased to produce for a time. Your uncle's loss, they could say, was only one of the losses, but after all that, the mines suddenly began to operate again. Somebody found a new lode of gold. Oh, they can say anything if they want to."

Mallory said, slowly, "I think I do trust Mr. Grenay."

Flo Bel was obviously shaken. "How can we be sure? He didn't act guilty. But a really clever man wouldn't. He might have a very urgent reason to kill Richard and...and try to kill you. Remember, you are Richard's heir. Mallory, I can only blame myself for not looking sooner and more minutely into Peter's financial affairs. I wasn't sure of anything except the letter Grenay denies sending. Then Richard arrived, and I liked him. I thought I would approach him at the proper time, that he would treat the matter fairly."

It explained Flo Bel; it explained her immediate cordiality toward Richard; it explained her ready consent to Mallory's marriage and prospective residence in a strange city, a city across a continent.

Flo Bel looked down at her still white and graceful hands. "Believe me, Mallory, it wasn't so much the money. More than anything, it meant something to my dear Peter's memory. Then Richard was killed."

Mallory said, "And that's why you believe they tried to kill me, too?"

Flo Bel's eyes glanced up. "I'm afraid—yes, afraid."

"But you agreed to let it be understood that Richard's death was due to an accident—"

"Certainly. Far better than the scandal of a trial. Dear Mallory, you are young. A story such as that can ruin a girl's whole life."

"But you do want to know who killed Richard and who tried to kill me."

"I want to see that you're in a safe place. It's too late to do anything about Richard. There's nothing I can do about that. But I can send you back to New York—"

Mallory sighed. "I'm not going."

"It's only for your protection. You ought to see that—"

"No, that is, yes. I can see it but I'm not going."

"This is unfair. But I am going to remind you of what your uncle—and I—have done for you. How can you refuse my . . . my request?"

Mallory felt as if Flo Bel had slapped her, as she had never done even in Mallory's sometimes rebellious childhood. The slap seemed to strike her heart and was as painful as if it were in fact a wound. "Flo Bel—"

"You think you've fallen in love with young Suydam. I was afraid of that on the train. But then I knew you were going to put young Suydam out of your thoughts and be happy—yes, happy, Mallory—with Richard. But now, that's why you refuse me the first thing I have ever asked you to do."

There was a soft knock at the door; at Mallory's word Su Lin came in. Her eyes were red-rimmed, her face downcast as she said she had come for their shoes. "Mr. Gorham says they must be cleaned. I'm to take them to him."

How like Gorham! Murder and fires and earthquakes, an eerie flight through rubble in the darkness—and Gorham was sure that their shoes needed cleaning. Mallory yanked off her shoes; Flo Bel actually gave a jerky kind of laugh and did the same. Su Lin took the four shoes in her arms, holding them against her black blouse, and slipped away.

Flo Bel seemed to consider resuming the argument, then to decide against it. She seemed to be listening to something, her neat head turned, her face as fragile-seeming and yet as strong as a well-cut cameo. "Someone has come back. There are voices. Have you got any bedroom slippers? Put on something. Your stockings are in ribbons."

Flo Bel groped in the small dressing case she had salvaged and drew out flat bedroom slippers, which she pushed at Mallory. "Never mind. I have extra stockings. Now, another thing—don't be afraid Gorham will lose Richard's will. He told me he would guard it and he meant it." She pulled out stockings—and a shocking, a paralyzing, conjecture darted into Mallory's mind and would not be turned away. Flo Bel had known about the will before Richard was shot.

Gorham must have told her at once, the same night he gave the envelope to Mallory on Scott's instructions.

Flo Bel had been, she had said, in her room, dressing, when the shot that killed Richard was heard.

Flo Bel was an excellent shot. She had gone hunting with Uncle Peter many times, and Mallory had heard him boast of her marksmanship.

Flo Bel had dismissed Mallory's flat statement that she would not marry Richard—but had she really dismissed it? Or had she taken swift and final action the instant she realized the unexpected opportunity?

Oh, no!

It was unthinkable.

Not Flo Bel! Where would she have obtained a gun?

But she had a will of steel. She had dauntless courage. But no—no, Mallory almost screamed to herself.

"Come along," said Flo Bel.

Mallory swallowed hard, her heart seemed to have got up into her throat; she tried to swallow, too, that dreadful question—and with a stinging conscience, walked slowly after Flo Bel. Murphy and Scott were in the long, low living room. Scott was obviously exhausted, there were deep lines in his face, but he brightened up slightly when Flo Bel, her elegant feet padding in stockings, and Mallory, shuffling a little in Flo Bel's pink slippers, came into the room. "I'm sorry," he said to Mallory. "I had to abandon the car. We ran out of gas. No way to get more. I expect people have already taken the Daimler for shelter. No use trying to get it back."

Murphy sighed. "I never liked the thing. That's why I put it out back of the stables. I had my beauties—I didn't want

175

that machine." He pushed his hands over his weary face. "Well, ma'am, it's gone now for sure."

"It went for a good purpose," Mallory said.

Murphy muttered something and went toward the kitchen.

Henry came in from outside, rubbing his eyes. "My place is in ruins. Lolo and Ernest say they can get some men to help, but I gave it up when I found this. In the rubble," he said, and extended a dirty hand holding a triangular piece of porcelain. He shoved it up and down on his coat, cleaning it, and looked at it. "Hawthorne," he said drearily. "I had three Hawthorne vases. Ever see such blues—or such white? See those plum blossoms." He put the piece of porcelain down on a table, and the translucent blues and whites seemed to gather all the light in the room. "Lolo is determined. She made Ernest and Gerald help her. They can't do much. I'll go back, though, as soon as I've eaten."

And have something to drink, Mallory thought tartly, for Henry lumbered off toward the pantry. Henry loved his gallery, but his first love was food and drink. Gorham announced luncheon with a cool air, quite as if it would be a feast, as it was not: corned beef and poached eggs. Cheng slouched sullenly around the table, serving.

Flo Bel ate thoughtfully. Scott had little to say. Henry gobbled his food, asked for more, and told such tales of horror of what he had seen or heard in the stricken city that at last Flo Bel said, in her iciest voice, that they could do nothing just then to help.

"But there is help. Already a committee has been formed. Mr. Spreckels and others—" There was a decanter of wine on the table; Henry poured another goblet himself. "Smoke, houses fallen apart, people without shelter, people killed and lying on the sidewalk—"

Scott finally intervened. "Places of shelter have been set up in the park."

"Ah, but they say sanitary conditions there will breed disease—"

"It hasn't happened yet," Scott said. "Eat something, Mallory."

She hadn't been able to eat during Henry's frightful tales. She took a mouthful, discovered that she was ravenous, and

176

closed her eyes and ears to Henry's gobbling, his loud slurping of wine and his talk.

But she heard it when Flo Bel said distinctly, "Mr. Suydam—Scott—may I have a few moments of your time?"

Scott looked up, startled. Flo Bel spoke to him, but her gaze was directed straight at Henry. "As I have told you, I hope you will act as my niece's representative and see to her interests here. My niece, as you know, is going back to New York. Perhaps you'll be able to assist her in getting to Oakland and getting a train. Now then, if you have quite finished your luncheon..."

Scott looked frozen. He rose, however, and drew out Flo Bel's chair. She swept out of the room. "Will you come, too, please, Mallory," she said and led them, her black-clad figure erect and slender, back to the rooms where she and Mallory had spent the night.

She started with no preamble. "Mallory is to return to New York. As you suggested last night. We can take no more chances with... with attempted murder." She was not one to dodge facts or mince her words. No, no, Mallory thought, how could she have wondered, even for a horrific second, if Flo Bel could have killed Richard! Flo Bel gave Scott a long look and added, "You'd better sit down. Here—"

She indicated the narrow sofa at the foot of the fourposter, and as he sat down, almost collapsing, she said, "You really ought to rest—this is no time to talk—"

"No, that's all right." Scott rubbed his hands over his forehead. "Yes, you know I agree with you about Mallory's going back to New York. But just now—honestly, I don't see how it can be done. Some people are still leaving the city by the ferries. But once in Oakland, there is considerable confusion about trains. At the moment, I was told, all passenger trains are being sidetracked for freight trains, expected from Chicago and other cities. Trains of food, clothing—that kind of thing. Desperately needed."

Mallory said again, almost wearily, "I'm not going..." She'd said it so many times that perhaps neither Flo Bel nor Scott now paid any attention to it. Scott rubbed his forehead again and said, "What do you mean about protecting Mallory's interests? I'll be glad to act for her, in the matter of the will, but—"

"That's not all." Flo Bel, sitting very erect and quiet on a footstool, said precisely, "Let me tell you the whole story—" And began.

As she told him her reasons for believing that someone in the Welbeck connection had deliberately deceived her husband, Peter Bookever, the lines of strain and fatigue seemed to leave Scott's face, as if he were gathering strength to tackle a new problem, certainly a different problem from some of the sad and tragic ones he had encountered since the city began to burn.

"Yes, I see," he said slowly when Flo Bel had finished. "You feel sure that Grenay knew all about this letter to your husband, saying that the mine was not in production?"

"I did feel sure—that is," Flo Bel said with her habitual accuracy, "it was my feeling. Now I'm not so sure. He insisted, saying he didn't know anything about it."

"Do you have the letter with you?"

"I left it with the bank in New York—in a vault, along with other papers, passports, things like that. But it is there."

"Can't be reached just now. Is the canceled check of your husband's in the vault, too?"

"Yes."

Scott nodded, frowning. "Best place for it." He looked directly at Flo Bel. "You feel that this...this deception has a relation to what we must consider attempts upon Mallory's life?"

"Yes," said Flo Bel flatly. "But I don't see what. Or rather, who."

"No." He considered, then said thoughtfully, "The attempt to pull her off the train can't have been made by anyone I know. I went through the cars several times. At the stops I watched—nearly got assaulted with a lady's umbrella one time when I peered under it." The faintest shadow of a grin touched his mouth. "But I simply saw nobody I knew. I don't see how anybody could have hidden in the train. I even looked in the washrooms. Of course, whoever did it could have been hired, but the argument against that is that such a bargain would have put the hirer in a very dangerous position. He'd have opened the way to being blackmailed for the rest of his life."

"Or her life," said Flo Bel.

"Dolores? I don't know. She damn near killed Richard dosing him with laudanum, trying to keep him an invalid and under her thumb. She didn't want him to marry, I suspect, although naturally, she never has admitted it. Oh, yes, I think she was and still is after the Welbeck money, but I can't see her actually turning on the gas jet in Mallory's room."

"Dolores is in it, somehow, I'm sure," Flo Bel said.

He considered this. "Henry is a big blundering fool—that is, he seems like a fool and a blunderer. He's really an astute businessman. I rather think he's got a very alert eye on his own prospects, and that means Dolores and her prospects. He wasn't on the train."

"Grenay..."

"He's very intelligent. Said to be honest. No question of that before this. The letter from his office could have been faked. Any number of ways. But there would have to be a way for the...the person who wrote it to get hold of money from your husband's shares. Of course," he said after a thoughtful pause. "That's not impossible. Embezzlement of far larger sums has happened. However, Grenay was not on the train, either. All these incidents, Richard's death, the attack on Mallory in Gary, the gas in her room could be *called* mere accidents. That's the remarkable efficiency about whoever it was who shot Richard."

"Richard would have seen to it that my husband's money was returned to me."

"Yes. Richard would have done that. He would have been horrified, shocked, but he'd have seen to it that whoever got away with that money was discovered and suitably punished and that restoration was made to you. Richard was like that. Never believed harm of anybody, but if he had to see that it *was* harm, it *was* wrong—oh, yes, he'd have tried to make it up to you. So, he was killed. That could be a reason. The other reason could be that his marriage must be prevented. It could be the double motive you suggest. Fear—money. But I don't know, I don't know a thing that can be proved."

179

Flo Bel rose suddenly, took the red eiderdown from the big bed, put her slim hand on Scott's shoulder and said, gently but firmly, "Lie down. You're almost sleepwalking. I'll call you, but sleep now."

"No—no, I—no—" said Scott and fell back on the small sofa at the pressure of Flo Bel's hand, sighed and slept.

"Worn out," Flo Bel whispered. "Be very quiet, Mallory."

Oh, yes, Mallory thought. I'll be quiet. Just watch him and be quiet.

Her thoughts were anything but quiet; they galloped furiously around in the same circles, as if she had got herself onto a race course and, as she flew around it, kept recognizing buildings, certain landmarks, certain faces—but before she could be sure of that recognition, she was whirled about again. One thing, however, she was sure about: she was not returning to New York.

Perhaps, she thought once, perhaps never. If Scott— No, she wouldn't dwell on that dimly seen prospect. She gazed out the window. Casa Madrone was built so some of the windows faced north, overlooking the Bay. The day was clear; she could see the ships and small boats surging back and forth, bringing water, supplies; often a cloud of smoke from the still-burning city drifted across, obscuring the blue waters of the Bay.

Flo Bel sat still, too; but her thoughts, too, Mallory knew, were swirling here and there, swiftly and with determination.

It grew chilly in the room as twilight came on; Mallory was still wearing only Flo Bel's thin slippers, and the floor gradually became so cold that she looked longingly at the fireplace and the stack of logs in an iron-grilled holder beside it, but even as she looked at it, Flo Bel guessed her thought and shook her head. Mallory tucked her feet under her and sat like a child—but thinking not at all like a child. Scott slept in utter, complete exhaustion. He slept and slept, and then all at once sat up, looked around him, seemed to come to full consciousness and grinned. "Whew! I needed that. Thank you." He clutched at the eiderdown as it started to slip off him.

Someone knocked softly at the door. Perhaps even in his

sleep Scott had been aware of the approaching footsteps. Flo Bel drew the bolt and opened the door. It was Gorham. He put their cleaned and polished shoes neatly beside the dressing table and said, "Thank you, madam. I see Mr. Suydam is here. I was sure of it. Mr. Suydam, I have drawn a hot bath for you and put out fresh clothes. I hope I found things in your wardrobe which you would wish me to select..."

Scott grinned again and scrambled to his feet; he yawned heartily, went over to Flo Bel and calmly kissed her. He glanced at Mallory as if he'd like to kiss her, too. The desire was so evident in his face that Mallory felt her cheeks turning pink. "Thank you, Gorham. I'll see you at dinner, Mallory, Mrs. Bookever. It must be nearly dinnertime."

He went away with Gorham. Gorham! Mallory's startled thoughts took a new and ugly swerve. Could Gorham have killed Richard because Flo Bel knew of the will?

Oh, no! Gorham was devoted to Flo Bel, but not in so deeply personal a way that he would commit murder to oblige her! He was loyal, he was a true and staunch support of the Bookever family. He was content, and attached to his lot as a strong, practical and efficient member of the Bookever household. But if Flo Bel had said go and kill somebody, he would have given her a look of disapproval; shaken his head and told her she ought to have a good lie-down and a cup of tea.

Gorham was one of Mallory's best and earliest friends. He wouldn't have tried to murder her, and indeed, if he had so far forgotten himself, he would have accomplished it with success!

Oh, what am I thinking of? she reflected, again with shame and a sting of conscience. Gorham wouldn't murder anybody. Besides being a dreadful and criminal act, he would consider it as revealing a shocking lack of conventionality!

While Mallory's fantastic speculation was flashing through her mind, Flo Bel had secured the heavy bolt.

"We might freshen ourselves up," she said, always a Spartan about behavior and appearances.

Again they used as little water as they could. Again Mallory put on the green dress, which reminded her of what now seemed enchanted hours on a train, moving westward. Again, to Mallory's amusement, Flo Bel adjusted Mallory's pearls safely below her white net collar.

They gave each other glances of approval, then opened the door and followed the aromatic scent of a wood fire, leading them to the living room. Dolores was there; Henry and Grenay were there; the blond-mustached Gerald was sitting glumly in a corner. From none of them did Mallory perceive the slightest glance of awareness that Flo Bel had accused Grenay—and thus, indirectly perhaps, Dolores and Henry— of stealing.

None of them had been accused of murder, Mallory thought coldly; yet one of them had to know too much of those murderous intents and attempts. They were summoned to dinner by Cheng, who was sulkier than ever.

What talk there was, was of the city and the burning. If there had been any further discoveries in the rubble of Henry's gallery, nothing was said of them. Henry may have done more than his usual hearty drinking; Grenay looked, if possible, even more drained and troubled—as well he might be, Mallory reflected, thinking of his interview with Flo Bel. Gerald was merely there, looking very tired, as all of them were. Only Dolores seemed rather fresh and content, although she did not wear the usual blue-green dress but a very stylish pale-gray one. Henry, holding his glass in one hand, continued to eye and fondly touch the one piece of lovely blue and white porcelain, which he had brought to the table—all that remained of the treasured Hawthorne vase.

Dinner was a silent affair. Su Lin did not help serve; only Cheng lounged sourly around the table. Gorham gave him unwontedly crisp directions. They were almost finished when Scott turned up, clean-shaven; he wore a spotless shirt, pressed and clean clothes. He did bring a slight air of normality to the table. Henry gave him an envious look. "Easy to see you've got your own clothes here."

"I live here," Scott said mildly.

"I only wish I could wear your size." Henry gave a kind of push at his bulging stomach. Dolores smiled. Grenay sighed and tried to straighten his wrinkled jacket. Gerald asked for more soup.

It was a fairly adequate meal, and they ate, all of them,

hungrily. Coffee and liqueurs were served in the living room by Gorham. Just as he put down the silver tray and started toward the fireplace as if about to add logs, a rat streaked across the room.

Sixteen

For the first time in Mallory's long knowledge of Flo Bel, she screamed. She also shot to her feet, gathered up her skirts and leaped as swiftly as a girl to the top of her chair. Dolores screamed, too. Mallory screamed and felt like a fool. The black streak had disappeared, dashing into the hall. Cho gave a startled bark and leaped after the rat, but Mallory caught him, so all he could do was growl frantically in the direction the rat had taken. Scott snatched the enormous iron fire tongs and ran into the hall. Gorham had already disappeared, flourishing a long iron poker.

Henry sagged back into a chair and said, panting. "A rat— that means—"

"What did you expect?" Flo Bel said tartly. She lowered her skirts and got herself down from the chair in one graceful movement, then sat down again, upright and dignified.

"Not so soon. Not all those rats in Chinatown! In the cellars! All over the city!"

"They seem to have got that one," Mallory said. And indeed they seemed to have got more than a rat, for men's voices rose angrily; someone yelled in a high voice in what sounded like Chinese. More voices! Finally Scott came back.

He was pale, not with weariness this time but with anger. "Dolores, how long have you known this man Cheng?"

Dolores widened her eyes until the white showed all around the pale iris. "Cheng?"

"Don't look at me like that. What do you know of him?"

"Why, I—dear me—he's a very skillful servant—"

183

"He's a liar and a thief. If you want to know, Gorham and I caught him sneaking out the back door with silver under his blouse and a basket of silver in his hand. My mother's silver, my grandmother's—Oh, the hell. He nearly got away with it. I'd like to strangle him."

Gorham came in and said, sedately, "He needs killing, Mr. Suydam, but I really wouldn't advise it. I've got him locked up in a wine room."

"He'll break the bottles."

Henry said, "Did you get the rat?"

"Which one do you mean?" Scott snapped at him.

Gorham intervened. "Yes, sir. The rat has been disposed of. But this man Cheng—we'll have to do something about him, and I'm very much afraid there's no chance of turning him over to the police."

Scott was still on the boil. "Turn him in to General Funston's soldiers for looting. They'll make short work of him."

Dolores turned toward him like a little cat. "Now see here, Scott—obviously he didn't get away with your precious family silver."

Mallory spoke up at that. "You saved your jewels! Scott certainly has a right to save anything in his own home."

Scott drew a long breath. "Gorham, that wine cupboard will never hold him. There's a woodshed with a good lock—"

"I'll see to it." Gorham put down the poker and went out.

They were silent, all of them listening to the sounds from the kitchen. What seemed to start to develop into a first-class brawl very suddenly, indeed rather ominously, quieted down. A door closed hard somewhere.

Scott sat down. "Sorry. But I don't like that slinking Oriental. Where did you find him, Dolores?"

Dolores' eyes were still very wide. "Why, someone told me of him and gave him a good reference."

"Who?"

Dolores hesitated for barely an instant. "Mrs. Galway."

"She's in Santa Barbara. I met her husband yesterday, trying to salvage something from their house. She's been in Santa Barbara for a month."

"She wrote to me," Dolores smiled, just faintly triumphant. "The letter, of course, was left in our house. Otherwise I'd show it to you."

Scott took another long breath. "How long has Cheng worked for you?"

"Why, for some time—"

"I'll ask Su Lin," said Scott. "Or Murphy."

Dolores waited a second or two, then smiled again. "My dear Scott! You are really so obstinate. Any woman will tell you how hard it is to keep servants. I found it necessary to dismiss the two we had left in the house while you and Kai Sing and Su Lin were in New York. They were most inconsiderate about Richard's illness and—" She lifted her shoulders daintily. "So there was nothing for me to do but get rid of them. I did. And employed Cheng."

"When?"

She made a little careless gesture of annoyance. "Why, as a matter of fact—"

Henry rumbled, "Now, Dolores—"

"You knew it," she snapped at him. "You agreed, you know you did. We had to put Richard's care first, didn't we? So I employed Cheng and told him exactly what to do—"

"When did he arrive at the Welbeck house?"

Again Dolores barely hesitated. Then she said, airily, "Why, it was just before you and Mallory and her aunt arrived. Cheng's first day—"

"Do you mean the first hour of his employment? Remember, Dolores, I have only to ask Murphy."

"As if it mattered. Why, yes, now you ask. He came to help Richard. Yes, it was the very day."

"Almost the hour?"

"What of that?"

"You're sure that he wasn't on the train with us?"

Cheng! Cheng trying to pull Mallory off the train? Cheng contriving stealthily to get his small wiry hands on the bottle of chloral hydrate? Scott had searched the train repeatedly, but he would not have recognized Cheng if he had never seen him before. Mallory watched Dolores, fascinated, yet at the same time struck with an ugly chill of terror.

"Oh, dear me," Dolores said. "What a bother about a servant."

185

"I do like to get these things straight," Scott said. "I can't help wondering if Cheng shot Richard."

Dolores jumped up again. "Cheng? Shot Richard? You don't know what you're saying!" She turned to Henry. "Do you think it at all possible that Cheng—why, I employed him!—could he have killed Richard?"

Henry was red-faced and sulky. "Don't know. Can't see any reason for it."

"Oh, I think there might be a reason," Scott began, and Ernest Grenay, who had prudently retired to the back of a high sofa, got gingerly down again and said, mildly, "If it hadn't been for the rat, you would not have caught Cheng, Scott. He'd have been gone by now. I do think, Dolores, that you might have been more careful about employing him."

Dolores' eyes flashed. "I had to have somebody who could help me see to Richard. He assured me that he would follow my orders. I am sorry that he has proved to be dishonest, Scott, but naturally, if I had had any reason to suspect him of anything, I'd never have employed him. Now, let's just forget…"

Gerald stirred. He, too, had prudently sought a chair until the rat was disposed of. He said, weakly, "I'm sure Cheng worked for Mrs. Galway. I must have seen him there."

Scott said, evenly, "Oh, certainly. You would back Dolores in anything she said. I don't think you ever saw him in your life before he came to work in the Welbeck house."

A dull pink rose in Gerald's delicately featured face. "Now, now, Scott. Don't talk like that. Of course I know that Dolores is telling the truth!"

Would Cheng follow Dolores' orders so precisely that he would get to New York, find out the time of the return of the private car, get on the train—and attempt to kill her? Mallory considered it coldly.

Gorham appeared in the doorway. "I think Cheng is secure for the time being. Murphy is sleeping in the room beside the kitchen. He'll know if Cheng makes a move. However"—one of Gorham's eyebrows lifted subtly—"he'll not make a move for some time, I fear."

Henry was pouring brandy into glasses. At Gorham's

words, his hands started to shake and his full face turned even redder. "You didn't kill him?"

Gorham was as shocked as if he had been accused of bad manners. "Really, sir! I only defended myself. By the way, I wonder how that rat got into the house."

Henry's face took on a shade of purple. He lifted a glass of brandy and swallowed convulsively. "My fault. I went out to take a look at the fires and—well, the fact is I left the door open behind me. Never thought of a rat. Really, I'm very sorry. But you'd not have found Cheng getting away with the silver if the rat hadn't got into the house."

Scott said, shortly, "I don't think you had that in mind. However, we'll forget it. I'll see what we can do about Cheng tomorrow. Mallory... Mrs. Bookever..."

Flo Bel said goodnight to nobody in particular. Mallory caught one sliding, yet somehow triumphant, glance from Dolores and followed Scott and Flo Bel out of the room.

Once they were upstairs, Scott searched all over the bedroom and dressing room, looking behind curtains, under furniture, everywhere.

"Nothing could get in here," he said at last, closing the door. "The whole house is solid. Henry's probably right—the rat must have come in while he was out in front. Now then, Cheng *could* have been on the train, but I can't be sure. There were several Chinese. Kai Sing might be able to remember his face. It's more likely he would recognize Cheng than I would. I was looking for—oh, I don't know what, but not a Chinese. But if Cheng was on that train, he could have taken—" Scott had brought his glass of brandy from the living room; he had put it down on a marble-topped table while he searched for any possible entry of another rat. Now he picked it up, swirled the brandy around for a moment and said, "That bottle of chloral hydrate. You see—it's my carelessness. It's disappeared again."

"Scott!" Mallory cried.

"Yesterday I took time to come here and put it in a desk in the room I use at the other end of the house. I locked the desk just because I usually do lock it. But it's not a hard lock to pick if anybody wanted to do it. I hid the bottle for what

187

I thought of as safekeeping. I didn't look for it again until this evening, when I was changing. It wasn't there."

After a time Flo Bel tipped her glass up to the last drop, lowered it and said, loftily but rather thinly, "The same dramatis personae."

That was indisputable. Mallory said in a small voice, "Cheng? He was stealing silver. He might have thought there were valuables in the desk."

Scott nodded. "But the fact is that damn bottle—I beg your pardon, Mrs. Bookever—I mean that bottle is gone." He sounded tired and discouraged. "You'll just have to be very careful."

Mallory said, almost in a whisper, "Then, as you said, it's possible that if Cheng were really on the train, he could have taken the chloral hydrate, and could have put it in a drawer in Richard's room. So if anybody wanted to use it or—"

"Yes. Possible." Scott gave Flo Bel a curiously absent glance, quite as if she were not there at all, came to Mallory and enfolded her in his arms. "I'll not let anybody, I'll not let— Mallory—"

"I know," she whispered, her lips against his face.

When he released her, Mallory was only vaguely surprised to note that Flo Bel had quietly retired to a window and was standing there, looking out toward the dim reddish glow still hovering over the sky. As Scott moved to leave the room, she drew the curtains across the window.

He said, "Remember the bolt," and closed the door after him. Mallory dropped the heavy iron bolt with a dull clang.

"No use talking," Flo Bel said.

It was her way of saying goodnight, don't worry—that is, try not to. But long after Mallory had gone to the small bed in the dressing room she made at least one firm resolution. She wouldn't take anything into which chloral hydrate could possibly be introduced. She had made that decision once before, on the train; it was rather difficult, really. But this time! Cheng *had* taken it! If only Su Lin could find her father, then he would almost certainly be able to prove or disprove Cheng's presence on the train.

Her last drowsy thought was that this had been the first reasonably quiet and peaceful night since the night of the opera. Then the memory of Scott's arms, holding her firmly, like a wall around her, at last permitted her to drift into sleep.

There were things to be done, things to be decided, but everything must wait as the city waited for rescue, for a return to its normal life.

The next morning she made a discovery she didn't at all like. The second little silver buckle was gone from her shoe. This one had not been pulled raggedly off. The threads holding it had been neatly cut.

She decided not to say anything to Flo Bel. At least she wouldn't tell her just yet. The buckle could have disappeared any time; she couldn't remember precisely when she had last noted it, shining quietly on the new-fashioned, low-cut but sturdy walking shoe.

Gorham came with their early tea. Su Lin, he said, had gone the night before. She was determined to find her father. "Dangerous, of course, but she's a fine girl. Sensible. She'll be all right, I think. I arranged for a basket of food, which she took with her for her father if she finds him. As I hope, indeed, that she does." He hesitated, a faraway look in his eyes. "Madam—Miss Mallory—you saw very few people, really, on the train coming west. But do you remember seeing Mr. Beaton—or anyone who looked like him? Or the young man with the mustache?"

"Gerald Flower!" Mallory said. "No, I don't remember seeing either of them."

Gorham sighed. "Or even Mr. Grenay? I realize that you wouldn't have recognized any of them, but Mr. Scott certainly would have. If one of them had been there," said Gorham cautiously.

Flo Bel said after a moment, "I don't think Scott Suydam would have wished to protect one of them."

Gorham considered it and shook his head. "I agree. Well, really—" He thought again and said, "It is possible, of course, that the attempt to drag Miss Mallory off the train was in fact made by a thief. But the bottle of chloral hydrate had to be taken by someone on the train." He sighed, bent and gathered up Cho, who was sitting at Gorham's feet. "I believe breakfast is about to be served. By Murphy," he said, a faint gleam of humor in his eyes, and departed, Cho under his arm.

What could be behind Gorham's carefully blank gaze? But there was never any use in questioning him; he always chose his own time to talk.

Only Flo Bel, Mallory and Gerald ate breakfast. Henry had gone, Gerald told them in a tired voice; Ernest Grenay had gone; Scott had gone. When Mallory asked him, he said he didn't know what they had decided to do about Cheng.

Murphy, his bald head glistening, laboring heavily but conscientiously around the table, offering coffee and toast and eggs, said, "Faith, miss, but he's still in the woodshed. He'll stay there till we can find a policeman. Although finding a policeman to take on a thief is like—like, well, there are too many thieves just now. Stealing anything they can get their dirty hands on. But we'll see to Cheng," he finished with determination in his solidly boned and pleasant Irish face. "Eggs, miss?"

Chloral hydrate, Mallory reminded herself, and tasted the coffee warily. Flo Bel had also sipped a time or two before she drank it. Gerald was drinking heartily. No, the coffee had to be all right. Mallory drank and felt better. She told herself not to yield to nightmarish apprehensions. Certainly boiled eggs were not likely to have been subjected to an introduction of any foreign liquid, either.

Dolores appeared in the doorway, nodded and beckoned to Gerald, who arose promptly and followed her out of the room. Mallory thought absently, He does seem to be tied to Dolores' apron strings.

Could he have been the one who tried to pull me off the train? Scott would have recognized him immediately.

It turned into a still and gloomy day. The fires were dying down, but clouds of smoke still drifted across the sky and the acrid smell of charred wood and burned wool persisted everywhere. Once Mallory thought, with a strange kind of remote recognition, Why, this is—it must be the twentieth, it was to have been my wedding day.

It seemed a long time since Richard had talked to her and given her pearls and then died—everything so far away, as if she were looking at all the events of those few days in the

Welbeck house from the wrong end of opera glasses. They must plan a religious service for Richard, a memorial service—something, yes, they must do that. But they could do nothing yet.

Su Lin did not return. Mallory dusted, polished, made the beds in the rooms she and Flo Bel had shared, thankful for something to do. It occurred to her that she might ask Gorham about the second silver buckle—if it had been on her shoe when he cleaned it.

Dolores departed without saying where she was going; from the living room Mallory had a glimpse of her walking down the path rather hurriedly, a veil over her black hair, her satin opera cloak, incongruous and smoke-stained, pulled tightly around her bluish-green dress, which trailed on the sooty cobblestoned path to the gate. The huge madrones that gave their name to the house leaned over as if protecting it.

Henry returned, still red-faced, still angry, as if the earthquake had been designed to strike at him personally. He immediately went for the liquor cabinet in the pantry. Once Mallory heard a series of thuds from outside, probably from the woodshed, for a shrill voice, no doubt shouting Chinese epithets, accompanied them. The whole noisy hubbub was subdued, again with rather ominous promptness. Gorham? Probably.

About noon Scott and Murphy arrived in a wagon, driving a tired-looking horse that drooped in the shafts.

"Mallory, we got hold of this wagon and a horse. Gorham tells me that he believes Mr. Grenay went to his home in Sausalito. Probably to look up the old Welbeck records. If he is, as we hope, an honest man, he will certainly wish to prove his integrity and his ignorance of your uncle's investment. So it seems to me sensible to follow him there. Because if he is honest, he'll hand over anything he can find in the way of financial records. But if he's not honest, then unless we can find him first, he'll have a chance to destroy anything proving your aunt's claim. As Richard's financée and now his legatee, you have the right to see Mr. Grenay and ask for any information he may have been able to discover. If he is intentionally concealing records— Well, we'll see."

"I'll go, too," said Flo Bel at once.

Scott vetoed this. "There's scarcely space in the wagon for three. Mallory is the logical person to go. So, Mallory, better get your coat. It's warm, but there are still cinders flying around. But the fires are being held, and it will be safe. Murphy—"

"I'll see to this horse," Murphy said, sadly eyeing the tired and ancient-looking horse.

When Mallory went back upstairs to get her coat, she was surprised to see Dolores, walking swiftly but gracefully along the opposite stretch of the hall leading to the added long wing of the house. Her back was to Mallory, who noticed that her heavy black hair was done up sleekly. She had changed clothes since she had gone out that morning. She now wore a fashionably tight-bodiced and full-skirted black dress. Obviously she, too, had managed to take some clothes with her when she left the Welbeck house. Suddenly she whirled into an open doorway. Mallory slowly continued on her way— puzzled.

It had to be Dolores, of course. Yet Mallory was struck by a weird fantasy: Dolores couldn't be in two places at once, but for an instant it had seemed to be so. She had seen Dolores leave, that morning, in her blue-green dress and the grimy satin opera cloak. Now she looked entirely different. Oh, well, Mallory thought, maybe she just hadn't happened to see her return.

She went downstairs, her coat over her arm, said goodbye to Flo Bel and went out with Scott. Murphy was already sitting in the rickety wagon, waiting for them.

Scott was accurate in saying there was little space in the wagon. It was very small, probably intended for carting vegetables; there was only a wooden seat across from side to side, with a narrow iron railing for a handhold. Scott put her on the outside, and slid his arm around her waist to give her balance as the horse started up at Murphy's urging and went stumbling over uneven cobblestones and cracks in what ought to be solid pavement—up and down in a seesaw movement which threatened at any instant to throw the wagon itself over on its side. Murphy held the reins firmly; he stood sometimes to look ahead and try to guide the horse around strange fissures, sometimes two or three feet in width, that

192

had developed in an instant or two the night of the earthquake.

There were people everywhere, some drifting along, some seeming to be urgently seeking for whatever had been lost—or what members of their families were missing. The wagon lurched past a church with the steeple aslant. Murphy muttered and crossed himself, but kept one stern hand on the reins.

Mallory had only imagined the devastation, but she could see now that the damage from the fires was unimaginable. She was horrified by what looked like the utter ruin of a city. Scott's arm drew her more closely against him. Once when a group appeared around a house which apparently had caved in, he said, "Don't look—we'll get out of this soon. They're putting up more or less permanent tents and huts, and places for food to be handed out. Funny little shacks where food is being cooked, too." Pride came into his voice. "You can't keep us down, you know. San Franciscans, they're a race of their own. They are different. Imaginative, sturdy, with a sense of humor. Oh, we'll get our city back again to what it was. Better building, of course."

The horse stumbled wearily on heaps of rubble, and Murphy pulled him up carefully. "Poor old fellow. He's worn out. He may get us down to the wharf all right, Mr. Scott, but he can't swim across the Bay."

Scott gave a brief laugh. "We'll not expect that of him. If we can get a fishing boat, we'll be lucky."

"Across the Bay?" Mallory asked.

"Sausalito. Marin County. Somebody will know where to find Grenay."

When they reached the Bay, Murphy pulled up the tired horse and they began their search for a fishing boat to take them across. There were people digging in ruins, talking, watching the Navy ships and fishing boats that filled the Bay. Every time they heard of a possible boat that could be hired, someone else got to it before they did.

Several men recognized Scott and nodded or spoke to him respectfully, Mallory noted. One, a young Navy ensign, trotting down the gangway of a Navy ship, saw Scott and hurried up to him. "Mr. Suydam, sir. We hailed your *Madrone Rosa* out of San Diego. She was going to offload her cargo and take on food and medical supplies."

Scott's face brightened. "Thank you. That's good news."

"Right, sir." The ensign hurried away. Scott said, affectionately, "The little old *Madrone Rosa.* First ship we had. She was laden with Honduras mahogany this time and some spices and coffee. She is small but sturdy. Does anything we ask of her. Fine for the coastal trade. Good captain, too. Shows sense. Well—shall we keep on trying?"

One of the men they paused to question was working at some rubble which had once been a fishing shack. He said, in a dreary voice, that young Antonio, one of the fishermen, had made several trips. "Last person I saw talking to him was a fine lady. Wore a funny kind of fancy big white coat, dirty, though. Veil over her face. Said she had to get to Sausalito, and gave him money. But then—" He sighed and looked around. "I don't see him now. I don't know whether he went or not. Everybody wants to hire our boats and get away."

Dolores, Mallory thought. Dolores? Yes, she would have tried to see the banker and get the records. Wouldn't she?

But she had returned; Mallory had seen her in the house before they left. The notion that Antonio's passenger might have been Dolores occurred to Scott, too. He spoke of it when at last they abandoned their pursuit of a boat and trudged back to the wagon and the dispirited horse. They hadn't given up easily; it was already late in the afternoon when they decided to go back to the Casa Madrone.

"I wonder if the lady in the white coat could have been Dolores," Scott said then, thoughtfully. "I wonder if she got there. I wonder—"

"She was at your house when we left. I saw her when I went back to get my coat."

"Then it looks as if she didn't succeed. In any event, I really don't think Grenay would have turned anything over to her. She has no legal claim. Murphy, we'd better get this horse back to the man that rented us the outfit before the poor animal drops dead."

They went on, past stark blackened ruins of once majestic houses, the window frames and door frames like snagged black teeth. Scott said, sadly, "They're all gone. Some of them—perhaps some were not built in the best taste. But the taste doesn't matter, the point is they were built by men of standing and men able to work. Men who liked work..." He went on with his tragic litany. "The Grand Opera House went like tinder. The Palace Hotel has only walls and twisted pipe left but"—again pride and determination came back into his voice—"but we'll rebuild."

They drew up at last—the horse now wobbling with fatigue—at the cobblestoned path that led to Casa Madrone, standing serenely below its guardian trees and shrubs.

Scott helped Mallory down, swinging her from the wagon seat, which had become unbearably hard during the futile journey. "I'll go with Murphy. Have to pay the man for wagon and horse. Mallory, go straight to your aunt. Take it easy..." He meant, Be very careful.

Mallory nodded and forced her cramped muscles to go up the path and open the wide door of the house.

As she walked into the hall she was struck by a sense of something different, something unusual in the house. Rather, it was a lack of anything at all—no sound, no feeling of any presence. Even little Cho did not come rushing to meet her.

Flo Bel was not in her room. Gorham was not hovering anywhere near. She went on through a neat and silent dining room, pantry, kitchen with its gleaming copper pots. The back door was open. She hurried through a small kitchen entry to look out—saw that the door to the woodshed was open. Cheng, then, was gone, too. Everybody was gone. She went back through the ominously silent and empty house. In the big bedroom, on the dressing table, was a note from Flo Bel: "Back soon. Gorham with me. Tea on table."

That was all.

But there *was* someone in the house. She had been mistaken. In the mirror over the dressing table she caught just a flicker of movement behind her.

Seventeen

She whirled around, and at the same instant the flicker of movement vanished. With the instinct of a hunted animal, not thinking, only acting, Mallory flung herself across the room, grasped the heavy door, swung hard to close it and dropped the heavy bolt in place.

Then she listened. Listened, and heard a small, muffled yelp from Cho. She ran to the dressing-room door, flung it open—no Cho. He yelped again, and she pulled open the door to a heavy armoire. Cho bounced out, stretched his fluffy legs luxuriously and, tail waving, gave her a reproachful look. "Who put you in there?" she cried.

Cho's attitude expressed an indignant dislike for being shut up in the darkness. He crawled on to the sofa and sat there eyeing her.

She wished he could talk. Somebody had shut him in the armoire, someone who had no desire to invite Cho's sharp teeth in his ankle? Lion heart, Richard had said.

Her heart had been hammering so hard that she was all but breathless. She sank down on the sofa beside Cho. She would wait, that was what she would do. In fact, she reflected dismally, there was nothing else she could do.

She looked around, trying to find something, anything that might give her a notion as to what had taken Flo Bel away, what had apparently taken everybody in the house away—except for that someone who had barely flashed in the doorway, and flickered out of sight again, swiftly and soundlessly. Dolores?

Cheng?

The open door of the woodshed which had confined Cheng was a sure indication he was no longer a prisoner, at least not in the woodshed. It seemed unlikely that any arrest by a policeman and the consequent jailing of Cheng could have been brought about just then.

Everything must wait, she thought again with a kind of sick emptiness. Everything had to wait. Waiting was hard. It was also frightening. Face it, she told herself, time gave anyone who really wished to kill her an opportunity to think and plan and perhaps accomplish the deed. No, she wouldn't let herself admit that—but couldn't check her fear.

She rose and moved about the room, pausing at the window to look out over the waters of the Bay, rapidly darkening now, although there was a pinkish glow from the setting sun—a glow that penetrated the ugly murky smoke clouds still drifting above.

An open bottle of brandy stood on the dressing table beside Flo Bel's too brief message. Nothing could have happened to Flo Bel, she thought wildly; not to Flo Bel.

The bottle had been considerably depleted; there were only a few inches of liquid remaining in it. A glass stood beside it, as if Flo Bel had, for some urgent reason, administered a swallow or two of brandy to herself. That was not like Flo Bel; on the other hand, nothing these days was at all like anything Flo Bel and Mallory herself had ever encountered. But the question was still there: Why had Flo Bel resorted to brandy? Tea— Oh, yes, there it was, scrawled hurriedly in the brief note. "Tea on the table." A cup of tea stood there, plain dark tea, no milk, no lemon; but, to her surprise, it was still hot. So Flo Bel could not have left too long before.

It was no use wondering where she had gone.

The tea looked inviting, and Mallory was very tired. The house was so still around her now that she began to think she had only fancied that flicker of motion in the mirror. She reached for the tea, thinking how very kind Flo Bel always was to see to her comfort. How foolish and indeed wicked she had been to allow herself even a second's wild suspicion that Flo Bel had resorted to murder! Whatever had called her aunt away from the house, clearly she hadn't had time to explain her absence. Anyway, Gorham was with her, whatever the errand was.

The tea was very dark, probably some unfamiliar Indian-Chinese mixture. She took up the cup and the hot liquid looked inexpressibly desirable. It had been a shocking day, seeing what she had only imagined but now had actually seen. She was exhausted; her muscles ached and her spirits were low—so low, she thought with a flash of schoolgirl humor, I'd have to reach up to touch bottom. They had accomplished absolutely nothing.

She could not suppress a mad notion that although she had seen Dolores in the house, at the same time Dolores had very probably been hiring a fishing boat to take her across the Bay to find Grenay before she and Scott could get to him. Dolores just might have convinced him that somehow she had a right to the Welbeck records.

The tea was steaming; she had barely touched it with her lips when all at once she remembered Su Lin's tiny nose sniffing at a glass of water on the dressing shelf in the train. She stared at the tea, frozen for an instant. Her lips weren't numb, just lips touched by hot tea, but she lifted the cup closer to sniff as Su Lin had done.

She couldn't smell anything but tea. Yet it was indeed unusually dark and strong. She shoved the cup back on the table, with a rattle of cup against saucer, and snatched up the brandy bottle. She sniffed that, too, even though she knew that the pungent odor of brandy could conceal anything else.

She jumped up, took cup and bottle to the bathroom and poured out the contents of both as fast as she could, almost as if otherwise she might be forced to drink them. Then she went back and began to search the big bedroom—searched very briefly, for she soon found a bottle, labeled "Mrs. Bookever, Chloral Hydrate, Take as Prescribed" under the hard little sofa. It might have been thought to have rolled there—after Mallory had killed herself. Why would she have killed herself? That was easy: grief for Richard, who was to have been her husband. Or, of course, an accident with an unfamiliar drug.

Accident: it was a repeated motif. Too successfully and dangerously repeated. Clutching the little bottle, she waited and listened. Surely somebody would come soon—if only, she thought coldly, to discover her body.

There was no sound at all—not a rustle of clothing, no footsteps, but abruptly Cho jumped down to the floor, his eyes on the door, and then began to crawl, belly low, tail swishing, blunt nose seeking. He crawled slowly, stalking. He reached the door and sniffed and snuffled a little. His nose traveled along the slight space between door and sill, and Mallory was sure she was going to scream. But a flash of cold terror caught her in a dreadful kind of paralysis. She couldn't scream. She couldn't move. She could only wait, trying to hear something above the jerky pounding of her heart.

No one tried to move the latch of the door. As far as she could see, no one tried to push against the door to make sure that the iron bolt was in place.

Still there was no sound. But after a time, which she could not and certainly did not try to measure, Cho sat down before the door and simply watched, ears and nose alert.

The bottle which had held chloral hydrate was in her hand. The note saying that Flo Bel would be back soon lay on the table. The scrawl was unlike Flo Bel's careful writing; if she had been in a hurry, she would have written "Back soon. Gorham with me." Someone else must have added "Tea on table." That was scrawled as if hurriedly, too, but now she was positive that Flo Bel had not written it.

No. Someone who had been in the room, someone who had brought the chloral hydrate, who had brought tea and brandy, and dosed each, she was sure, with what was intended to be a lethal liberality.

Dolores? Had it been Dolores in her satin cloak—hiring a fishing boat to cross the Bay? And, at almost the same time, Dolores in a black dress—in the house? Nothing seemed to make any sense any more.

Cho looked at Mallory and gave a slight wave of his tail. He appeared to be satisfied that all was well. Still she wouldn't open the door, she wouldn't move—

But she did move. She sprang up and ran to the door when she heard Scott shout, "Mallory, here we are—" and Flo Bel's sweet, high voice mingled with Gorham's serious "Yes, madam, certainly, madam." Mallory tore back the bolt so it rasped her fingernails. "Oh, Scott—"

She didn't fall into his arms; she could do nothing but stand there and look at him.

Flo Bel came up beside him. "For heaven's sake, Mallory! You look like—"

"Look!" Mallory held out the deadly, but now empty, little bottle.

Gorham came running from the hall. "Cheng is gone! What's wrong?"

"There was tea. There was brandy. You said in your note—"

Flo Bel swept past her and snatched up the paper. "I didn't write this. That is, I did write 'Back soon, Gorham with me.' I said nothing about tea. Oh, Mallory, you didn't drink it. Or— There's a brandy bottle. No brandy in it. Mallory—"

"No, I barely tasted the tea. Then I remembered Su Lin, and the gas jet and . . . and the hands on the train, and I poured out the tea and the brandy . . . and I'm so glad you're home. Nobody is here. Somebody was here, but . . . oh . . ." She started to sob, and leaned against Scott.

Scott drew her back into the room. Cho jumped up importantly on the sofa. Flo Bel stood like an elegant statue, turning the paper around in her slim fingers. Gorham reached out and closed the door.

"Who's here?" Scott kept his arm close around Mallory. "Dolores? Henry? Who—"

"Oh, I don't know! I didn't hear anybody. I thought the house was empty. So I looked everywhere, even in the kitchen and the back entry, and then I saw that the door to the woodshed was open, so I knew Cheng was gone. But I didn't see him—"

"You didn't see anyone?"

"No! But I saw a kind of movement, something, in the mirror. When I turned around, nobody was there. I closed the door, but Cho thought something was outside it, too. He went and sniffed and— But I didn't hear anybody at all."

"They've got to get out of here! Every one of them!" Scott's eyes blazed. "One of them tried to murder Mallory! Tried again to make it look like suicide or an accident." He tried to collect himself as he turned to Flo Bel. "If Grenay and Henry had anything to do with the deception about your husband's money, Mrs. Bookever, then, as I said before, there might be a double motive for Richard's murder. Fear—and greed."

Gorham said, thoughtfully, "It does seem as if one of your guests—"

"Guests!" Scott said explosively.

"Well, the people here in the house. And if one of them *is* responsible for Mr. Richard's murder, as well as the attacks upon Miss Mallory—then it seems to me wiser, possibly safer, to let them stay here. Until—that is, in order to observe them and also to protect Miss Mallory." Gorham reached down for Cho. "This fellow wants dinner and a walk. I'm sorry I had to shut you in the wardrobe, lad. But I couldn't run the risk of your following us."

"Oh," Mallory cried. "It was you who did that."

It gave her an altogether disproportionate sense of relief. Closing Cho in the big wardrobe was merely a measure of safety for Cho, not a means of protecting an intruder's ankles from his sharp teeth.

"You may be right, Gorham," Scott said.

"I agree with Gorham, let them stay," Flo Bel said, "and watch them."

Scott gave her a harried look. "All right, then. But we've got to do something."

"We will, I'm sure," Gorham said sedately.

Scott was still white with anger—and with fright. "I ought to have disposed of that bottle right away. I thought I had hidden it safely, but—"

"Never mind," Mallory said. "It's empty now. And I barely tasted the tea—no more."

Gorham tucked Cho, wagging and happy, under one arm. "I'll see about dinner; we really must eat, you know."

"I'll help you." Mallory started toward the door.

Flo Bel said, "She does very well, you know, Gorham. Since my husband died..."

Gorham didn't lift an eyebrow. He said, only, "Indeed, madam, Miss Mallory does try."

Faint praise, Mallory thought. Gorham continued, "Now, madam, you really must rest, you know. It was a very tiring effort. I'll get an unopened bottle of brandy. I'm sure a drink

201

would relax you. With your premission, sir." He addressed Scott, who nodded automatically.

"Where were you?" he asked Flo Bel as Gorham disappeared, Cho's brown tail waving from under one arm.

Flo Bel sighed. "I had to see for myself—about the ferry, I mean, and how to get Mallory away from all this—"

"And you found you couldn't," Scott said. "You shouldn't have tried. You went down into the city—"

Flo Bel's voice was just a little uneven. "Oh, yes. I know you wouldn't have wanted me to see all that."

"You must have walked."

"There was no other way we could go. Once Gorham tried to hire a little cart, but someone else got it away from the man who, I suppose, owned it. Yes, I am tired. But Scott is right, Mallory. You can't go back to New York now. The ferries are running, but they're overcrowded—and even if you get across to Oakland, there's no way to get to a train. No, you'll have to stay here for...for a day or two," she said, summoning up her special brand of steely determination. "Then you can leave."

Mallory said, "I'm going now to help Gorham."

"I'll go with you." Scott turned to Flo Bel. "You'll be all right here?"

"Why not?" Flo Bel said tartly, but then quietly lay down flat on the bed. She didn't close her eyes; she only lay there, neat and dignified.

When Scott and Mallory entered the hall, Gorham was already at the dining-room door, with a bottle and glass on a small silver tray in one hand. He gave them a nod. "If you can't keep your spirits up, put some down," he said gravely, but surely, yes, surely, with the slightest twinkle in his eyes.

"How right!" Scott led the way toward the dining room and the cupboard for wines and liquors. But at the door he paused to stare. Mallory paused, too, for there was Dolores, her back turned toward them, again walking along the narrow hall leading to the added bedroom wing of the house; her once-elegant satin opera cloak floated around her, sweeping the floor, and a veil covered her black hair.

"It's Dolores! We thought she might be the woman who

hired a fishing boat, before we got to the wharf. But I saw her here—just before we were leaving!"

There was a sharp click as the door to Dolores' room closed.

Scott said, soberly, "We didn't actually see the woman the man talked about. Did you say she was wearing black when you saw her here?"

"Yes. I never saw Dolores in black before, but I'm certain the woman I saw had on a black dress."

"Did you see her face?"

"No. She was turned away from me."

Scott's face cleared a little. "It must have been my house-keeper. Come back to see how things were going. Yes, I think that likely. There can't be two Doloreses. One is enough. More than enough. I'd like to kick them all out."

"But you said you'd...wait."

"I don't see how I *can!* I can't stand Dolores and Henry and Grenay and that little pal of Dolores', Gerald Flower, in my home for a minute longer!" He looked around him. "It's my house and I love it and I don't want them in it."

"They'll be here tonight for a meal, just the same," Mallory said practically. "Come on! Nothing can happen while you and Gorham and— We have to eat."

Scott scowled, but he took her hand and they walked together through the big dining room with its white walls, dark and shining table, chairs and long buffet, its red curtains over windows, shutting out the night. A beautiful room, Mallory thought, and unbidden: Would she sometime preside at that table? They went through the pantry with its neat shelves that had survived the earthquake; some of the glasses had been turned over, but if any had been broken, Gorham or Su Lin had cleared away the shattered pieces. The kitchen also seemed to speak a welcome, long and low-ceilinged, like the living room, gleaming with copper pans hung from a rack above a long white-scrubbed table. Even the cooking stove seemed to glimmer, not only with polish but with a kind of friendly greeting.

Scott's face was sober. "I thought I had to find out who killed Richard. I still think I must do that. But I don't know how. There can't exist much proof that I could take to a jury. The gun that killed him—that's undoubtedly gone, somewhere in the rubble of the streets. As for whose gun—we're not far removed from the gold-rush days. Probably everybody in the city has access to one. We know that you were in your room when you heard the shot. That leaves Grenay, Dolores, Henry, Gerald, Murphy and me, somewhere nearby. Even your aunt. Oh, and Cheng, I suppose. I didn't see him then. And Su Lin. And who opened the woodshed door to let Cheng out? But anybody could have released Cheng. And anybody could have hired Cheng, sent him to New York, set him watching you."

"Scott, you may not be able to find out who killed Richard. But Dolores heard you say that you were going to stop my marriage to him. Dolores heard you say that. No matter when or where, as soon as she can, Dolores will accuse you."

He looked at her for a moment, his eyes grave. Finally he picked up a long cooking spoon from the table and turned it absently in his fingers. "Oh, yes. She heard the things I told you. And I meant every word. Oh, I don't know how I was going to stop your marriage. But I did have one faint hope. If I told Richard how I felt about you, he might—he just might have postponed the wedding, or something. Richard was like that. He was fair. He would not have demanded it if he thought you didn't want to marry him."

"But who will believe that if Dolores repeats your words? And the will!"

"I know that Dolores wanted to get her hands on the money. By the way, have you ever noticed what large and ugly hands she has? But that's beside the point. I did advise Richard to make a will. I also intended to tell him about us. Yes, cold logic would conclude that I advised him to make the will because I hoped to marry you myself, and then killed him in order, as Dolores says, to get the money and the girl."

"No—"

"No, I didn't. And as to the will, on the train coming out here, almost as soon as I met you, I had already realized that Richard ought to make the kind of will that would protect you. But then, the night of the opera when I came to talk to Richard, I tried, but I simply couldn't tell him about us, or suggest that he postpone the wedding or anything. He was pathetic that night."

"I remember."

"I did get him to make a will. I was beginning to lose heart about stopping the wedding. But the will would have protected you whatever happened. As for me—honestly, I was in such a state that I didn't have any very clear ideas about anything. I couldn't let you marry him. Yet I couldn't bring myself to tell him the truth."

"You believed that Richard was in danger—"

"I couldn't be sure even about that. I did believe that he was being systematically doped. I thought the intention of that was to work on him so thoroughly that he wouldn't be in a condition to—oh, so much as get to the altar. I felt that Dolores was behind all that drugging. Who else? As for the chloral hydrate, it had to get from the train to the drawer in Richard's room. I don't know how. Dolores was not on the train. But now we've found and lost and found again that damned little bottle— Well, obviously, it didn't walk from the train."

He paused for a moment, turned the long spoon in his hands and said, "Of course, I could have taken it myself. I could have—but, Mallory, I didn't!"

The arguments against him would be convincing in the chilly light of a courtroom and a trial: inducing Richard to make a will, after stating flatly, within Dolores' hearing, that he intended to stop the marriage. Mallory had also experienced Scott's remembered feelings of regret, no certain knowledge of what to do or when, the conflict of loyalty to Richard and a whirlwind of confused reluctance to rob him of his evident happiness, so she understood, but strangers in a courtroom wouldn't be so sympathetic.

She put up her arms to Scott, who said, against her face, "But you'll be safe here."

Gorham, entering quietly, cleared his throat politely but firmly. "If you'll peel the potatoes, Miss Mallory, I'll see to the other things."

So, she thought, Gorham relegated her to the lowliest of kitchen chores! "I was going to make an omelet," she said crossly, but Gorham gave her a mild glance. "I wouldn't if I were you, miss. I really wouldn't. An omelet," he added

205

coolly, "requires a certain cooking ability. Here are some potatoes and a knife."

She was sitting at the table, Scott was carving a big ham under Gorham's eagle eye, when a door was flung open and Su Lin came running from the narrow hall leading to the back door. Her black blouse and trousers were wrinkled; her face was pale. "A man," she gasped. "He came for me. A man—"

Scott was already on his way to the back door, the carving knife still in his hand. Gorham stopped him. "A moment, Mr. Scott! Who was the man, Su Lin?"

The girl leaned, half sobbing, across the table. "I think it was Cheng. But Cheng was locked up in the woodshed. I don't know who. He's out there—"

Scott had disappeared.

"Cheng!" Gorham cried and went after Scott.

"Sit down, Su Lin. Get your breath."

"Oh, miss. My father..." Su Lin was trying not to cry, but enormous tears ran down her round cheeks. "I think he's dead, miss. I got to Chinatown—it's all ashes and broken-down timbers still smoking, and it's terrible. I couldn't find my father anywhere. Mr. Gorham gave me some food to take to my father—if I could find him. Somebody got the basket, just snatched it away from me."

"Dear Su Lin. Now listen. Your father has good sense. He probably has gone to Golden Gate Park or some other place of refuge."

Su Lin wiped her face on a wide black sleeve. "Do you really think so, miss?"

"Yes," Mallory said stoutly and hoped she was right.

Scott and Gorham came back, breathing heavily; both looked frustrated and angry. "He got away," Scott said. "I think it *was* Cheng."

Gorham got his breath. "Perhaps. Now I ought to just make sure that Madam is all right."

Scott said, gently, "Su Lin, you couldn't see the man who frightened you?"

"Oh, no, sir. I just heard him coming after me, running. It's almost dark now, you know. I heard him and I ran."

"All right, Su Lin. Go and change your dress. You'll feel better."

Su Lin gave him a grateful little bow and trotted away. Scott looked after her. "Dress? Maybe I ought to have said— But no, really, I couldn't say pants or—"

"I think she understood." There was the smallest catch of laughter in Mallory's throat. But then she thought again: Cheng!

"Scott, do you think Cheng *was* on the train?"

"Su Lin's father could have told us. I think. I still wonder if Dolores got to Grenay. If she got the records, we'll soon know that—"

Suddenly Dolores herself was in the room, black hair smooth around her catlike face. But she was not wearing the blue-green dress; she was dressed in a stylish narrow-waisted, wide-swinging black silk. Mallory stared for a moment and then turned to Scott. "It wasn't your housekeeper! It was Dolores!"

Scott understood instantly. "But the woman at the docks— Yes, I see. Dolores, where were you this afternoon?"

"Why, right here, Scott. In the house."

But a woman very like Dolores, in a bedraggled opera cape, had tried and perhaps succeeded in getting to Marin County. Mallory and Scott had seen her return, still in the cloak, only a few minutes ago. And Mallory had seen her dressed in black when she had returned to her own room to get her coat and leave for the wharf.

Dolores couldn't be in two places at once.

Scott said, bluntly, "You went to Marin County this afternoon. You returned five minutes ago."

"Me! I certainly did not go to Sausalito. Isn't it about time for dinner?" She widened her eyes—yet surely not quite in her usual confident way. Indeed, now that she looked closely at Dolores, Mallory was surprised to see that she, too, seemed to be under some kind of strain; nervous tension showed in her tight mouth, in her wide eyes, which were even wider than usual, showing large dark pupils. Even her hands were restless, fussing at her belt, changing the white ruffle at her throat. At last Dolores had lost her air of assured authority.

She gave Mallory what was almost a placating glance and said, mumbling a little, "Dinner—we must eat. I suppose."

Mallory said crisply, "Then help. Peel these potatoes. Here's a knife." She thrust the knife at Dolores, then had a fleeting sense of uneasiness as she did so. Dolores with a small sharp knife was not a really comfortable sight.

Suddenly, surging from the living room, there was the sound of men's voices, loud, a spatter of high-pitched Chinese and one shrill howl of pain. Dolores, knife in hand, ran out of the kitchen. Mallory dashed after her. She ran into Gerald, staggering toward the bedroom wing, his hand at his face. Gorham was struggling with Henry. A lamp had been lighted in the long room. Mallory had just a glimpse of Cheng at the front door; he whisked out of sight and was gone. Scott rushed after him.

Dolores cried, shrilly, "Cheng wouldn't hurt anybody! Come back, Scott!"

The open door was only an empty black space. Every trailing scrap of pinkish-yellow glow from the sunset had vanished.

Gorham landed a fist into Henry's bulging middle. Henry yelled and sank into a chair.

Scott came back into the room and went to Dolores. "That was Cheng! You let him out of the woodshed this afternoon!"

Henry rubbed his middle. Gorham rubbed an eye. Dolores said, calmly, "Of course I let him out. Why, the woodshed might have caught fire. Everything else has."

"What was he doing? Did he come back to rob me again, or was he meeting someone here?"

Ernest Grenay had entered so quietly that he was not noticed until he spoke. "I encountered Cheng just now. I take it you were after him. The poor man is terrified. He said he came only to apologize, to say he was sorry he tried to steal anything."

Scott stared at the little gray man. *"Sorry!"*

"Well." Ernest Grenay smoothed his thin hair. "You see, he wants to come back here. He has no place to stay. And he's hungry."

"But—but—" Scott stopped helplessly.

"I know." Ernest Grenay smiled faintly. "You do have a

rather unwelcome set of guests on your hands. I did try to get to Sausalito today, but as you see, failed. So really, I don't know where else I—or any of us—could go."

"There are huts," Scott said.

"Oh, Scott!" Dolores widened her eyes. "You wouldn't make us leave until...until we have found some kind of shelter."

Murphy ended it, for he came in through the dining room and said, very solemnly, "Mr. Suydam, I must speak to you. Alone."

Eighteen

Scott went back toward the kitchen with Murphy.

An unexpected, if fragile kind of everyday quiet settled upon them all. Henry muttered something about washing, struggled out of his chair, rubbing his stomach, and went off along the narrow hall leading to the extra bedrooms. Grenay muttered something, too, and followed him. Dolores still had the sharp paring knife in her hand; it turned jerkily and caught quick gleams of light from the lamp. She said, "Well then—potatoes."

Scott and Murphy were in the dining room, both with very serious faces. Scott said, "She'd better know now, Murphy. Mallory—"

He drew her back into the living room, Murphy following them, his kind face grave. Scott said, "He had to tell us. I think it's right, Mallory. Richard would have liked it—"

"Richard—"

Murphy said, "I'll tell her, Mr. Scott. You see, miss—well, I'm a Catholic. Mr. Richard—he wasn't. I hope you'll not think it a liberty. But Father Connor thought it was right, and he consented— There were several others. Three others, I believe, at the same time." He watched her, troubled.

"I see," Mallory said after a long moment.

Scott said, "Murphy thought it was for the best. There are so many religious services, and they have not yet been organized—can't be, with the city in the present state of confusion. Murphy acted without consulting any of us but—"

"I did it for the best, Miss Mallory," Murphy said. "It was done this afternoon while we were at the wharf. Everything, I'm sure, was...was...as Mr. Richard would have wanted it."

"Yes," Mallory said after another pause. "Oh, yes. Thank you. And thank Father Connor."

Murphy didn't pull a forelock, probably deterred by the fact that he didn't have one to pull. But he gave a kind of sketchy bow of acknowledgment and turned to Scott. "Miss Dolores?"

"We'll not tell her now. That can wait. Everything all right, Mallory?"

"Yes," she said steadily.

"The way I feel," Scott said, understanding her.

Murphy suddenly put out a hard, strong hand. Mallory put her own hand in his grasp and said again, "Thank you."

Murphy turned away.

There was a clatter from the kitchen. "Mallory," Scott said. "Dear Mallory."

"You had known him much longer than I did. It's been hard for you."

Scott said, soberly, "It was like Murphy to think of a religious ceremony. Richard would have approved of that."

"Yes." They went together, soberly, back to the kitchen, where voices and clatter seemed for the moment almost normal.

Dinner, however, was a peculiar, even preposterous, kind of disorganized eating, whenever anyone seemed to feel he wanted food. Gorham had, rather absently, it struck Mallory, opened two bottles of whiskey. Glasses began to turn up here and there, on tables, chairs, wherever the user felt inclined to put them. Nobody said much, but everyone seemed to want to talk, which itself was strange. Certainly Mallory heard nothing but short and interrupted or half-said comments, nothing that concerned anybody. Gerald did not appear at all. Scott came out of his distraction to scowl at Henry, who certainly never dropped his glass anywhere but moved only to refill it; Scott also scowled at Dolores, who had quite efficiently got the kitchen fire going and the hated potatoes boiling. She left the peelings and the knife on the table.

Mallory helped Gorham, whose eye was now completely shut, prepare a tray for Flo Bel, who had decided to remain in her room. The dinner itself wasn't much, but enough. Indeed, no one of them, except perhaps Ernest Grenay, who prepared a neat plate for himself, seemed interested in doing more than cutting off bread from a huge loaf and sandwiching it with ham. When Gorham and Mallory went to see Flo Bel, she was sitting in a chair, hair brushed and tidy, looking quite herself. She asked what all the fight had been about, and then, noting, with a swift look, Gorham's eye, said, unbelievably, "I hope the other fellow got a worse one."

"He did," Mallory said. "But he's recovering. Cheng came back, he wants to stay. He has no place to go. Scott went after him. And then— I don't really know what happened. Henry—"

"Poked me in the eye, madam," said Gorham austerely. "I don't really know why, unless he had his mind set on a bottle and I got in his way. Temper! However"—a reminiscent gleam came into his one open eye—"I doubt if he will take such a liberty again. Now, madam, there's something—" He adjusted the tray, glanced at Mallory and said, "You might look at these, madam." He dug into a pocket and pulled out a small silver buckle.

Flo Bel and Mallory both stared. Mallory cried, "But it's mine—"

"Certainly, miss. I cut it off for comparison with the other one."

"The other— But it was pulled off my shoe in Gary!"

"Yes, miss. I happened to find a buckle in Mr. Henry Beaton's pocket. I thought it belonged to you, but wasn't sure. I left that one, naturally, in Mr. Beaton's pocket, for I did not wish to remove it without a witness to state where I had found it—"

"Gorham!" Mallory cried. "Henry *wasn't* on the train! I told you! Mr. Scott would have seen him and told us."

"Y-yes..." Gorham's one open eye looked rather smug. After all, he had had the pleasure of sinking his fist into Henry's middle. "Yes, I think so. All the same—Well, Mr. Henry was troubled about his clothing. He asked me to try to give his coat at least a brush—and one little silver buckle was in a pocket. So I matched it with this one."

No one spoke for a long, long moment. Henry! Cheng? Cheng might have been on the train. Henry, no.

Gorham said, thoughtfully, "Mr. Henry does strike one as being rather a fool. He may not be a remarkably successful businessman, but he may have more brains than he seems to have." Gorham's eye was turning a deeper red. He touched it cautiously.

Flo Bel said, absently, "If we only had steak," revealing an unsuspected knowledge of fistic encounters. Then she got back to the subject at hand. "What about this wispy young man, Gerald, who's always hanging around Dolores? Her lover, I suppose," Flo Bel added, surprising Mallory again with her calm Victorian acceptance of the facts of life, as long as this particular fact was not found out.

Gorham thought it over and shook his head. "I fancy not, madam." He was as thoroughly Victorian as Flo Bel. "Something about the way she looks at him. Annoyed, so to speak. But, yes, there is something proprietorial in her attitude."

Flo Bel thought it over and nodded. "She does order him to do this and that. Remember"—she turned to Mallory—"when she didn't know what to do with those jewels she managed to save—not that I really blame her for that, I must say— However, when she wanted someone to take care of them she spoke to this...this Gerald, not to her husband."

"True," Gorham said, then was silent for a moment. "I do wonder," he said at last, "what has happened to the various records which the city must have."

"Burned," Flo Bel said flatly. "If what we saw of the city is any indication."

"Possibly some records exist in the bank vaults, which are still unopened—cannot be opened until the fire damage has been repaired."

"If you mean birth records, I don't think such records are required here. Perhaps. I don't know. But I honestly don't

212

think so," said Flo Bel, as if once she had unleashed outspokenness, she might as well continue to make her meaning perfectly clear. "If you're thinking that this young man is Dolores' bastard, I don't. Too old."

"I don't believe I was thinking of that. Possibly in other cities— No, such records may not exist. Expecially if under another name. Certainly, just now there is little opportunity to explore even if one knew where and what to explore. I understand he worked for a time for Mr. Grenay, then went into Mr. Henry's store—gallery, as Miss Dolores calls it."

"You're thinking that possibly he was hired to...to kill Mr. Richard, and to kill my niece."

"The thought did occur to me. Yet Mr. Scott searched the train, not only once but several times. No, I'm not sure just what I'm thinking," said Gorham sourly and touched his swollen eye.

There was a hard knock at the door, and Scott flung into the room, stopped, stared at Mallory and wiped his forehead. "I didn't see you leave the kitchen! I was— Never mind, you're safe here." He looked relieved, wiped his forehead again and said, rather sheepishly, "I let Cheng stay. He's locked in the woodshed again, but at least I know where he is. Unless someone lets him out again. But I honestly don't think he wants out again. He really was hungry and scared and no shelter and—"

"You've let all the others stay for much the same reason," Flo Bel said astutely.

"Only for the night. And as Gorham suggested—to watch them. What else can I do! You've seen what's left of the city. You've seen the makeshift shelters and— Yes, I let them stay. It may be safer, I don't know. Even if"—he sobered then—"even if one of them murdered Richard. And one of them must have," he finished.

"If only we knew which one—" Flo Bel began, and Mallory said, "What could we do? Right now, we couldn't even get a policeman. Besides, we need proof."

All at once, Gorham's one eye looked fishy. "It has just occurred to me," he said rather enigmatically, "perhaps we have been too ready to take the truth to be lies."

Mallory stared at him. "What on earth do you mean by that?"

"I don't know, miss. I really—I don't know what I mean."

"Of course you know what you mean!" Mallory was not going to accept this evasive reply from someone whose properly striped legs she had kicked valiantly on an occasion when he had pulled her down from the pantry shelf and a cake box she was after; true, that was some years ago, but still! She snapped, "You've got that dreamy look on your face as if you are thinking and— And what are you thinking? Who killed Richard? Who tried to kill me? Who—"

"And how did the accident happen to Mr. Richard? He fell on the stairs. We must remember that." Gorham made a gesture of a bow in Flo Bel's direction and walked with undiminished dignity out of the room.

"Well!" Mallory cried. "He's too bossy! Acts as if he knows everything!"

"Never mind," Scott said "Your Gorham has given me an idea. Yes, that accident. Richard could have been killed then." With that, he, too, walked out of the room.

Flo Bel sighed and lifted her fork.

"You may as well eat," Mallory said. "Not much of a dinner but—"

"Far better than hundreds of unfortunate people are having tonight."

Mallory was still ruffled. "It never has made me feel any better to think that other people feel worse."

"Dear Mallory! Do control your temper. At all times." Flo Bel munched on bread and cheese.

"Do you know where Gorham has Richard's will? And your jewels?"

"Not my jewels, Mr. Jacobsen's jewels. Oh, I'm sure Gorham has them safe. And the will, too."

Flo Bel was almost as infuriating as Gorham and Scott. The trouble is, Mallory thought, I've been terrified! I've nearly been killed! I'm about to cry. Flo Bel glanced up and said, "Tears never helped anything."

Cho, a dog who believed firmly in the power of the canine eye, sniffed at Flo Bel's dinner tray and went to sit before

214

her, fastening what he obviously hoped would be a magnetic gaze upon her.

Mallory thought, I'm hungry, too. And edgy and still frightened. It would be a good idea to get some food, even some drink, into me.

She left Flo Bel to her dinner, which all at once seemed rather appetizing. The wide door from the living room to the path between the madrones was open; she hoped, off on a tangent, that no rat would slide into the house. The pale light from the living-room lamp streaked out so she had a glimpse of Gorham and Scott pacing outside, then gradually vanishing into the darkness.

They seemed to be talking, but she could not even hear the murmur of their voices. When she reached the kitchen no one was there. There was only the dreary sight of unwashed plates and silver, some scraps of food here and there, smeared glasses, an empty bottle of whiskey; even the little heap of potato peelings still lay on the table. The sharp paring knife, however, had been put away; at least, it wasn't there. She noted its absence briefly.

She found bread and some cheese left on the broad cheese tray. The whole house was extraordinarily quiet, as it had been during the afternoon. She munched on the bread and cheese and decided to find another bottle of something that would brace her spirits.

She went to the liquor cabinet, which was open. As she reached for a bottle of brandy which stood on a shelf, there was the faintest rustle of sound, a near sound. She whirled around, caught one glimpse of Dolores' greenish-blue dress and felt a hard strong grip on her throat. Out of the corner of her eye, she had the barest look at a flashing, sharp knife.

She couldn't scream. She tried to, but the only sound she could make emerged as only a kind of choking gasp, and the strong hands gripping her throat exerted a sudden force that dragged her, on her heels, back to the dark little entry and back door. She tried and tried to cry out, she kicked, as she had done at Gary, but she could feel her breath going, her heart pounding too hard. She writhed with all her strength, but couldn't escape the iron grip on her throat. Her flailing hands went up and back, trying frantically to claw at Dolores' face. Then a most horrible thing happened—the top of Dolores' head came off and into her hands. Dolores screamed.

But the scream did not come from behind her; it was close beside her. Someone tugged at the hands on her throat. Someone kept on screaming. Words were mingled with the scream. "No! No! Don't—you mustn't. No—no—I tell you. I won't have it. No!"

Feet came pounding through the kitchen. Men's voices shouted. The hands on her throat dropped, or were torn away. She took a long, shaky breath and stared at the top of Dolores' head, in her own hands. But it wasn't Dolores' head, it was only like it. It was a heavy black mass of hair. She was dazed; she was numb with terror. She thought wildly, It's a black wig, dressed and arranged the way Dolores arranges her hair.

Dolores, herself, in her black dress, was, unbelievably, sobbing, but she had the sharp paring knife in one of her own strong hands. "He shouldn't have done it! He shouldn't have pushed Richard. He shouldn't have tried to kill her! I never meant him to do all that—"

He? Mallory thought wildly. He? But she had seen Dolores' familiar blue-green dress.

Scott had her in his arms, feeling all over her throat, touching her gently. The wiry mat of hair in her hands felt loathsome; she flung it wildly away.

The lamp shone yellow upon the young man dressed in Dolores' dress, his own blond hair disheveled, his face smooth, with no mustache now. Even without the wig, he looked astonishingly like Dolores. Gorham held him with his arms crooked behind his back. Dolores sobbed, "I never meant him to kill anybody!"

"Your confederate, Mrs. Beaton—or something more?" Gorham asked and held Gerald's arms firmly. Henry came lumbering into the room, followed by Grenay, looking anything but neat. "What—" Henry began, and Dolores sobbed, "I didn't know until today! I didn't even suspect."

"You knew he went to New York," Gorham said as if merely stating a fact.

"He wanted to go! He said there was something he wanted to look at, and perhaps buy for Henry's gallery—"

216

"Are you talking about Gerald?" Henry said dazedly. "He told me he had gone down into the peninsula—"

"Actually, he was on the train returning from New York," Gorham said, quietly again. "I suspect he was the one who tried to drag Miss Mallory off the train. When the silver buckle came off her shoe during the attack, he kept it—I can't imagine why, unless it was to cast suspicion on someone else at a later time. I found it in your pocket, Mr. Henry."

Henry looked stunned. "In my pocket? I never heard of— Dolores, is this young man something to you? Did he kill Richard?"

"I didn't mean him to do that! All I wanted was for Richard to postpone his marriage indefinitely—remain dependent on me. I never dreamed that he would ask Mallory to come out here for the wedding—that's when Gerald must have become desperate." Dolores lowered her head, her hands over her eyes.

Henry went to her and put a kind hand on her shoulder. "I don't understand. He was always around, pleasant, helpful; he worked in the bookkeeping department for Ernest—"

Grenay said, sharply, "A slick young man. I never liked him, but I knew he was a friend of Dolores', and Richard had recommended him. I let him go—oh, two years ago. I never actually caught him doing anything wrong, although I had my suspicions. Then he went to work for you, Henry. I kept my mouth shut about him, but I never could understand why Dolores had him around so much."

Henry cried, "Lolo? Does Gerald have some connection with you? I never questioned your interest in him; he was good at his job for me. That T'ang horse last year—"

"Which he procured for you, so bravely, you said, dressed as a peasant woman." Scott shook his head. "That ought to have suggested how he dressed on the trip to New York."

Henry uttered an explosive sound and looked grimly at Dolores. She cried, jerkily, "How could I tell you, Henry? How could I tell anybody? He's my brother, my half brother. Illegitimate, of course. A disgrace to to me and— But my father—oh, he's long gone. Gerald came up from Mexico and proved he was my half brother and . . . and I had to help him. He'd have told everybody if I didn't. Besides, I was truly fond

217

of him. Blood is . . . a bond. Oh, I told Richard. His cousin, too! I knew Richard would never tell. We got him the job in Ernest's office. Then a job for you, Henry."

"You said that it was only today when you began to suspect him," Scott said.

"Well, yes. But yesterday I happened to overhear that there was a question about some money while he was working for Ernest. I began to wonder. I knew that he had been in the house the day Richard fell. He could have waited and watched and given Richard even the slightest push down the stairs and then run away, down the back stairs. And then— and then today he took my dress and cloak. I didn't know why he took them; then I saw him leaving in them. I was sure that he was trying to get to Ernest's house and get some records about the missing money, and— Don't you see, everybody would want to help a poor distraught woman." She cried, sobbing but coherent, "Richard's money was supposed to come to me—who else? That is, if Richard should die. And . . . and he knew that I'd have shared with him. All the time, Scott, you had such a strong motive! I truly believed you shot Richard." She fell back into Henry's arms. "I never dreamed he would do such . . . such dreadful things."

"But what happened this afternoon?" Scott's voice cut into Dolores' frenzied sobbing.

She lifted her face, tear-streaked. "I wasn't even aware of it when he returned—and that horrible chloral something— I heard you talking later. He tried to murder Mallory! He told me, Scott, that you and Mallory had seen him go into my room and he was sure you thought it was me. When I accused him of trying to follow Ernest to Sausalito this morning, he put on his own clothes and his mustache and ran out again. But then he returned. He said he'd been attacked just outside in the street by someone who pulled off the fake mustache. He was furious. He must have hurried into my dress again and hung around the back door, hoping for a chance and— Why!" Dolores' eyes were huge circles of dark pupils and white rims. "Why, he used my dress to protect his own clothes from bloodstains, and also, so if anyone saw him, they'd think I killed Mallory."

Gorham observed, remotely, "Blood from a cut throat
218

would have been found on your dress. And if anything had gone wrong at Mr. Grenay's, you would have been blamed for that, too."

Dolores gave a choked scream. Scott said, almost mildly, "When the fire reached the Welbeck house and we came here, I remember thinking how odd it was—Gerald saving his opera hat. But it was a wig."

Grenay strode over to Gerald. "*You* wrote that letter to Mrs. Bookever on my office paper. *You* told her the mine was no longer in operation! Oh, I admit that I was at fault. Careless. Trusting. Embezzlement, false information, all that has happened, but never before in my office. I don't know exactly how you did it, but I'll find out! Where is Mrs. Bookever's money? What about other people?"

Gorham said, "I do blame myself, too. I suspected that his mustache was false the first night we were here at dinner. He got it tangled with soup and I brought a napkin to his assistance and I couldn't help noting— But I really thought it only a matter of a young man's vanity. Until tonight, when I got a good yank at it."

Gerald suddenly shrieked, "You nearly took my face off, too!" And indeed there was a red patch above his weak and now trembling mouth.

"I never suspected a woman had tried to drag Mallory off the train." Scott seemed to be talking to himself. "I looked at the face of every man in every car. But the women— He was dressed as a woman, of course. And I suppose he stole into Richard's private car late that night looking for another opportunity to attack Mallory, and he stumbled on that bottle of chloral hydrate. It must have seemed like a gift from heaven. I wouldn't be surprised if he had added a lethal dose to the glass of water in Mallory's stateroom. With no success again, fortunately. When we arrived in San Francisco, he adopted his mustache. Didn't you think that was strange, Dolores?"

"I only thought he was vain. He likes the mustache; thinks it makes him look less boyish."

Mallory cried, "But he sat in my room when the fires started! He sat there and sobbed—"

"Scared. Like the rest of us," Gorham said succinctly.

"Scared. But he wanted money more. So he slipped out and shot Mr. Richard. Dear me, fear of discovery and the love of money. He must have taken the chloral hydrate, and I daresay he put it in a drawer in Mr. Richard's room in the hope that Mr. Richard would take it by accident. Or that he could kill Mr. Richard with it so it would look like suicide. But then—the earthquake, the chance to do away with Mr. Richard at once, finally. No questions asked, he must have believed. Not really very smart. Very little intelligence, but much fear and much greed."

Scott interrupted. "But that didn't solve his problem, because Richard's will unexpectedly left everything to Mallory. Maybe he turned on the gas in her room. Maybe it really was an accident. We'll probably never know. Anyway, the chloral hydrate must always have been in the back of his mind. He learned I had the bottle during that unpleasant discussion at dinner the last night in the Welbeck house, so later the logical thing for him to do was to search my room until he found it again."

Henry bestirred himself and took Dolores out with him. Gerald suddenly wriggled and squirmed out of Gorham's grip and slid for the back door. Gorham dashed after him. Ernest Grenay ran, too, displaying surprising agility.

Scott said, "We'd better tell your aunt—"

"You needn't," Flo Bel said from the doorway. "I see now what Gorham meant when he said we were taking the truth to be lies. Dolores, Grenay, even I suspect, Cheng, were really telling the truth all the time. Not all the truth, but some of it. Dolores was really devoted to Richard, mistaken in dosing him, yes, but in her view, the cautious and right thing to do."

"But she did want control of Richard and the Welbeck money," Scott said.

Flo Bel looked amused and grave at the same time. "Well, that's all settled now. Richard's will takes care of the money. My niece is going to get it."

"No!" Mallory lifted her head from the warmth of Scott's shoulder. "I'll keep enough to pay you back, Flo Bel, for the money you've spent, but—"

"We'll talk about that another time. Let's get back to Dolores. I can understand that she wanted to keep the knowledge that she had an illegitimate brother a secret. Oh, yes, she would protect him. She had some affection for him. Now, this afternoon—"

"Yes," said Scott. "He tried again. He never got to Grenay's house. So he came back and found that, aside from Dolores, no one was here. He read your note to Mallory, added words of his own, arranged the tea and the brandy and waited to see what would happen. Later we saw him in the hall and thought he was Dolores. Oh, it's all clear enough. But we have to get jury evidence—"

"You'll get evidence," Flo Bel said grimly. She had Cho under one arm. Now she shoved the little dog at Mallory and went sedately back toward her room.

"Dolores did save my life," Mallory said.

"Yes—oh, yes." Scott sighed. "It will take time. The courts, the evidence. Somehow we'll see to all that."

Cho waddled ahead of them into the living room. A log fire glowed; the red curtains were drawn like a shield against the world.

Scott said, soberly, "Everything will take time. Rebuild the city—steel and concrete this time. But we'll rebuild. This beautiful undefeatable city—oh, we'll rebuild."

He added, dreamily, "The hills are still here. The ocean, the Bay are still here. And the people. San Franciscans," he said proudly. Then he looked at Mallory. "We'll live here. At Casa Madrone."

ABOUT THE AUTHOR

MIGNON G. EBERHART'S name has become a guarantee of excellence in the mystery and suspense field. Her work has been translated into sixteen languages, and has been serialized in many magazines and adapted for radio, television and motion pictures.

For many years, Mrs. Eberhart traveled extensively abroad and in the United States. Now she lives in Greenwich, Connecticut.

In April 1971 the Mystery Writers of America gave Mrs. Eberhart their Grand Master Award, in recognition of her sustained excellence as a suspense writer, and in 1977 she served as president of that organization. She recently celebrated the fiftieth anniversary of the publication of her first novel, *The Patient in Room 18*.